PENGUIN BOOKS

CORNISH SHORT STORIES

Denys Val Baker is well known as a short-story writer and novelist and is the author of a series of autobiographical books about life in the county which has been his home for the past thirty years. These include *An Old Mill By the Stream, Spring At Land's End* and *Sunset Over the Scillies*. He was the founder and editor of the *Cornish Review* (1949–74) and is editor of various anthologies.

Denys Val Baker is married and has six children. His wife, Jess, has embarked on a new career as a mature student in psychology at London University, after twenty years as a studio potter.

CORNISH SHORT STORIES

*

EDITED BY

DENYS VAL BAKER

PENGUIN BOOKS

Penguin Books Ltd, Harmondsworth, Middlesex, England
Penguin Books, 625 Madison Avenue, New York, New York 10022, U.S.A.
Penguin Books Australia Ltd, Ringwood, Victoria, Australia
Penguin Books Canada Ltd, 41 Steelcase Road West, Markham, Ontario, Canada
Penguin Books (N.Z.) Ltd, 182-190 Wairau Road, Auckland 10, New Zealand

First published 1976

Made and printed in Great Britain
by Richard Clay (The Chaucer Press), Ltd
Bungay, Suffolk
Set in Linotype Granjon

CONTENTS

ACKNOWLEDGEMENTS

Frank Baker: 'Tyme Tryeth Troth' first published in *The Uncertain Element*, Jarrolds, 1950.

Charles Causley: 'Looking For Annie' first published in *Hands to Dance*, Carroll & Nicolson, 1951; copyright © Charles Causley, 1951.

Jack Clemo: 'The Clay Dump' first published in *One And All*, Museum Press, 1951; copyright © Jack Clemo, 1951.

Ronald Duncan: 'When We Dead Awaken' first published in *A Kettle of Fish*, W. H. Allen, 1971; copyright © Ronald Duncan, 1971.

Daphne du Maurier: 'The Lordly Ones' first published in *The Breaking Point*, Victor Gollancz, 1959; copyright © Daphne du Maurier, 1959.

Winston Graham: 'Jacka's Fight' first published in *Argosy*, 1971; copyright © A. W. M. Graham, 1971.

Charles Lee: 'The Defeat of the Amazons' first published in *Cornish Tales*, J. M. Dent & Sons Ltd, 1941.

Ruth Manning-Sanders: 'John Pettigrew's Mirror' published in *One and All*, Museum Press, 1951.

'Q': 'Once Aboard the Lugger' first published in *Old Fires and Profitable Ghosts*, J. M. Dent and Sons Ltd, 1927.

Donald R. Rawe: 'The Deep Sea Dream' first published in the *Cornish Review*, 1950; copyright © Donald R. Rawe, 1950, 1976.

A. L. Rowse: 'The Curse Upon The Clavertons' first published in *Cornish Stories*, Macmillan, 1967, copyright © A. L. Rowse, 1967.

Howard Spring: 'Corporal Strike' first published in *Eleven Stories and a Beginning*, W. M. Collins Sons & Co. Ltd, 1973; copyright © Marion Howard Spring, 1973.

Anne Treneer: 'Sheep May Safely Graze' first published in *Happy Button*, Westaway Books, 1950; copyright © Susan Treneer, 1950.

J. C. Trewin: 'Carriages Ten-Thirty', copyright © J. C. Trewin, 1976.

Denys Val Baker: 'The Discovery' first published in *A Summer to Remember*, William Kimber, 1975; copyright © Denys Val Baker, 1975.

C. C. Yyvyan: 'The Witch of Tregonebris' first published in *Gwendra Cove*, 1931; copyright © C. C. Vyvyan, 1931.

David Watmough: 'Ashes' first published in the *Cornish Review*, 1972; copyright © David Watmough, 1972.

INTRODUCTION

Cornwall has always been one of the creative centres of the British Isles. In the times of the Celts and right up until the Middle Ages it was a land rich in cultural traditions, noted for its miracle plays and other open air drama. In those days, of course, there was a Cornish language, spoken by large numbers of people living in the region. Unfortunately, though, whereas like Wales and Scotland and Ireland, Cornwall has preserved many of its traditions, unlike those countries it has completely lost its native language. The consequence is that there is not today a strong and clearly defined native Cornish literary movement in the same sense as can be observed, for instance, in Wales. There is, indeed, an Old Cornish movement, sponsoring a revived and developing Cornish Gorsedd, an annual gathering of bards held at various Cornish centres. At these gatherings titles are conferred on Cornish men and women in recognition of some manifestation of the Celtic spirit in work done for Cornwall. Such awards were conferred on the late R. Morton Nance and the late A. S. D. Smith ('Caradar'), both prolific writers in the Cornish language – and similar recognition has been given to native writers, such as the poets Jack Clemo and Charles Causley, who have preferred to write in English (and thereby, incidentally, reach a much wider audience). However, it has to be admitted that if Cornwall's literary output was to be measured merely by the work of native-born writers then this would be a slim volume.

Fortunately, while Cornwall may not have produced many of its own writers and artists, it does seem, almost hypnotically, to entice others into its possession. Many famous authors have lived either temporarily or permanently in Cornwall, and they would hardly have been human if they had not been stimulated into writing about their adopted land. From the past one thinks of such eminent figures as D. H. Lawrence, Thomas Hardy, Hugh Walpole, Compton Mackenzie and, more recently, the late Howard Spring; in present times authors of the stature of Winston Graham and Hammond Innes have written extensively about Cornwall – while the name of Daphne du Maurier is almost synonymous with Cornwall! Less well-known writers have also contributed a formidable share to Cornwall's literature, one of the most outstanding figures being Charles Lee, who paid his first visit to Cornwall when he was in his early twenties and stayed on to make those shrewd observations of life and character that produced such minor masterpieces as *Mr Sampson* and *The Widow Woman*.

Cornish Short Stories, then, is a selection of some of the best stories about Cornwall written either by Cornish-born authors or by 'furriners' who have come to live in, or learned to love, England's most westerly county. In many ways it is a case of getting the best of both worlds: some outstanding work from such Cornish authors as A. L. Rowse, Jack Clemo, Charles Causley, J. C. Trewin and Ronald Duncan – plus the added lustre of Daphne du Maurier, Winston Graham, Frank Baker and others. Because there are so many excellent living authors to choose from I have aimed largely at a contemporary anthology, but it seemed only fair to include one or two representatives of a distinguished past era. Finally, may I express the hope that not only will the volume provide entertaining reading, but also some solid evidence to support a strong case for Cornwall – like Wales, Scotland and Ireland – remaining very much 'its own place'.

Denys Val Baker

Jack Clemo

THE CLAY-DUMP

Lucy Gribble, the caretaker of Pengarth school, was forty years old. She was already much bowed, her left shoulder drooped; she was also lame. A withered stem of her former self, Miss Gribble had been dogged all her life by troubles.

Her first mature sorrow had made her a spinster. It occurred when she was twenty-two.

She had developed a fervent love for Roger Lean, a neighbour of the Gribbles during Lucy's childhood. He was eight years her senior, and though he had felt a tender regard for the girl he was a shy man and never expressed his feeling or guessed hers. He had worked as a loader in a clay-pit near Pengarth, and one winter's day he had been crushed by a skip-waggon. Less than a week later he died from his injuries, still unattached emotionally and without the comforting assurance that Miss Gribble would want him to kiss her in heaven.

This tragedy overwhelmed Lucy with grief, and while she was prostrated by it other blows were showered upon her for no apparent reason. Her father died suddenly from a heart attack, and, becoming crazed by the shock, his wife shut herself in the parlour where Mr Gribble had passed away, and refused to leave it even for sleep. She was soon removed to the asylum, and it was during the nightmare interval at the cottage that Miss Gribble first became aware of the clay-dump as a menace.

This clay-dump dominated the village and was a landmark for miles around. By day it dwarfed to insignificance the cluster of dour houses and their little defiant puffs of chimney smoke, while in the darker evenings the homely glow from the cottage windows looked pale and timid compared with the cold, baleful glare of the floodlight on the tip.

The Gribbles' home stood nearest the dump – so near that one side of the white pyramid loomed up from the garden hedge. Mrs Gribble had eyed it strangely during the last few days that she spent in the house, and Lucy too became fascinated, aroused to a certain identification of the gravelly dune with the heaping up of afflictions in her life. All her hope of enjoyment had been like the flowers that pushed out so pitifully through the turf fringing the dump's base – soon to be burst and flattened and buried by the descending vomit of sand and stone. The wooden tip-structure under which the waggon appeared as it spilled its load two hundred feet above the cottage, looked like a fantastic window in heaven, and Lucy's thoughts would grow darkly religious as she watched the inexorable movements up there.

'Tis like sand poured out over everything in my life,' she would say bitterly. And at times the bitterness swooped dangerously, biting at the brain.

'Tis like God up there on the tip,' she told herself. 'Tis God creeping out sly under they tip-beams ...'

But when her mother was gone from the house Miss Gribble turned her mind to more wholesome and practical affairs. In casting about for some additional means of support after obtaining the post as school caretaker, and also for some relief from the loneliness at home, she decided to let the front room as a furnished apartment. It was a cosy room, and though the district did not attract tourists – for it was the least Celtic part of Cornwall – there were occasional visitors who might like to remain a while amid the bleak, half-rural, half-industrial solitude.

Miss Gribble advertised her accommodation in the local paper, and soon received inquiries from interested folk. The villagers, who had pitied her, became envious and sought some way of venting their disapproval. They felt that she was taking an unfair advantage of them, trading upon her bereavements in a most callous manner. In many of the surrounding houses violent quarrels arose as wives proposed to follow Miss Gribble's example. Finding that limitation of space forbade this, they watched the progress of Lucy's venture suspiciously and with dark expectations.

Their hopes kindled swiftly, for the first visitor to lodge with Miss Gribble – and he stayed all the winter – was a bachelor of fifty who was sly in manner and regular in his attendance at church.

Vulgar curiosity in a remote Cornish village can go to lengths that seem incredible to those to whom scandal is not the whole spice of life; and the neighbours' ingenuity rose to the occasion.

While this gentleman – a Mr Wardler – was Miss Gribble's guest, the parents in Pengarth found for their children a pleasant sport. This was nothing less than setting them to spy at Lucy's parlour window whenever a light was shining there during the dark evenings, and to report what they saw. It was not regarded as in any way an improper pastime. If the parents themselves indulged in such activities they might indeed be considered rather ill-bred, but children were excused, and in reporting the behaviour of dubious persons they were providing necessary information by which the moral standard of Pengarth, and the extent of hypocrisy – for Miss Gribble was a chapel-goer – could be judged.

As far as the children were concerned the whole excitement lay in the daring approach to Miss Gribble's cottage, the tiptoeing across the garden and the furtive glimpses through the window, over which the curtain was drawn loosely; for nothing in the least scandalous was ever perceived within. Mr Wardler was always alone, poring over his books. There was a more piquant interest for the youngsters in spying through the kitchen window into the tiny room where Miss Gribble sat brooding, often so close to the fire that her clothing was almost singed. She usually held her cat on her lap, a black tom which she had named Roger, to which she would confide her troubles and over which she would frequently weep, wiping her eyes in its fur.

Mrs Goudge, the cobbler's wife, who lived just across the road from Miss Gribble and from her bedroom could observe the movements behind Lucy's curtain at bedtime, was understood to declare that Miss Gribble always dressed and undressed alone and that Mr Wardler was never seen to enter her bedroom.

But though Miss Gribble's morals defied impeachment, misfortune continued to sour her path. For several years things seemed to run smoothly, occasional lodgers coming and going without mishap. But a turning-point came with the arrival of Albert Lark, a young man from Falmouth who announced himself as a journalist who wished to get first-hand knowledge of the clay district. Within a week of Mr Lark's appearance in Pengarth the village constable called at Miss Gribble's home and stated that her lodger answered the description of a man wanted by the Falmouth police on a charge of housebreaking. Mr Lark had left Pengarth in custody and Miss Gribble never ceased to regret admitting him into her cottage. Her neighbours now had good cause to rejoice against her, and took it upon themselves to warn every stranger who came to the village of the evil that had befallen Mr Lark. Somewhere about the place – usually in the 'King's Arms', from which the chimneys of Miss Gribble's home were visible – prospective lodgers were told that 'the last bloke that lodged wi' Lucy Gribble went straight behind prison bars from her doorpost, 'a did'. The tone and manner in which this information was given implied that Miss Gribble was entirely to blame for this downfall, and that a similar fate would befall any man who accepted her hospitality, however innocent he might be when she received him.

As a result of these warnings Miss Gribble's apartment remained vacant for some years, during which time the view from the window became much restricted by the swelling of the clay-dump. Miss Gribble watched day after day as the sand spilled down, a cold gritty crust, pouring as from the sky and blocking the field of her vision. As she tidied her parlour she scowled through the window up at the clay-tip, growing mutinous against it.

'He's still throwing down the old sand,' she would mutter, and would clench her hands, impotent.

But at length there came a measure of relief from the lonely friction of her spirit with the encroaching refuse. A strange woman alighted one summer evening at the Pengarth bus stop, and, meeting Miss Gribble before any of the neighbours could drop cautionary remarks, she found the little front room exactly suited to her taste and agreed to take it for six months. She described herself as a Plymouth woman, Miss Lydia Jauncey – stout, dark-haired, in the early thirties. Miss Gribble welcomed her and for some time the two ladies lived together pleasantly, learning much of one another's sorrows and feeling drawn by mutual sympathy and respect.

But just before Christmas a letter arrived for Miss Jauncey which obviously caused her great agitation. She left Pengarth for two days, and then returned with an infant which she admitted was hers and which she had meant to abandon as its father had abandoned her. She insisted that the child should be allowed to remain with her in the cottage, but Miss Gribble naturally refused to expose herself further to the contempt of the villagers. There was a scene, during which Miss Jauncey used a great deal of bad language and Miss Gribble threw her lodger's suitcase out of the doorway.

Since then Miss Gribble alone had occupied the house under the clay-dump. The dump edged closer and Miss Gribble more resentful, writhing under the vague menace. She rebelled against the fate it seemed to impose upon her. In retaliation she ceased to attend chapel.

'No good sheltering there – the old sand is still coming down,' she complained.

And when at last this revolt broke through into her actions and she put forth her hand to crime, Miss Gribble felt the clay-dump to be the sinister, impelling agent.

The first crime that Miss Gribble committed was theft. She had become very poor and winter began with heavy rainstorms and icy gales sweeping the bare Cornish uplands. Miss Gribble often found her cottage a cheerless place, for she couldn't afford to buy enough coal to keep a fire burning all day long. There was plenty of charred furze, and even a little peat, on the surrounding moors, and she could have procured this fuel as some of her less prosperous neighbours were forced to do. But to be seen gathering sticks on the down would disclose her straightened circumstances to the whole village, and at all costs this must be avoided.

Early one Wednesday morning in November Miss Gribble lit the fire in the infants' classroom of Pengarth school, which stood less than a hundred yards from her home. Rain lashed pitilessly against the windows and the wind howled, reminding her that when she had finished baking that day she would have to let the fire die out in the cottage, as the little coal that remained in her scuttle had to last until Friday.

Miss Gribble brooded among the empty desks, peering miserably through the high, blurred windows. The clay-dump loomed vaguely across the road, its pinnacle and tip-frame hidden in mist. Through the mist the waggon was gliding out, full of sodden refuse. She heard the crash of its load, and, as she watched the lava-like stream emerge, coming inexorably down the slope, she felt the old terror seize upon her. Someone was moving amid the clouds, pouring a gritty, sour crust upon the earth, shutting her off from all warmth and pleasure ... She made a swift, blind decision, almost in panic.

Miss Gribble carried home a large lump of coal from the school coal-shed, wrapped in newspaper and concealed under her coat.

The winter passed and the thefts were repeated. Miss Gribble became more stealthy and secretive in manner, but she also experienced a warped, cunning flicker of satisfaction. She was taking her revenge. She felt sure that the removal of these small quantities of coal, once or twice a week – sometimes in her pail, carefully covered by her floor-cloth and scrubbing-brush – would not be observed.

And then came the day which marked the climax of Miss Gribble's rebellion against the movements on the clay-tip.

One dull, windy afternoon in January the headmaster, Mr

Eggardon, caught her in the act of filling a brown-paper bag with coke in the fuel-house. She had supposed that he had left the school with the other teachers half an hour earlier.

Mr Eggardon was a small, middle-aged man, rather nervous, but he showed in his shocked surprise something of the official sternness which the situation required.

'You know what might happen if I reported you,' he said, frowning through his glasses at Miss Gribble as she cowered back upon the heaped coal.

Miss Gribble didn't even nod; she was paralysed with fear, showing a hint of her mother's crazed look in her glittering eyes and blank, pinched features.

'You could be summoned – perhaps fined – as well as dismissed from your post,' said Mr Eggardon.

Lucy peered wildly, like a trapped rat, about the coal-shed, then at Mr Eggardon's face. She grew calmer.

'I know 'twas foolish – and wrong o' me,' she faltered. ''Twon't happen again, Mr Eggardon – I can promise 'ee that. But it's been so hard to manage . . .'

Through the tense silence came the crash of refuse slithering down the clay-tip, loose stones battering the trees of the hedge and bouncing into a bramble-thicket near the road. Mr Eggardon heard the boulders settle heavily. His face smouldered, but not with anger.

'I quite understand, Lucy. I don't think it'll be necessary to report you. There's a way in which you can escape that.' He smiled cunningly, moving closer to her over the bag and the spilled coke. 'Do you know, Lucy, that you are a pretty woman?'

He spoke to her as to a child, and this was a clue to his mood. The day's work had left him – as it often did – with a cloudy sensual uneasiness produced by the girl children with whom he had been cooped up for so many hours and whom he had gloatingly watched at play. He was inclined to blame the clay-dump for this obsession. It towered above the school like an obscene dribbling breast, throwing upon the classrooms a dank, clammy shadow, or reflecting sunlight in sharp dazzling splashes, unnaturally white and fervid. He felt stifled by it, his emotions pressed back upon the near-adolescent girls like a sort of refuse, a squashed, muddy awareness of young female bodies. This perverse emotion had not yet focused on any particular girl, but he had known for some time that his wife alone could not release him from the vague infantile infatuation.

And now, suddenly, the thing had pounced – the recoil towards normal adult passion with the requisite tang of the lawless and forbidden. He looked feverishly at Miss Gribble, aware of his mastery.

There could be no doubt that Miss Gribble understood his meaning. He saw first the frightened look of a child on her face – then the fascination. She had no will against him, he knew. In stooping to the lesser crime she had brought this thing upon herself. She shivered, groping with her smutted hand along the wall.

'Come back to the classroom with me, Lucy,' said Mr Eggardon, in a strained tone. 'It's warmer there and we can talk things over.'

He stepped from the doorway – furtive but with an air of deliberation. His brown overcoat flapped in the wind, but his bald head was erect and defiant.

Miss Gribble limped slowly out under the drab sky. She stared dazedly up at the clay-tip as she followed Mr Eggardon across the yard.

'Tipping more sand over me,' she whispered. 'Thee be still tipping sand ...'

Charles Lee

THE DEFEAT OF THE AMAZONS

We know not whether the rest of the world is better enlightened, but to us at Porthjulyan the ways of womankind are a profound mystery. That man's destined mate should be utterly incomprehensible to him is as strange as it is true. All Sam Jago's brilliant epigrams on the sex are, when you come to analyse them, only witty confessions of the fact. I have heard tell of a wise conclave of lawyers and doctors who once decided that a man was in no way akin to his own mother; and surely they were right. We won't deny a certain superficial resemblance as to language, diet, the disposition of features, and so forth; but probe below the surface, and what do you find? An unimaginable discrepancy. What is man? To deal, for convenience's sake, in the concrete, what is Bessie's Tom? Bessie's Tom is a rational creature, a creature of noble ideals and lofty imagination, a deft logician, a humorist of the first water – in short, Nature's masterpiece. And as Bessie's Tom is, so are we all at Penticost's, more or less. Deprive us of our ideals, our imagination, our logic, and our humour, and what should we be but gibbering apes, whom humanity would disown straightway? Has woman any of these qualities? Take humour. We go home from the club and tell our wives a merry tale of Penticost and his stool, and a bit of codgy-wax intervening. Do they laugh? I trow not. As like as not they only villify us for tormenting an inoffensive old man in his own shop. As for logic, their notorious deficiency in this respect has long been the discourse of the nations; it can only be paralleled by their utter lack of imagination. I'll give you an insight. After the great debate was over, James-over-to-shop, defeated but not convinced, carried home his cherished cat-pie and set it before his wife, seeking sympathetic support. What was the result? At the outset she caught him up and would hear no more, declaring that Thomas and Simons were both respectable men, and would never betray their customers in so senseless and disgusting a fashion. No imagination, you see. And when he tried her with his other argument, the one by which he proved that smoking wadn' no good, she showed her crass ignorance of the nature of logic by suggesting that he should at once cast his pipes in the fire, and a good riddance too.

We grant their possession of ideals of a sort – but ideals so ignoble that they are unworthy of the name. Take home life. A man's domestic ideal is a purely spiritual one – comfort; a woman's is cleanliness, which is grossly material. No wonder that spirit and matter clashing as they inevitably must, we, the heirs of the ages, take off our sea-boots on the caunce, and smoke our precious pipes in cold, draughty back kitchens. But there! as Sam Jago says:

'Woman! You read all about her in Genesis, and a pretty job she made av things, sure 'nough. Scat creation first go-off, b'lieve, and been dancing on the shards ever since. If 'twadn' for she, you and me'd be in the Garden this day, stroking the lions and tickling the tigers.'

We notice this, that women do markedly resemble cows. Take them singly, and they are more or less amenable, if not to reason, at least to gentle persuasion and tender discipline. But in the herd they are all horns and hoofs; on the least provocations, on no provocation at all, it's up heels and a mad cooce round the field. Then there's no holding them; over the gate with you, unless you've a mind to be gored and trampled. In my brief description of our little town I omitted all mention of Juliana's; purposely, since Penticost's, of which I aspire to be the humble mouthpiece, has reason to regard Juliana's as a public nuisance, a foul blot or excrescence on our community, about which, for our fair fame, it were best to keep silence before the world. But now I have a tale to tell of grievous peril, of siege, of seeming rout and glorious victory, wherein Juliana's figures as the fell adversary. So of Juliana's I must speak perforce, or leave my tale untold.

Juliana, with the noblest mangle in the place, does the washing for our aristocracy and our go'bout women. At her gate the feet of all our wives are stayed when scandal is hatching. In fact, Juliana's is a kind of distorted feminine counterfeit of Penticost's; and over against Penticost's it is set, with the width of the street between. But while Penticost's, with characteristic male modesty, burrows half underground, Juliana's looks brazenly down on the street from an altitude. The rites of the mangle are performed in an inner room, of which, as no man is allowed to penetrate to it, I can give you no description, only hinting darkly that more things than sheets and towcers are mangled there; but the washing is done in the front yard, in the sight of all the world. Now this yard is planned on the model of a fortified place; it is approached by steps, which are barred at the top by an iron wicket, and round it runs a goodly rampart of stone, breast-high within, and towering over the heads of those without. From this commanding situation the fair garrison can not only pour their broadside on the adversary as he passes, but rake him fore and aft as he approaches, and retreats, from the inn far up the street right down to the edge of the sea. And they have the advantage of attacking from above – an advantage you will be quick to appreciate if you have ever parleyed from the pavement with a cabman on his lofty perch. Add to this that the general of the Amazons, Juliana herself, is a big woman, whose perpetually rolled-up sleeves display a pair of muscular arms, whose voice is of extraordinary volume and penetration, and whose temper the fumes of the washing-tray have not mellowed, to say the least, and you will realize what a power in the land Juliana's can be in times of excitement.

Now, while our sweet enemies confine themselves to the fashioning and adorning of true tales about one another and ourselves we make no complaint. 'Tis the pretty way of the sex, and can no more be helped or hindered than spring tides or kittens. But, as I hinted before, they are subject to periodical fits of dementia, during which the orderly life of the town is disorganized, domestic peace takes wing, and even the cloistral seclusion of Penticost's is not exempt, as you will see, from peril of disturbance.

Some time ago Orlando Chynoweth – stuttering Orlando – had the misfortune to come into a legacy of seventy pounds. Straightway Minnie Trupp up and married him. A dashy piece was Minnie, of the variety known to us as 'crame 'pon pilchards' – a flower garden in her hat, and generally enough mud on her boots and petticoats to teel the same in. We didn't expect great things of the match, and we were not disappointed. We are accustomed to give bridegrooms at least a month's leave from club attendance; but barely a fortnight had elapsed from the wedding-day when Orlando reappeared at Penticost's. We rallied him wittily, and the sickly grin which was his only answer spoke volumes to every married man among us. Bessie's Tom cried truce to raillery, and made sympathetic inquiry.

'Tongue, Orlando?'

'Tongue 'tis,' stammered Orlando. 'T-tongue till c-cows come ome, and then she t-talk in her sleep be-bezide.'

'Ah,' said Tom, winking on the company. 'And your speech being afflicted, like, you can't answer back so smart as you might; edn' that so, Orlando?'

'Haven't spit a c-clean word out for a week,' said Orlando. 'Don't get t-time.'

'Ah,' said Tom. 'A man with your affliction didn' ought to marry, Orlando, that's plain. "Just cause or impediment," the Prayer Book say; "impediment" – that's aimed at 'ee straight. Have 'ee tried swearing? I mind your dees were always gressed, like, than your Christian speech.'

'T-true,' said Orlando mournfully, 'they were. But n-now they'm like the rest – snails c-crawling through t-tar.'

'I've heard tell,' said James-over-to-shop, putting his ponderous shoulder to the joke, 'av a man that was plagued that way, and he put his wife snug in the asylum in a year. Never said nothing, frall her holling and balling, but just sissed like a cat all the while – like this, *ftts!* – to everything she said.

And in a year she was as mad as a curley. Sim'me you could do that easy, Orlando.'

Orlando shook his head hopelessly.

'Try the stick,' said somebody.

Again Orlando shook his head. 'She'd have me up,' he said.

'Smash the cloam,' said another.

'Aw no, don't 'ee do that, my dear,' cried Penticost, his hammer suspended in mid-air. 'There's a man up to Tregarry did that, and the woman put a crust round the shards, and baked 'em and give 'em to him to carr' to his work. They call en the Shardy-pasty man to this day, and the last state av that man is worse than the first.'

Sam Jago looked up, his eyes twinkling.

'Orlando,' he said, 'how don't 'ee put her head in a sack?'

Orlando peered doubtfully at Sam.

'N-no, Sam,' he said, 'you d-don't mane that, do 'ee?'

It was a treat to see how serious Sam made himself of a sudden.

' 'Tis the only course for 'ee to steer, Orlando,' he said with grave emphasis, 'your natural weapon (that's your tongue, Orlando) being av no use. The stick – that's assault and battery; but a sack – a commojous flour-sack, now – 'tis warm and soft and soothing. Heave en over her head, and pull en well down over her arms, and skip out av the way av her legs, and you'm all right. She can't holler and she can't use her fistes; lev her be so for a bit, and she'll soon see the error av her ways.'

Orlando pondered, while we contained ourselves as best we could.

'I've a t-terrible mind to try,' he said finally.

'Do 'ee now,' urged the persuasive Sam; 'and if so be all do go well, we'll bless 'ee, and lay in a stock – a sack to every man. 'Twill be the salvation av the town.'

Orlando sat in deep meditation. Then, suddenly, without another word, he got up and went out.

'My life!' exclaimed Bessie's Tom. 'He'll do ut! He've gone to fetch the sack! Sam Jago, you'm a masterpiece!'

How we laughed! But a peep into futurity would have twisted our faces the other way.

Orlando did it, sure enough. From Penticost's door he went straight over to shop, and thence emerged with mild determination on his face and an empty flour-sack on his arm. Home he went. The sack caught Minnie's eye; and her instant and particular inquiries, remaining unanswered, resolved themselves into a flood of comprehensive vituperation. Orlando gave her two minutes' law, and then proceeded gravely and faithfully to carry out Sam's instructions – not without difficulty, for the sack was none of the largest, and Minnie was a stout young woman and well set up. Then he went out and shut the door behind him. Presently a neighbour, hearing mysterious sounds, peeped in and beheld a strange headless figure curiously gyrating round the room in an accompaniment of muffled squealing music, as of distant bagpipes. After some labour Minnie was extracted, breathless, dishevelled, and ghastly white; for the flour-sack had not been entirely emptied of its contents. Powdered as she was from head to waist – an incomplete image of Lot's wife – she rushed into the street, tore down-along, and captured Orlando just as he was turning into Penticost's again to report progress. I am not going to tell you what happened next. It is the reverse of creditable to our town that such a spectacle of manly humiliation – humiliation of the grossest kind – should have taken place before the public eye; though at the time, to be sure, we laughed as we had never laughed before.

Next day we met to laugh again, heedless of a certain murmurous agitation that buzzed and swelled about Juliana's yard, as about a hive in swarming time. For, as we knew presently, the sex was up in arms, and the little domestic incident we were quietly chuckling over had been elevated across the way into grave political importance. In the talk overnight, some indiscreet male had divulged the source of Orlando's action. That was enough; by the mysterious alchemy of the feminine brain Sam Jago's innocent bit of waggery was transmuted into a deep organized plot against wifely rights and privileges. The suspicious hatred of clubs natural to women, and the rankling jealousy of Penticost's which, thanks to Penticost himself, is always ahead of Juliana's in the matter of news, were ready at hand to feed the flame.

The first mutterings of the storm passed, as I said, unnoticed. But presently, as we sat placidly chewing the cud of the joke, we heard a smart shower of taunts and execrations come pattering down from above, and immediately afterwards Bessie's Tom came hastily in, shaking his ears.

'Pip-ph!' he exclaimed. 'The women's gone clean mazed, I think. Such profaning I never heard in all my married days. Hark to 'em – like a passel av gulls on a rock!'

'What is it?' was asked.

'What is ut? Minnie Chynoweth 'tis, and Orlando, and a flour-sack, and all av us. And Minnie's all Foxe's Martyrs complete, and we'm the persecuting Papishers. That's av ut.'

We reconnoitred. To the door we did not venture, but by leaning over the table and peering up through the lower panes of the window we could just take in the top of Juliana's rampart. We saw a row of bobbing heads with swiftly moving jaws and red, furious faces, ever and anon turned menacingly in our direction; and not a man among us but jerked discreetly back after the first peep. We looked at one another, and as we looked, the silence in the shop, which was as the silence of interstellar space, was pierced by shrill meteors, imperfectly discerned, but obviously of dire import.

'There's trouble brewing, b'lieve,' said James-over-to-shop, weakly enough.

'The sperit av the devil's in their stummicks!' exclaimed Sam Jago, whose concise vigour of speech never deserts him.

'The time av war and tribulation is at hand,' prophesied Penticost, 'when your owld men shall not slumber in their beds and your young men shall hear voices in the night.'

'Tay-time's at hand anyway,' said Bessie's Tom, with a brisk effort to disperse the gloom. 'Who's going home-along out av this?'

Nobody stirred, and James remarked that we were safest where we were.

'Don't be so sure o' that, my dears,' said Penticost, who was peeping out of window. 'If that edn' Juliana coming across – '

There was a confused sound of shuffling feet as we rose to escape. But Juliana's commanding figure already blocked the doorway. With mottled arms akimbo she stood, contemptuously surveying us. Then she spoke, with a sudden scream that jumped us. I venture to punctuate a speech that was innocent of all stops save those that exhausted nature demanded.

'Men! Call yourselves men? A nest av hadders! Stuffle your lawful wives, will 'ee, you blaggards-worse-than-heathen-Turks? Ben't lef to spake in our own houses, ben't us? Give us the sack – that's av ut, eh? Ah-h we've ben too soft with 'ee! But stank on us agin, and we'll bruise your heels proper, I assure 'ee. Neighbours!' she turned about, dramatically beckoning, 'step up and look upon 'em.' Maenad faces geeked through the window; 'twas like a horrid nightmare. 'Look upon 'em, neighbours. They came to us soft-soaping and putting their heads under their wings, the hadders, so's you don't know which way they'm going to fly next, and when they've catched us they put us into sacks – into flour-sacks they put us, and so whiten our heads before their time, the scheming hadders! Don't grin upon me, Sam Jago!' Sam had donned the patient smile of the good man frowned on by fortune. 'The likes of you edn' fit to to look a h-honest woman in the face, lev alone mock her. You'm the worst o' the bunch, and if I was Sarann Jago I'd lev 'ee know. Put 'ee in a sack yourself, I would – ess, a coal-sack; and then you wouldn' be blacker'n what you be already. Eyah-h! A nest av grizzling hadders!'

' 'Ere, missus!' It was Bessie's Tom who spoke, with a courage born of desperation. ' 'Ere, missus, this won't do. Agin regulations, you see.'

'What do the lazy pauper mane?' inquired Juliana.

Bessie's Tom turned very red, and it was a trembling hand that he raised and pointed to our club rules hanging on the wall.

'Rule three,' he stammered. 'No women allowed. There 'tis.'

Juliana strode across the shop, taking no more notice of

Penticost, as she upset him, than if he had been a worm. The next moment Tom's own rules were cast in his face in the shape of a crumpled ball.

'That for your rules,' remarked Juliana, as the missile flew. She strode back to the door and faced on us again.

'Sim'me you'm mazed!' gasped Tom.

Juliana dropped a mocking curtsey.

'A wake woman if you plaise,' she said, 'but sound in body *and* in mind. Siss so long as you've a mind to, hadders! You waan't drive *me* to the asylum.' Her eye was on the guilty, squirming James-over-to-shop. Was nothing hid from this terrible person? 'A wake woman, but my conscience is clane, and I can stand up agin the lot av 'ee, and call 'ee heathen Turks and hadders and everything but men, and there edn' one among 'ee that can flip out his tongue to call me out av *my* name. Fah! I scorn 'ee. Not one av 'ee edn' fit to look a h-honest woman in the face.' Here Juliana, with a fine sense of dramatic effect, began to back out. 'Not one av 'ee but what 'ud steal his wife's dead shoe-strings, give en the chance. No women allowed? We'll see 'bout that, won't us, neighbours? We've borne with you and your club long enough.' Light streamed through the unobstructed doorway, but Juliana's voice still assailed our ears. 'A nest av roaring hadders, and call itself a club! We'll club 'em, as I'm a Christian woman!' The voice grew faint, as Juliana and her following retired to their fortress; but still we caught fragments:

'Sacks! ... Stuffle their wives! ... Turks! ... Hadders!'

We sat and stared at one another in blank silence. James forced a weak laugh.

'He-he! Amoosing to hear her! Quite amoosing, I should say.'

'That woman,' exclaimed Bessie's Tom, the sting of an injurious appellation rankling within him, 'is a complete venom; that's what she is – a complete venom. Mind what I say; a complete venom, that woman is.'

'What did I tell 'ee, my dears?' cried Penticost. 'A time av war and tribulation, those were my words; you heard me spake.'

'My missus,' said Sam Jago, 'sent my Sunday shirt to the wash this week. My name's stitched on the tail av ut in red cotton for all to see. My heart do ache for that shirt.'

Bessie's Tom turned savagely on him. 'That's very well, Sam Jago,' he said. 'You're a smart joker, no doubt, but I ask you this. Who landed us in this here mess, with his smart jokes? Where's our refuge in time av trouble now? That venom's ben here once; she'll be here agin; and I put the fault on you – ess, I condemn 'ee to your face!'

A fresh gust of invective shook the windows.

'Another hadder coming,' said Sam the imperturbable. 'Ah! The deaf hadder this time,' he added, as Archelaus Trudgeon entered, beaming and boisterous as usual.

'Hullo!' he roared – he has to roar to hear himself speak. 'What's up with you all? You'm looking like you done a roguery, and were having it out with owld Conscience. Wisht you'm looking: stick a knife into 'ee, you'd get no blood. What's up?'

'Why, Archelaus,' said James, 'didn't you notice nothing as you come along, no commotion, like, up over?'

No; Achelaus had noticed nothing unusual. We enlightened him briefly. He laughed.

'Bless my poor ears!' he shouted. 'They do me good sarvice, frall they edn' no use. The women can beller till the cows come home, frall I care. They can't reach me – I'm blockaded, like.'

We found it in our hearts to envy the impenetrable armour which had brought Archelaus unscathed through storm and tempest.

Suddenly Sam Jago slapped his knee.

'I have en!' he cried.

'What have 'ee?'

'A way out av this. Come 'ee here, Archelaus.'

Archelaus is so deaf that whispers and shouts are all one to him. But let him watch a man's mouth, and he can tell what that man is saying by the movement of his lips. Sam, who loves an impish mystification, now baffled our curiosity by making a completely voiceless communication to Archelaus, who punctuated it with tantalizing nods and explosions of laughter. The colloquy ended, Sam rose and said:

'Me and Archelaus is going outside. They that want to go home can go; they that want to see a bit of fun can stay. Now, forlorn hope, forward!'

Sam and Archelaus marched out. The storm burst forth anew; for a few moments it raged, and then we heard the bellow of Archelaus above it, dominant, supreme, like the sound of thunder over pelting rain.

'Ah, Juliana, my dear, good afternoon. How's your health? Sim'me you edn' looking so well as you might. You women drink too much tay, that's the truth. I say tay,' he added in an aside to Sam – his asides are louder, if anything, than his direct speech – 'I say tay to save the woman's feelings; but brandy's the true tale, as all the world do know.'

A petrified silence. Then Juliana collected herself, and Archelaus's private character fell in rags about his feet.

'Did Juliana speak?' asked Archelaus, all affability. 'Would 'ee mind saying that over again, Juliana, and spake up, if you plaise. I'm a bit deafer than usual to-day – or else,' he bawled in Sam's ear, 'or else the woman's too far gone to speak plain.'

The raving incoherence of Juliana's reply betrayed her plight, like the disorderly rally of half-defeated troops. Archelaus only shook his head wistfully.

'I know 'tis something int'resting, Juliana; but I'm properly deaf to-day, sure 'nough. Poor woman!' he murmured, and a stentorian murmur it was. 'Local option – that's what we want.'

'She glazed,' said Sam, describing the scene afterwards, 'she glazed, and guggled, and swayzed her hands, and then, flop! indoors, and door shut home.'

Archelaus smiled pensively and singled out another Amazon. But I needn't describe the details of the combat. As ultimate victors we can afford to be generous, and to be sure Archelaus was not nice in his choice of weapons. The buried scandals that saw the light in the next few minutes had best be buried again in decorous silence. The fight was over. Deserted by their leader, and finding their adversary absolutely invulnerable against their only weapon, the rebels soon broke and fled within doors, leaving us – we were all outside by then, even Penticost in apron and shirt-sleeves – masters of the field. Archelaus received our congratulations, nor were we backward in thanking the ingenious Sam.

Up to now we have had no further trouble with Juliana's.

Daphne du Maurier

THE LORDLY ONES

I

Ben was thought to be backward. He could not speak. When he tried to form words sounds came, harsh and ugly, and he did not know what to do with his tongue. He pointed when he wanted something, or fetched it for himself. They said he was tongue-tied, and that in a few years' time he would be taken to hospital and something could be done. His mother said he was sharp enough, he took in what you told him all right, and knew good from bad, but he was stubborn, he did not take kindly to 'no'. Because of his silence they forgot to explain things to him, arrivals and departures and changes of plan, and his world was made up of whims, the whims of older people. He would be told to dress for no reason, or to go out into the street to play; or some toy was denied him that had been given him an hour before.

When the stress became too great to bear he opened his mouth, and the sound that came out of it alarmed him even more than it alarmed his parents. Why did it rise? How did it come? Then someone, usually his mother, picked him up and shut him away in the cupboard under the stairs, amongst the mackintoshes and the shopping baskets, and he could hear her calling through the keyhole, 'You'll stop there until you're quiet!' The noise would not be quelled. It did not belong to him. The anger was a force that had to have its way.

Later, crouched beside the keyhole, spent and tired, he would hear the noise die away, and peace would come to the cupboard. The fear would then be that his mother would go away and forget to let him out, and he would rattle the handle of the door to remind her. A flash of her skirt through the keyhole meant reassurance, and he would sit down and wait until the grinding of the key in the lock spelt release. Then he would step out into the daylight, blinking, and glance up at his mother to gauge her mood. If she was dusting or sweeping, she ignored him. All would be well until the next moment of anger or frustration, when the performance would be repeated – either the cupboard again, or his bedroom with no tea, his toys taken from him. The way to ensure against their anger was to please his parents, but this could not always be done, for the strain was too great. In the middle of play, absorbed, he forgot their commands.

One day suitcases were packed and he was dressed in his warmest clothes, although it was early spring, and they left the house in Exeter where he had been born and went to the moors. There had been talk about the moors for some weeks past.

'It's different up there from what it is down here,' his parents would say. Somehow cajolery and threats were combined: one day he was to be lucky, another he had better not get out of sight once they moved. The very words 'the moors' sounded dark and ominous, a sort of threat.

The bustle of departure added to fear. The rooms of his home, suddenly bare, were unfamiliar, and his mother, impatient, scolded him ceaselessly. She too wore different clothes, and an ugly hat. It clung round her ears, changing the shape of her face. As they left home she seized his hand, dragging it, and bewildered he watched his parents as they sat, anxious themselves, among the boxes and the packing-cases. Could it be that they were uncertain too? That none of them knew where they were going?

The train bore them away, but he could not see out of the windows. He was in the middle seat between his parents, and only the tops of trees told him of country. His mother gave him an orange he did not want. Forgetting caution, he threw it on the floor. She smacked him hard. The smack coincided with a sudden jolt of the train and the darkness of a tunnel, the two combined suggesting the cupboard under the stairs and punishment. He opened his mouth and the cry came from it.

As always, the sound brought panic. His mother shook him and he bit his tongue. The carriage was full of strangers. An old man behind a newspaper frowned. A woman, showing her teeth, offered him a green sweet. No one could be trusted. His cries became louder still and his mother, her face red, picked him up and took him into the rattling corridor. 'Will you be quiet?' she shouted. All was confusion. Fatigue seized him, and he crumpled. Rage and fear made him stamp his feet, clad in new brown-laced shoes, adding to the clatter. The sound, coming from his belly, ceased; only the gasp for breath, the stifling sobs, told him that the pain was with him, but for what reason he could not tell.

'He's tired,' somebody said.

They were back again in the carriage, and room was made for him by the window. The world outside went past. Houses clustered. He saw a road with cars upon it, and fields, then high banks swaying up and down. With the gradual slowing of the train his parents stood up and began to reach for their belongings. The fluster of departure was with them once again. The train ground to a standstill. Doors opened and clanged, and a porter shouted. They tumbled out on to the platform.

His mother clutched him by the hand and he peered up at her face, and at his father's too, to try and discover from their expressions whether what was happening was customary, expected by them, and if they knew what was to happen now. They climbed into a car, the luggage piled about them, and through the gathering dusk he understood that they were not back again in the town from which they had come, but in open country. The air bit sharp, cool-smelling, and his father turned with a laugh to him and said, 'Can you smell the moors?'

The moors ... He tried to see from the window of the car, but a suitcase balked his view. His mother and father were talking amongst themselves. 'She'll surely have put on a kettle for us, and give us a hand,' said his mother; and, 'We'll not unpack everything tonight. It will take days to get straight.'

'I don't know,' said his father. 'It's surprising how different it will seem in a small house.'

The road twisted, the car swaying at the corners. Ben felt sick. This would be the final disgrace. The sourness was coming and he shut his mouth. But the urge was too strong, and it came from him in a burst, splaying out over the car.

'Oh, no, that's too much,' cried his mother, and she pushed him from her knee against the sharp end of the suitcase, bruising his cheek. His father tapped the window. 'Stop . . . the boy's been sick.' The shame, the inevitable confusion of sickness, and with it the sudden cold so that he shivered. Everywhere lay the evidence of his shame, and an old cloth, evil-smelling, was produced by the driver to wipe his mouth.

On again, but slower now, standing between his father's knees, and at last the rutty, bumpy road came to an end and a light was in front of them.

'It's not raining, that's one blessing,' said his mother. 'Don't ask me what we'll do here when it does.'

The small house stood alone, light in the windows. Ben, blinking and shivering still, climbed down from the car. He stood looking about him as the luggage was lifted out. For the moment he was ignored. The small house faced a green, smooth as a carpet in the dark, and behind the house, which was thatched, were humped black hills. The sharp sweet smell he had noticed on leaving the station was stronger still. He lifted his face to sniff the air. Where were the moors? He saw them as a band of brothers, powerful and friendly.

'Come on in, my handsome,' said a woman from the house, and he did not draw back when she bore down upon him, welcoming and large, and led him into the paved kitchen. A stool was drawn up to the table and a glass of milk put in front of him. He sipped it slowly, his eyes sizing up the flagged kitchen, the scullery pump, the small latticed windows.

'Is he shy?' asked the woman, and the whispers began, the grown-up talk, something about his tongue. His father and his mother looked embarrassed and awkward. The woman glanced back again, in pity, and Ben dipped his face in his glass of milk. Then they forgot him, the dull talk passed him by, and unwatched he was able to eat bread and butter without hindrance, help himself to biscuits, his sickness gone and appetite returned.

'Oh yes, watch out for them,' the woman said. 'They're

terrible thieves. They'll come by night and raid your larder, if you leave it open. Especially if it continues cold like this. Watch out for snow.'

So the moors were robbers. A band of robbers wandering by night. Ben remembered the comic paper that his father had bought him, with the ogre's face upon the cover. Yet they could not be like that, for the woman was saying something about their fine looks.

'They won't hurt you,' she said, 'they're friendly enough.' This to Ben, who watched her, puzzled. Then she laughed, and everyone got up to clear the tea, to unpack, to settle.

'Now then, don't wander off,' said his mother. 'If you don't behave you'll go straight to bed.'

'He can't come to harm,' the woman said. 'I've latched the gate.'

When they were not looking Ben slipped out of the open door and stood outside. The car that had brought them had disappeared. The silence, so different from the noise of the street at home, was like the silence that came when his parents were not angry. It wrapped itself about him. The little lights winking from the other cottages, away down the green, were distant as stars. He went and rested his chin on the gate, and stared into the peaceful darkness. He felt himself at rest. He had no wish to go indoors, to unpack his toys.

There must be a farm somewhere close, for the smell of manure mixed with the cold air, and a cow lowed from a stall. These discoveries were pleasing to him. Mostly he thought about the moors, the thieves of the night, but somehow they did not frighten him: the reassurance of the woman's smile and the way his parents had laughed showed that the moors were not to be feared. Anyway, it was to come to the moors that they had packed their things and left home. It was this that had been discussed now for so many weeks. 'The boy will like the moors,' people had said, back at home. 'He'll grow strong, up there. There's nothing like the moors for giving appetite.'

It was true. Ben had eaten five pieces of bread and butter and three biscuits. Already the band of brothers had shown power. He wondered how close they were to the house, if they lurked, smiling encouragement, beyond those dark humped hills.

A sudden thought occurred to him. If food was put out for the thieves, they would not steal. They would eat it and be thankful. He went back inside the kitchen, and voices from upstairs told him that his parents and their helper were unpacking and out of the way. The table had been cleared, but the tea-things, unwashed, were piled in the scullery. There was a loaf of bread, a cake still uncut, and the remaining biscuits. Ben filled his pockets with the biscuits, and carried the loaf of bread and the cake. He went to the door, and so down the path to the gate. He set the food on the ground, and concentrated upon the task of unfastening the gate. It was easier than he had expected. He lifted the latch and the gate swung back. Then he picked up the loaf and the cake and went out on to the green. The thieves made for the green first, the woman had said. They prowled there, looking for odds and ends, and if nothing tempted them, and no one shouted and drove them away, they would come to the cottages.

Ben walked a few yards on to the green and set out the food. The thieves could not miss it if they came. They would be grateful, and go back to their lair in the black hills well satisfied. Looking back, he could see the figures of his parents moving backwards and forwards in the bedrooms upstairs. He jumped, to try the feel of the grass under his feet, more pleasing than a pavement, and lifted his face once more to feel the air. It came, cold and clean, from the hills. It was as though the moors knew, the thieves knew, that a feast was prepared for them. Ben was happy.

He ran back to the house, and as he did so his mother came downstairs.

'Come on, bed,' she said.

Bed? So soon? His face protested, but she was not to be moved.

'There's enough to do without you round my heels,' she complained.

She pulled him up the steep little stairway after her, and he saw his own bed, miraculously brought from home, standing in a corner of the small room lit by candlelight. It was close to the window, and his first thought was that he would be able to look out from his bed and watch when the thieves came. This interest kept him quiet while his mother helped him to undress, but she was rougher than usual. Her nails got caught in a button and scratched his skin, and when he whimpered she said sharply, 'Oh, be quiet, do.' The candle, stuck in a saucer, threw a monster shadow on the ceiling. It flounced his mother's figure to a grotesque shape.

'I'm too tired to wash you tonight,' she said. 'You'll have to stay dirty.'

His father's voice called up the stairs. 'What did you do with the bread and the cake?' he called. 'I can't find them.'

'They're on the scullery table,' she answered. 'I'll be down in a minute.'

Ben realized that his parents would search for the food to put it away. Instinct warned him to make no sound. She finished undressing him, and he went straight to his bed without delay.

'Now I don't want to hear any more from you tonight,' she said. 'If you make a sound I'll send your father to you.'

She went downstairs, taking the candle with her.

Ben was used to darkness, but, even so, the room was unfamiliar. He had not yet had time to learn the shape. Was there a chair? A table? Was it long or square? He lay back in bed biting at the blanket. He heard footsteps underneath his window. Sitting up, he looked between the curtains, and saw the woman who had welcomed them walk down the path, through the gate, and away down the road. She was carrying a lantern. She did not cross the green. The lantern danced as she moved, and soon she was swallowed up in the darkness. Only the bobbing light betrayed her passage.

Ben lay back again in bed, disturbed by the flickering lantern and voices raised in argument below. He heard his mother come upstairs. She threw open the door and stood there, holding the candle, the monstrous shadow behind her.

'Did you touch the tea-things?' she said.

Ben made the sound his parents understood as a denial, but his mother was not satisfied. She came to the bed and, shielding her eyes, stared down at him.

'The bread and cake have gone,' she said. 'The biscuits too. You took them, didn't you? Where did you hide them?'

As always, the rising voice brought out antagonism. Ben shrank against his pillow and shut his eyes. It was not the way to question him. If she had smiled and made a joke of it, it would have been different.

'Very well,' she said. 'I'll settle you, young man.'

She called for his father. Despair seized Ben. It would mean a whipping. He began to cry. Explanation was beyond him. He heard his father stump up the stairs and come into the room, his shadow monstrous too. The pair of them filled the small, unfamiliar room.

'Do you want a hiding?' his father asked. 'Now then, what did you do with the bread?'

His father's face was ugly, worn with fatigue. The packing and unpacking, all the hustle of removal, of starting the new life, had meant strain. Ben sensed this, but he could not give way. He opened his mouth and yelled. The cry roused the full fatigue and anger of the father. Resentment, too. Why must his son be dumb?

'That's enough of that,' he said.

He jerked Ben out of bed and stripped the pyjama legs. Then he laid the wriggling child across his knee. The hand found the flesh and hit hard, with all its force. Ben screamed louder still. The relentless hand, so large and powerful, smote and smote again.

'That's learned him, that's enough,' said his mother. 'There's neighbours across the green. We don't want trouble.'

'He must know who's master,' said his father, and it was not until his own hand ached with the force of the blows that he gave up and pushed Ben from his knee.

'Now holler if you dare,' he said, rising abruptly, and Ben, face downwards on the bed, his sobs long ceased, heard them withdraw, felt the candle go, knew that the room was empty. Everything was pain. He tried to move his legs, but the movement sent a warning message to his brain. The pain travelled from his buttocks up his spine to the top of his head. No sound came from his lips now, only a trickle of tears from his eyes. Perhaps if he lay quite still the pain would go. He could not cover himself with the blanket, and the cold air found him, bringing its own dull ache.

Little by little the pain numbed. The tears dried on his cheeks. He had no thoughts at all, lying there on his face. He had forgotten the cause of his beating. He had forgotten the band of brothers, the thieves, the moors. If in a little while there could be nothing, let nothing come.

2

He awoke suddenly, every sense alert. The moon shone through the gap in the curtains. At first he thought that everything was still, and the movement from the green outside told him they were there. They had come. He knew. Slowly, painfully, he dragged himself across his bed and so to the window. He pulled at the curtains. The white night showed him the wonder. The thieves were there, the lordly ones. Not as the woman had described them, but more beautiful. A little group, intent upon his offering. There was the mother, with two children, and another mother just behind, with a taller child, playing by himself. Two others ran round in circles, delighting in the snow, for with them the snow had come, turning the green white. That must be the father, watching. But he was not angry, like Ben's father: he was beautiful like the mothers and the children, beautiful and wise. He was staring at the window. He had already seen Ben, and then, to show his appreciation of the cake placed ready for him, he touched it gently and moved away, letting the son play with it instead.

It was the time of night when no one moves. Ben knew nothing of time, but instinct told him that his parents had long been in bed, and that morning would not come for many hours.

He watched them, the moors, the lordly ones. They were not thieves at all, they were far too proud. They ate with delicacy what Ben had given them, and they did not attempt to come near to the house, or prowl, as the woman had said. Like Ben, they did not speak. They talked by signal. The father, in command, moved his head, and leaving the food the mothers summoned their children, and the whole company settled themselves on the green, in the snow, to wait for morning. Their supreme disdain of the sleeping houses showed itself to Ben as contempt of authority. They made their own laws.

Ben lowered himself from his bed. His buttocks and back were still very sore, and the cold night had stiffened him, lying as he had done without a cover. Nevertheless, he began to put on his clothes. He dressed slowly, not yet accustomed to doing it quite alone, but finally he satisfied himself that he was ready, although his jersey was back to front. Luckily his wellington boots were in the scullery. They had been among the first things to be unpacked.

He could see his room clearly now, for the moonlight turned it to day. There were no strange bulges or shapes. It was just a room, small and plain. The door-latch was high above his head, so he dragged a chair beneath it and stood on it to lift the latch.

Cunningly he crept down the narrow stair. Below in the kitchen it was still dark, but instinct led him to the scullery, and to the corner where his boots waited. He put them on. The larder was only a cupboard, part of the scullery, and the door was ajar. His mother, in her anger, must have forgotten to close it. Deliberately he took the last loaf, intended for breakfast, and then repeated his performance with the chair beneath the latch of the front door. There were bolts here too to be withdrawn. If his parents heard him, he was lost. He climbed down from the chair. The door lay open. The white night was before him, the great moon benign, and the lordly ones were waiting on the green. It was green no longer, but glistening white.

Softly, his boots lightly crunching the snow, Ben tiptoed down the path and lifted the latch of the gate. The sound roused the watchers on the green. One of the mothers looked up, and although she said nothing her movements warned the father, and he too turned his head. They waited to see what Ben would do. Perhaps, thought Ben, they hoped for further gifts: they had not brought food with them, and were hungry still.

He walked slowly towards them, holding out the loaf. The mother rose to her feet, and the children too. The action roused the others, and in a moment the little company, who had settled themselves for sleep, seemed ready to march once more. They did not try to take the bread from Ben. Some sense of delicacy, perhaps, forbade it. He wanted to show generosity to them and to flaunt his parents at the same time, so, tearing the loaf in two, he went to the smallest child, not much taller than himself, and offered him part of it. This surely would be understood.

The little moor came forward and took the bread, watching Ben when he had eaten it, and then he shook his hair out of his eyes, for he was wild and unkempt, and glanced at his mother. She did not do anything, she did not speak to him, and Ben, encouraged, offered her the other half of the loaf. She took it from him. Their silence pleased Ben, for it was something he understood and shared with them.

The mother had gold hair, like her ragged son, but the older boy was dark. Relationships were confusing, because there was another mother – or could it be an aunt? – who was standing quite close to the father, and a little apart, not taking much notice of anyone, was surely the gran, so grey and thin, who looked as if she did not care for the snow, but would have been more at her ease before a good warm fire. Ben wondered at their roaming ways. What made them wander, rather than stay at home? They were not thieves, he was sure they were not thieves.

Then the father gave a signal. He turned, and slowly, majestically, led the way down the green. The others followed, the children dancing, glad to be on the move again, and the old gran, hobbling, brought up the rear. Ben watched them, then glanced back at the sleeping house. Decision came to him. He was not going to stay with the parents who did not love him. He was going to follow the moors, the lordly ones.

Ben ran across the crunching snow in the wake of his chosen companions. The old gran looked over her shoulder as she heard him coming, but she did not mind. She seemed to accept him. Ben ran until he caught up with the mother he liked best, the one with the golden hair and the ragged son, and when he was beside her she gave him a friendly nod of the head to show that he was now of the company. Ben trudged beside her in the snow. The father, still in front, was making for the hills, but he had a fine instinct for avoiding the deeper snow. He picked his way along a track, drifts on either side, and came at last to a high ridge where the world stretched wide and far on either side. The green was a long way below. Soon it was lost to sight. There were no houses in this wild country, lit by moonlight. Ben was warm from his climb, and so were his companions. Their breath went from them all like smoke in the frosted air.

What now? They looked to the father for instructions. He seemed to debate the move within himself. He glanced to right and to left. Then he decided to continue along the ridge, and once more led the way, with the family following.

The children dragged a little, for they were getting tired, and Ben, to encourage them, jumped and skipped, forgetting his bruised, stiff back. The pain made him cry out, and the cry startled the golden mother, who, staring at him, spoke to him. Was she asking a question? Ben did not understand her language. He thought that the noises in his throat must have told the mother that his back was stiff, for she seemed reassured and slowed her walk to his. Ben was relieved. He did not want to have to hobble in the rear with the old gran.

Presently the ridge sloped to an old trackway, banked high on either side with snow, and the father stopped here, making as though to camp. He stared across the wastes to the line of distant hills, and did not move. He must be thinking very deeply, decided Ben; he did not want to talk to the others. The mothers wandered around in circles, and then found a resting-place for the children on firm ground against a bank of frozen snow. The old gran, discontented, could not settle. She found the night air cold. Ben wondered what he should do. His legs were aching and he was as tired as the gran. He watched the children curl up in a patch of snow. If they can do that, he thought to himself, I suppose I can too. But they are used to sleeping on the ground, and I am not.

Then the mother, the one he liked, decided to settle by her son. Her broad, comfortable body reminded Ben of the woman who had welcomed him and his parents the night before at the thatched house on the green. She had been kindly too. But this mother was beautiful, more beautiful by far than his own mother. He hesitated a moment, then he crept forward and crouched against her. Would she be angry? Would she push him away?

She did not look at him. She did not speak. She let him understand that he could lie there, against her, and receive her warmth. Her good body smell was comforting. He snuggled close, his head against her shoulder, and put up his hand to touch her hair. She shook her head gently, and sighed. Ben closed his eyes, eased by the warmth, the comfort, the tender understanding of the mother and the reassurance of the father, still watching the far hills. He was the guardian of his sons, he would never beat them. They were all of one company, these moors, not the band of brothers he had imagined, but a family, a tribe, belonging one to the other. He would never leave them, the lordly ones.

3

The sun came over the hills in splendour, and Ben opened his eyes. In a moment it was broad day. Already the old gran was on the move, hobbling about on her stiff legs. Her example put the others to shame, and they rose in turn, the children reluctantly, for they could have done with an hour or two more of sleep. No one had breakfast, and Ben was hungry. What was to be done about food? The bread he had brought with him had all been finished on the green. Uneasily, he remembered that the woman had called them thieves. Perhaps, after all, it was true. They were going to wait until night, and then descend to a village and either beg for bread or steal it. What about the children? Would they last through the day?

Ben stood up and stamped his feet for warmth. Then he stared. The little ragged son, who must surely be of an age with himself, was feeding from his mother. Only babies did that. Was it because the lordly ones were wanderers that they had such wild ways? The mother did not hide herself with her son to do this, as a friend of his own mother's had once done in their back kitchen, but she let it happen now, in the open, with the others looking on. Then abruptly she pushed the small son away, showing him that he had had enough. She began to walk after the father. The long trail started, and Ben stumped along by the mother's side. After all, if it was their custom ...

He began to wish the mother had fed him too. The ragged son, filled and happy, danced up to him, suggesting play, and Ben, forgetting his hunger, ran after him, laughing, pulling at his hair. They ran in circles, calling to one another. And the ragged son, as he might have done himself, pranced back to tease the gran. He skipped in front of her, mocking the hobbling gait, and nobody minded, thought Ben, nobody told him it was rude.

The sun was high now, the warmth of it melting the snow beneath, and with it came the gnawing pain of hunger in Ben's stomach, and there was nothing to eat, for the lordly ones gave him nothing. Quelling his shyness, he went to the mother and pointed, showing by the sound in his throat that he wanted to feed. She moved away, though, she would not let him. He understood that she kept her food for the son.

They went on walking, they followed the father. He was some way ahead when he suddenly stopped, and, looking back, called to the mothers. They halted, and the mothers returned his cry. Then they waited. Instructions had been given not to move. There was a sound of running in the far distance, and over the hill came another moor, a stranger. He stopped when he saw the father, and the pair of them stared at each other. The mother beside Ben murmured something to her companion, and the company formed a little circle, wondering what the father was going to do.

Ben watched, apprehensive; he did not like the look of the threatening stranger. The newcomer advanced again, and then, without warning, hurled himself upon the father, and the pair of them wrestled there together in the snow, fiercely, without weapons, the watchful father turning of a sudden to a savage. There was a time of anger, and stamping feet and strangled sobs, and the mothers, watching, huddled together for comfort, Ben in the midst of them. Their fear bred fear in Ben, and he began to cry again, remembering his own angry father. Would the battle never be done? Suddenly it was over. But the result was terror. For the father, the kind leader who had watched over them all night, began to run. Not towards his own family, the mothers and the children, but away across the snow to the distant hills. He was afraid of the stranger. The stranger had defeated him. As Ben watched he saw the trail of blood on the snow.

Ben put out his hand and touched the mother. He tried to tell her that they must follow the wounded father, follow their leader, but she shook herself away impatiently. She was looking at the conqueror. Slowly he advanced towards them. Ben shrank back against the ragged son, as frightened, surely, as he. The old gran turned away in disgust. She would have nothing to do with it. Then the mother, the golden mother beside whom Ben had slept, walked slowly towards the stranger, and Ben realized, by the way she touched him, that she acknowledged him as leader. He would be the father from now on. What if it happened in his own home? What if a neighbour came to fight with his father, and, beating him, drove him away from home? Would his mother mind, would she go to the neighbour?

Ben waited and watched, and then the stranger, who was brown-haired and broad, less graceful than the defeated father, but younger, jerked his head in signal to the mothers to follow him, and meekly, without a word, they obeyed, the children with them. Only the old gran looked backwards across the snow, where, in the distance, stood the smudged figure of the defeated leader, lost and alone.

The battle was over. The day went on as before. As Ben trudged beside his companions through the snow he became accustomed to the new father, the new leader. By afternoon he might have led them always. Perhaps after all he was a relation, an uncle – there was no way of telling what customs they had, the moors.

The sun travelled across the sky and began to sink on the other side of the hills. The company paused once more, and the new father, not so watchful as the first, walked round about the other mother, the aunt – he seemed to like her best. He did not stay on guard as the first father had done. They murmured together, sharing some secret, and when one of the children ran to join them the new father drove him away. He was not going to be so easy of temper as the first.

Ben was faint from hunger now. He went to the mother, the one he knew, the mother of the ragged son, and this time she was patient while he tried to feed, and did not push him away, but suffered him to stay. Ben managed to feed a little, but it was hard. He was not certain of himself, and he was clumsy. After a moment or two the mother moved, and then, as she had done the night before, she settled herself in the snow with her son, and Ben lay down beside her. The others waited around, but Ben had already closed his eyes, his head once more against the shoulder of the mother, his hand in her hair, and whether or not they settled he did not know. Nor did he bother about it, for all that mattered was to be warm and sheltered, protected and cherished by the one he loved.

The angry shouts brought the company to their feet. Bewildered, Ben rubbed his eyes. The moon was full. There, running across the snow, was a crowd of men with sticks, his own father among them, and they were shouting and yelling, waving their sticks at the lordly ones.

This time there was no battle. The leader ran. And with him galloped the mothers, the children, the old gran. They galloped quickly under the moonlight across the frozen snow, and Ben, deserted by his mother, the chestnut mare, deserted by his brothers the moors, the lordly ones, uttered a great cry. He heard the cry tear his chest, and he shouted, 'No ... no ... no ...' for the first and the last time, and he fell face downwards in the snow.

'Q'

'ONCE ABOARD THE LUGGER'

Early last fall there died in Troy an old man and his wife. The woman went first, and the husband took a chill at her grave's edge, when he stood bare-headed in a lashing shower. The loose earth crumbled under his feet, trickled over, and dropped on her coffin-lid. Through two long nights he lay on his bed without sleeping and listened to this sound. At first it ran in his ears perpetually, but afterwards he heard it at intervals only, in the pauses of acute suffering. On the seventh day he died, of pleuro-pneumonia; and on the tenth (a Sunday) they buried him. For just fifty years the dead man had been minister of the Independent chapel on the hill, and had laid down his pastorate two years before, on his golden wedding day. Consequently there was a funeral sermon, and the young man, his successor, chose II Samuel, i. 23, for his text – 'Lovely and not divided.' Himself a newly-married man, he waxed dithyrambic on the sustained affection and accord of the departed couple. 'Truly,' he wound up, 'such marriages as theirs were made in Heaven.' And could they have heard, the two bodies in the cemetry had not denied it; but the woman, after the fashion of women, would have qualified the young minister's assertion in her secret heart.

When, at the close of the year 1839, the Rev. Samuel Bax visited Troy for the first time, to preach his trial sermon at Salem Chapel, he arrived by Boutigo's van, late on a Saturday night, and departed again for Plymouth at seven o'clock on Monday morning. He had just turned twenty-one, and looked younger, and the zeal of his calling was strong upon him. Moreover he was shaken with nervous anxiety for the success of his sermon; so that it is no marvel if he carried away but blurred and misty impressions of the little port and the congregation that sat beneath him that morning, ostensibly reverent, but actually on the pounce for heresy or any sign of weakness. Their impressions, at any rate, were sharp enough. They counted his thumps upon the desk, noted his one reference to 'the original Greek', saw and remembered the flush on his young face and the glow in his eyes as he hammered the doctrine of the redemption out of original sin. The deacons fixed the subject of these trial sermons, and had chosen original sin on the ground that a good beginning was half the battle. The maids in the congregation knew beforehand that he was unmarried, and came out of chapel knowing also that his eyes were brown, that his hair had a reddish tinge in certain lights; that one of his cuffs was frayed slightly, but his black coat had scarcely been worn a dozen times; with other trifles. They loitered by the chapel door until he came out in company with Deacon Snowden, who was conveying him off to dinner. The deacon on weekdays was harbour-master of the port, and on Sundays afforded himself roasted duck for dinner. Lizzie Snowden walked at her father's right hand. She was a slightly bloodless blonde, tall, with a pretty complexion, and hair upon which it was rumoured she could sit if she were so minded. The girls watched the young preacher and his entertainers as they moved down the hill, the deacon talking and his daughter turning her head aside as if it were merely in the half of the world on her right hand that she took the least interest.

'That's to show 'en the big plait,' commented one of the group behind. 'He can't turn his head t'ward's her, but it stares 'en in the face.'

'An' her features look best from the left side, as everybody knows.'

'I reckon, if he's chosen minister, that Lizzie 'll have 'en,' said a tall, lanky girl. She was apprenticed to a dressmaker and engaged to a young tin-smith. Having laid aside ambition on her own accord, she flung in this remark as an apple of discord.

'Jennifer Hosken has a chance. He's fair-skinned hissel', an' Lizzie's too near his own colour. Black's mate is white, as they say.'

'There's Sue Tregraine. She'll have more money than either, when her father dies.'

'What, marry one o' Ruan!' the speaker tittered spitefully.

'Why not?'

The only answer was a shrug. Ruan is a small town that faces Troy across the diminutive harbour, or perhaps I should say that Troy looks down upon it at this slight distance. When a Trojan speaks of it he says, 'Across the water,' with as much implied contempt as though he meant Botany Bay. There is no cogent reason for this, except that the poorer class at Ruan earns it livelihood by fishing. In the eyes of its neighbours the shadow of this lonely calling is cast upon its wealthier inhabitants. Troy depends on commerce, and in the days of which I write employed these wealthier men of Ruan to build ships for it. Further it did not condescend. Intermarriage between towns was almost unheard of, and even now it is rare. Yet they are connected by a penny ferry.

'Her father's a shipbuilder,' urged Sue Tregraine's supporter.

'He might so well keep crab-pots, for all the chance she'll have.'

Now there was a Ruan girl standing just outside this group, and she heard what was said. Her name was Nance Trewartha and her father was a fisherman, who did in fact keep crab-pots. Moreover, she was his only child, and helped him at his trade. She could handle a boat as well as a man, she knew every sea mark up and down the coast for thirty miles, she could cut up bait, and her hands were horny with handling ropes from her childhood. But on Sundays she wore gloves, and came across the ferry to chapel, and was as wise as any of her sex. She had known before coming out of her pew that the young minister had a well shaped back to his head and a gold ring on his little finger with somebody's hair in the collet, under a crystal. She was dark, straight, and lissom of figure, with ripe lips and eyes as black as sloes, and she hoped that the hair in the minister's ring was his mother's. She was well aware of her social inferiority; but – the truth may be told – she chose to forget it that morning, and to wonder what this young man would be like as a husband. She had looked up into his face during sermon time, devouring his boyish features, noticing his refined accent, marking every gesture. Certainly he was comely and desirable. As he walked down the hill by Deacon Snowden's side, she was perfectly conscious of the longing in her heart, but prepared to put a stop to it, and go home to dinner as soon as he had turned the corner and passed out of sight. Then came that unhappy remark about the crab-pots. She bit her lip for a moment, turned, and walked slowly off towards the ferry, full of thought.

Three weeks after, the Rev. Samuel Bax received his call.

He arrived, to assume his duties, in the waning light of a soft January day. Boutigo's van set him down, with a carpet-bag, band-box, and chest of books, at the door of the lodgings which Deacon Snowden had taken for him. The house stood in the North Street, as it is called. It was a small, yellow-washed building, containing just half a dozen rooms, and of these the two set apart for the minister looked straight upon the harbour. Under his sitting-room window was a little garden, and at the end of the garden a low wall with a stretch of water beyond it, and a barque that lay at anchor but a stone's throw away, as it seemed, its masts stretching high against the misty hillside. A green-painted door was let into the garden wall – a door with two flaps, the upper of which stood open; and through this opening he caught another glimpse of grey water.

The landlady, who showed him into this room, and at once began to explain that the furniture was better than it looked, was hardly prepared for the rapture with which he stared out of the window. His boyhood had been spent in a sooty Lancashire town, and to him the green garden, the quay-door, the barque, and the stilly water, seemed to fall little short of Paradise.

'I reckoned you'd like it,' she said. 'An' to be sure, 'tis a blessing you do.'

He turned his stare upon her for a moment. She was a benign-looking woman of about fifty, in a short-skirted grey gown and widow's cap.

'Why do you say that?'

'Because, leavin' out the kitchen, there's but four rooms, two for you an' two for me; two facin' the harbour, an' two facin' the street. Now, if you'd took a dislike to this look-out, I must ha' put you over the street, an' moved in here myself. I *do* like the street, too. There's so much more goin' on.'

'I think this arrangement will be better in every way,' said the young minister.

'I'm glad of it. Iss, there's no denyin' that I'm main glad. From upstairs you can see right down the harbour, which is prettier again. Would 'ee like to see it now? O' course you would – an' it'll be so much handier for me answerin' the door, too. There's a back door at the end o' the passage. You've only to slip a bolt an' you'm out in the garden – out to your boat, if you chose to keep one. But the garden's a tidy little spot to walk up an' down in an' make up your sermons, wi' nobody to overlook you but the folk next door; an' they'm church-goers.'

After supper that evening, the young minister unpacked his books and was about to arrange them, but drifted to the window instead. He paused for a minute or two with his face close to the pane, and then flung up the sash. A faint north wind breathed down the harbour, scarcely ruffling the water. Around and above him the frosty sky flashed with innumerable stars, and over the barque's masts, behind the long chine of the eastern hill, a soft radiance heralded the rising moon. It was a young moon, and, while he waited, her thin horn pushed up through the furze brake on the hill's summit and she mounted into the free heaven. With upturned eye the young minister followed her course for twenty minutes, not consciously observant; for he was thinking over his ambitions, and at his time of life these are apt to soar with the moon. Though possessed with zeal for good work in this small seaside town, he intended that Troy should be but a stepping-stone in his journey. He meant to go far. And while he meditated his future, forgetting the chill of the night air, it was being decided for him by a stronger will than his own. More than this, that will had already passed into action. His destiny was actually launched on the full spring tide that sucked the crevices of the grey wall at the garden's end.

A slight sound drew the minister's gaze down from the moon to the quay-door. Its upper flap still stood open, allowing a square of moonlight to pierce the straight black shadow of the garden wall.

In this square of moonlight were now framed the head and shoulders of a human being. The young man felt a slight chill run down his spine. He leant forward out of the window and challenged the apparition, bating his tone as all people bate it at that hour.

'Who are you?' he demanded.

There was no reply for a moment, though he felt sure his voice must have carried to the quay-door. The figure paused for a second or two, then unbarred the lower flap of the door and advanced across the wall's shadow to the centre of the bright grass-plat under the window. It was the figure of a young woman. Her head was bare and her sleeves turned up to the elbows. She wore no cloak or wrap to cover her from the night air, and her short-skirted, coarse frock was open at the neck. As she turned up her face to the window, the minister could see by the moon's rays that it was well-favoured.

'Be you the new preacher?' she asked, resting a hand on her hip and speaking softly up to him.

'I am the new Independent minister.'

'Then I've come for you.'

'Come for me?'

'Iss; my name's Nance Trewartha, an' you'm wanted across the water, quick as possible. Old Mrs Slade's a-dyin' to-night, over yonder.'

'She wants me?'

'She's one o' your congregation, an' can't die easy till you've seen her. I reckon she's got something 'pon her mind; an' I was to fetch you over, quick as I could.'

As she spoke the church clock down in the town chimed out the hour, and immediately after, ten strokes sounded on the clear air.

The minister consulted his own watch and seemed to be considering.

'Very well,' said he after a pause. 'I'll come. I suppose I must cross by the ferry.'

'Ferry's closed this two hours, an' you needn't wake up any in the house. I've brought father's boat to the ladder below, an' I'll bring you back again. You've only to step out here by the back door. An' wrap yourself up, for 'tis a brave distance.'

'Very well. I suppose it's really serious.'

'Mortal. I'm glad you'll come,' she added simply.

The young man nodded down in a friendly manner, and going back into the room, slipped on his overcoat, picked up his hat, and turned the lamp down carefully. Then he struck a match, found his way to the back door, and unbarred it. The girl was waiting for him, still in the centre of the grass-plat.

'I'm glad you've come,' she repeated, but this time there was something like constraint in her face. As he pulled-to the door softly she moved, and led the way down to the water-side.

From the quay-door a long ladder ran down to the water. At low water one had to descend twenty feet and more; but now the high tide left but three of its rungs uncovered. At the young minister's feet a small fishing boat lay ready, moored by a short painter to the ladder. The girl stepped lightly down and held up a hand.

'Thank you,' said the young man with dignity, 'but I do not want help.'

She made no answer to this: but as he stepped down, went forward and unmoored the painter. Then she pushed gently away from the ladder, hoisted the small foresail, and, returning to her companion, stood beside him for a moment with her hand on the tiller.

'Better slack the foresheet,' she said suddenly.

The young man looked helplessly at her. He had not the slightest idea of her meaning, did not in fact know the slightest difference between a foresheet and a mainsail. And it was just to find out the depth of his ignorance that she had spoken.

'Never mind,' she said, 'I'll do it myself.'

She slackened and made fast the rope, and took hold of the tiller again. The sails shook and filled as they glided out from under the wall. The soft breeze blew straight behind them, the tide was just beginning to ebb. She loosed the mainsheet a little, and the water hissed as they spun down under the grey town towards the harbour's mouth.

A dozen vessels lay at anchor below the town quay, their lamps showing a strange orange yellow in the moonlight; between them the minister saw the cottages of Ruan glimmering on the eastern shore, and over it the coastguard flagstaff, faintly pencilled above the skyline. It seemed to him that they were not shaping their course for the little town.

'I thought you told me,' he said at length, 'that Mrs – the dying woman – lived across there.'

The girl shook her head. 'Not in Ruan itsel' – Ruan parish. We'll have to go round the point.'

She was leaning back and gazing straight before her, towards the harbour's mouth. The boat was one of the class that serves along that coast for hook-and-line as well as drift-net fishing, clinker-built, about twenty-seven feet in the keel, and nine in beam. It had no deck beyond a small cuddy forward, on top of which a light hoar-frost was gathering as they moved. The minister stood beside the girl, and withdrew his eyes from this cuddy roof to contemplate her.

'Do you mean to say,' he asked, 'that you don't take cold, wearing no wrap or bonnet on frosty nights like this?'

She let the tiller go for a moment, took his hand by the wrist, and laid it on her own bare arm. He felt the flesh, but it was firm and warm. Then he withdrew his hand hastily, without finding anything to say. His eyes avoided hers. When, after half a minute, he looked at her again, her gaze was fixed straight ahead, upon the misty stretch of sea beyond the harbour's mouth.

In a minute or two they were gliding out between the tall cliff and the reef of rocks that guard this entrance on either side. On the reef stood a wooden cross, painted white, warning vessels to give a wide berth; on the cliff a grey castle, with a battery before it, under the guns of which they spun seaward, still with the wind astern.

Outside, the sea lay as smooth as within the harbour. The wind blew steadily, off the shore, so that, close-hauled, one might fetch up or down Channel with equal ease. The girl began to flatten the sails, and asked her companion to bear a hand. Their hands met over a rope, and the man noted with surprise that the girl's was feverishly hot. Then she brought the boat's nose round to the eastward and, heeling gently over the dark water, they began to skirt the misty coast with the breeze on their left cheeks.

'How much farther?' asked the minister.

She nodded towards the first point in the direction of Plymouth. He turned his coat-collar up about his ears and wondered if his duty would often take him on such journeys as this. Also he felt thankful that the sea was smooth. He might, or might not, be given to sea-sickness: but somehow he was sincerely glad that he had not to be put to the test for the first time in this girl's presence.

They passed the small headland and still the boat held on its way.

'I had no idea you were going to take me this distance. Didn't you promise me the house lay just beyond the point we've just passed?'

To his amazement the girl drew herself up, looked him straight in the face and said –

'There's no such place.'

'*What?*'

'There's no such place. There's nobody ill at all. I told you a lie.'

'You told me a lie – then why in the name of common sense am I here?'

'Because, young man – because, sir, I'm sick o' love for you, an' I want 'ee to marry me.'

'Great heaven!' the young minister muttered, recoiling. 'Is the girl mad?'

'Ah, but look at me, sir!' She seemed to grow still taller as she stood there, resting one hand on the tiller and gazing at him with perfectly serious eyes. 'Look at me well before you take up with some other o' the girls. To-morrow they'll be all after 'ee, an' this'll be my only chance; for my father's no better'n a plain fisherman, an' they're all above me in money an' rank. I be a Ruan girl, an' my family is naught. But look at me well; there's none stronger nor comelier, nor that'll love thee so dear!'

The young man gasped. 'Set me ashore at once!' he commanded, stamping his foot.

'Nay, that I will not till thou promise, an' that's flat. Dear lad, listen – an' consent, consent – an' I swear to thee thou'll never be sorry for't.'

'I never heard such awful impropriety in my life. Turn back; I order you to steer back to the harbour at once!'

She shook her head. 'No, lad; I won't. An' what's more, you don't know how to handle a boat, an' couldn't get back yoursel', not in a month.'

'This is stark madness. You – you abandoned woman, how long do you mean to keep me here?'

'Till thou give in to me. We'm goin' straight t'wards Plymouth now, an' if the wind holds – as 'twill – we'll be off the Rame in two hours. If you haven't said me yes by that maybe we'll go on; or perhaps we'll run across to the coast o' France –'

'Girl, do you know that if I'm not back by daybreak, I'm ruined!'

'And oh, man, man! Can't 'ee see that I'm ruined, too, if I

turn back without your word? How shall I show my face in Troy streets again, tell me?'

At this sudden transference of responsibility the minister was staggered.

'You should have thought of that before,' he said, employing the one obvious answer.

'O' course I thought of it. But for love o' you I made up my mind to risk it. An' now there's no goin' back.' She paused a moment and then added, as a thought struck her, 'Why, lad, doesn' that prove I love 'ee uncommon?'

'I prefer to consider the question. Once more – will you go back?'

'I can't.'

He bit his lips and moved forward to the cuddy, on the roof of which he seated himself sulkily. The girl tossed him an end of rope.

'Dear, better coil that up an' sit 'pon it. The frost'll strike a chill into thee.'

With this she resumed her old attitude by the tiller. Her eyes were fixed ahead, her gaze passing just over the minister's hat. When he glanced up he saw the rime twinkling on her shoulders and the star-shine in her dark eyes. Around them the heavens blazed with constellations. Never had the minister seen them so multitudinous or so resplendent. Never before had the firmament seemed so alive to him. He could almost hear it breathe. And beneath the stars the little boat raced eastward, with the reef-points pattering on its tan sails.

Neither spoke. For the most part the minister avoided the girl's eyes, and sat nursing his wrath. The whole affair was ludicrous; but it meant the sudden ruin of his good name, at the very start of his career. This was the word he kept grinding between his teeth – 'ruin', 'ruin'. Whenever it pleased this mad creature to set him ashore, he must write to Deacon Snowden for his boxes and resign all connection with Troy. But would he ever get rid of the scandal? Could he ever be sure that, to whatever distance he might flee, it would not follow him? Had he not better abandon his calling, once and for all? It was hard.

A star shot down from the Milky Way and disappeared in darkness behind the girl's shoulders. His eyes, following it, encountered hers. She left the tiller and came slowly forward.

'In three minutes we'll open Plymouth Sound,' she said quietly, and then with a sharp gesture flung both arms out towards him. 'Oh, lad, think better o't an' turn back wi' me! Say you'll marry me, for I'm perishin' o' love!'

The moonshine fell on her throat and extended arms. Her lips were parted, her head was thrown back a little, and for the first time the young minister saw that she was a beautiful woman.

'Ay, look, look at me!' she pleaded. 'That's what I've wanted 'ee to do all along. Take my hands: they'm shapely to look at and strong to work for 'ee.'

Hardly knowing what he did, the young man took them; then in a moment he let them go – but too late; they were about his neck.

With that he sealed his fate for good or ill. He bent forward a little and their lips met.

So steady was the wind that the boat still held on her course; but no sooner had the girl received the kiss than she dropped her arms, walked off, and shifted the helm.

'Unfasten the sheet there,' she commanded, 'and duck your head clear.'

As soon as their faces were set for home, the minister walked back to the cuddy roof and sat down to reflect. Not a word was spoken till they reached the harbour's mouth again, and then he pulled out his watch. It was half past four in the morning.

Outside the Battery Point the girl hauled down the sails and got out the sweeps; and together they pulled up under the still sleeping town to the minister's quay-door. He was clumsy at this work, but she instructed him in whispers, and they managed to reach the ladder as the clocks were striking five. The tide was far down by this time, and she held the boat close to the ladder while he prepared to climb. With his foot on the first round, he turned. She was white as a ghost, and trembling from top to toe.

'Nance – did you say your name was Nance?'

She nodded.

'What's the matter?'

'I'll – I'll let you off, if you want to be let off.'

'I'm not sure that I do,' he said, and stealing softly up the ladder, stood at the top and watched her boat as she steered it back to Ruan.

Three months after, they were married, to the indignant amazement of the minister's congregation. It almost cost him his pulpit, but he held on and triumphed. There is no reason to believe that he ever repented of his choice, or rather of Nance's. To be sure, she had kidnapped him by a lie; but perhaps she wiped it out by fifty years of honest affection. On that point, however, I, who tell the tale, will not dogmatize.

Charles Causley

LOOKING FOR ANNIE

During the first four years I was in the navy, I was easily the worst sailor in the fleet. As soon as I got in, I discovered that I was one of those people who suffered from sea-sickness. I often used to wonder why I had joined the navy at all.

Being a Cornishman, of course, may have had something to do with it. I suppose I thought at the time that all Cornishmen 'belonged', as we say, to go to sea. That is, if they didn't join the then Duke of Cornwall's Light Infantry. But my father had been in the trenches in France in the First World War, and from what I'd heard about it, I didn't fancy the army. Another thing: when I was about eight I went to stay with my Auntie Elsie for a summer holiday, and she lived near an army barracks. I can still hear the non-commissioned officers bawling at the recruits on that dusty parade-ground. Not for me, I thought.

The sailors I'd seen ashore in Cornwall, and on the streets of Plymouth, on the other hand, were a different matter. They all seemed to my childlike vision to be strong, smart, handsome, healthy, merry. I thought that if ever I put on that magic uniform, my dough-like complexion, thin arms and legs, spectacles, and general incapacity for games and doing anything remotely practical would all fade away and that I should somehow become as they were.

Further, such was my general state of arrested development and full-flowering ignorance, when the war finally did come in my nineteenth year, I thought that if I opted for the navy I should be based in Devonport and that I would be able to get home to Cornwall at week-ends. As it turned out, I spent only ten days in what to me was the hell's kitchen of the barracks in six years, and those were ten days too many. Another thing: the one element I failed to take account of when I joined the navy was the sea. But once I was in, it was too late to bother about reasons. Early in 1940 I was drafted to *H.M.S. Sunburst.*

The ship was stationed about as far from Cornwall as it could possibly be while still in the British Isles. I can see myself now being welcomed by the coxswain, a huge puffy man with warts and a thin spiky beard sticking out like the rays of the sun all round his face as I stood anxiously with my kit-bag and hammock on the heaving slippery narrow steel deck of the destroyer in the green sea of Scapa.

'Name?' growled the coxswain. My arrival had interrupted his tea.

'Trethewey,' I squeaked. 'D/JX 197950. Ordinary Coder.'

The coxswain looked at me like a scientist across whose microscope some fabled insect has suddenly crawled.

'Ordinary *what*?' he said.

'Coder, sir,' I said. 'Decoding and deciphering signals. It's a new branch.'

'Never 'eard of it,' said the coxswain. 'You're in Number Two Mess. That's the watch-keepers' mess, down forrard. You'll find it. Abandon ship station: Carley Float Number Four, port-side. And remind the Leadin' 'nd o' the mess we're sailin' in 'alf an hour. Seventeen-thirty. All right?'

Dismally I gathered up my kit-bag and hammock and trudged forrard.

'Oh, an' – what's s-yer-name!' the coxswain called after me.

'Sir?' I said.

'You want a shave.'

I did, too. I hadn't had a proper wash for three days, and it felt like three years. I was so miserable it's a wonder I didn't take a jump over the side. But I'm glad I didn't, because if I had I should never have met Annie.

There he was: down in the mess, sitting on the end of a form under the radio speaker, drinking grey tea made with thick, condensed milk and reading the births and deaths column in an old copy of the *North Cornwall Echo*.

Naturally, Annie wasn't his real name. Annie was called Mark Annear, and he came from the fishing village of Port Treloar on the long, sandy estuary of the River Polwenner that runs off Bodmin Moor into the sea on the north coast of Cornwall. 'Annie', of course, came from his surname: Annear. Nobody in Cornwall, or anywhere else in the West Country for that matter, would have dared to call him this. It would have outraged politeness, propriety. In the navy, though, with its passion for nicknames, it was inevitable, but had nothing whatever to do with personal characteristics. 'Hookey' Walker, 'Dolly' Grey, 'Bungy' Williams, 'Clara' Bow, 'Brigham' Young, were all attached as automatically as official numbers. 'Annie' Annear was a name I heard nowhere else but in *Sunburst*. Most important, he didn't appear to mind the nickname. Anyhow, I remember thinking, when I first heard it, that it was wildly inappropriate.

He was, in those days, a man of about twenty-six: tall, hefty, very big-boned. His wrists and fingers seemed to me to be constructed on an entirely larger, looser principle from my own. To look at, Annie was by no means what many people take to be a typical Cornishman. He wasn't short, thick-set, dark-haired, Celtic-eyed. Yet his Cornish surname – Annear – should have given me a clue: it comes from *an hir*, the tall or the long. His height, his large, open, freckled face and sandy thatch of hair was something you would expect to find on the prairies of Canada or on the sheep-farms of Australia, not in his father's boat-building yard at Port Treloar.

As I scrambled down the metal ladder the rest of the members of the mess – arguing, scuffling, singing, writing, playing uckers (ludo), even somebody shaving – ignored me. But Annie picked up my kit-bag. 'Hello,' he said in a slow, easy West Country voice. 'My name's Mark Annear. Supply Assistant. I'm in the stores. Everybody calls me Annie. Have some tea. Shockin' stuff, but there's nothing else.'

After the unexpected greeting in familiar Cornish tones, I began to feel that life in the *Sunburst* mightn't be so bad after all. It was, of course. I might have known what to expect from the boat journey between the mainland at Thurso and Lyness. I seemed to be the only person on board being ill. It was quite a fine day in early summer, and, to make things worse, I was the only passenger in naval uniform. A priest and a couple of young children paused in a ball game and gazed at me with some concern: not so much, I imagine, for me as for the future of the country.

If the passenger-boat was bad, the *Sunburst* was worse. Apart from rolling, she used to leap forward like an electric hare, and – shut as we were inside – we would seem for a short while to be in some kind of spaceship on our way to the moon. Then she would suddenly change her role. Like a miners' cage, she would drop flat on the sea with a dreadful metallic bang that seemed to rattle every separate screw and nut and bolt in the ship. It was terrifying; something out of a flooding Inferno. And, naturally, my sea-sickness didn't get any better.

Everybody, especially the new hands who knew nothing about it, was full of advice. Lie down, close your eyes, drink cold water, they said. It's a sort of spirit-level in your ears: keep them steady. Stand up. Sit amidships with your back to something warm. Keep your eyes open. Don't look at the sea. Keep working, and (this was a favourite one) it's your imagination. I resorted to rum, pills, fasting, injections, prayer. All no good. I just went on being ill. The only person who didn't give me the benefit of his opinion was Annie. In fact, he never mentioned sea-sickness.

Annie had almost only one topic of conversation: the fishing village of Port Treloar where he lived. Up to the outbreak of war, he had spent all his life around the bay and the estuary there, working for his father, and sailing. One day he produced a faded photograph of himself. The resemblance wasn't a good one, and it was badly out of focus: Annie, grasping a tiller with giant paws and gazing sternly but dimly from the cardboard. Nevertheless, that photograph – obviously – was a talisman; a reminder of another reality. 'You must come and see me,' he said. 'And my wife. You can get a train from Dunborough. Change at Port Isaac. When you get to Port Treloar, come across on the ferry. It's a motor-boat; Tom Hocken runs it. At least, he did when I was home last: that's eight months ago. When you get to the other side of the river, our boat-building yard's facing you. "Denzil Annear and Son" – that's me – "Boat Builders, Port Treloar". Blue letters on a white ground; you can see it for half a mile. There's a steep hill, and about a hundred yards up on the left is our house. It's whitewashed. You can't miss it; it's the only one on that side. Come any time.'

'I will, Annie,' I said. 'It sounds all right.'

'It *is* all right,' he said. 'Of course, I don't use the ferry. I row over in my own boat. Got a little boat-house almost underneath the landing-stage. I keep my things there. Funny, my boat's tied up on the other side of the river waiting for me now. And I'm here. In Freetown. Don't know how long she'll have to wait.'

I laughed; but Annie looked serious. 'And don't wait till the end of the war,' he went on. 'Anyhow, it looks like going on for ever.'

'Supposing you're not at home?' I said.

'Doesn't matter,' said Annie. 'I've written home about you. By the way, my wife's expecting. Perhaps you'll see the baby before I do. You never know.'

I never forgot that conversation with Annie. We were sitting outside the canteen by the King Tom Jetty at Freetown. Just then the liberty-boat came in, and by the time we returned to the ship it was quite dark. The coxswain was waiting for me on the gangway.

'Trethewey, Ordinary Coder?' he said, giving me that old scientific look.

'Sir?' I said.

'You're going on draft. Tonight,' he said.

'Ashore, Cox?' I said hopefully: white man's grave or no white man's grave.

'The *Lifton*. Cruiser. Shake yer up,' he said encouragingly. 'Boat'll be 'ere for yer in twenty minutes. Git flyin'.' And he vanished back into his office like a wicked fairy.

Annie helped me pack my kit-bag and lash my spare books

in my hammock. In an hour, I had left the *Sunburst* for ever and was in the *Lifton*, making for Simonstown, Fremantle, Sydney, the Pacific. Years later, I heard that the *Sunburst* had stayed in Freetown three weeks, then returned to Londonderry.

Annie and I wrote a letter or two. But he wasn't what might be called a writing man. And I was often too ill, too far away, to bother. Anything might have happened to him. It was a long war for those who had been at sea since 1939. One Christmas – it must have been in Brisbane, we were there four days in 1943 – I nearly sent him a cable. But it seemed, at the last minute, absurd. He might have been dead. I had heard that the *Sunburst* had been at Crete. So I didn't really think much more about Annie until nearly a year later.

I was home in Cornwall, at Dunborough, on forty-eight days leave. I was tired of people asking me when I was going back, and telling me how thin I was. Secretly, I was worried about my next draft. I'd left the *Lifton* and was wondering how long my inside would last if I went back to destroyers. So, to take my mind off it, I decided to go down to Port Treloar and find Annie.

Once I got started, I couldn't help wondering why I hadn't gone before. The feeling of excitement, of expectancy, soon wore off, though. I began to wish I'd stayed at home. The train rattled along the tiny branch line past scruffy little fields, mud, bare trees. It was beastly cold November weather, and I felt it pretty badly after three years in the Pacific. The railway line hugged the coast, and now and then, through the mist, you could catch a sight of the grey, cold heaving line of the north Cornish sea. Dreadful. There was practically nobody else on the train. Increasingly, I wished I hadn't come, and began to wonder how I was going to get back to Dunborough that night. Looking for Annie! Annie was probably dead; comfortable at the bottom of some ocean. And what should I say to his wife?

The train stopped violently, as though we had hit something. The wind from the sea came sawing up the platform like a blade of ragged ice. I pulled my coat about me and wished for the fiftieth time I'd worn my uniform. So this was Port Treloar.

It was just as Annie had described it. Climbing into the motor-boat to cross the river, five minutes later, I felt I had known Tom Hocken for years. 'Mr Hocken?' I said. Like many Cornish people dealing with a supposed foreigner, he professed to show no surprise. 'Everybody d'knaw me,' he said, and we shot in a thick spray of muddy water across the estuary. I spent the journey mopping my face and my thin coat. I was the only passenger. As I got out of the boat on the other side, I thought I would try again. 'A friend,' I said, 'told me about you. In Africa, Mr Hocken.'

'That'll be sixpence,' he said. 'Look slippy out o' the boat now, my sonny. I got to be on t'other side in a few minutes.'

I gave up, gave him the money, stepped on the wooden jetty. I was absolutely alone. The mist and the rain were still blowing in from the sea; and the sea itself was now invisible. I could hardly see the houses on the other side of the river. I might have been a traveller on the landscape of an unknown planet. Then I noticed the signboard.

There it was: painted in blue and white. 'Denzil Annear and Son. Boat Builders. Port Treloar.' Just as Annie had said. My throat seemed to close up. I felt, surprisingly, that I might easily burst into tears. But a voice startled me from my line of thought.

'You came, then,' it said: and laughed. There was no mistaking that easy, West Country voice. I looked down from the jetty to the edge of the river beneath me. There, standing in a rowing-boat and tying her up, was Annie. He wore his naval uniform, a thick scarf, gloves, and – I remember thinking this rather odd – a balaclava helmet. At the bottom of the boat was a black, wooden box with his name and number painted on it in white. He must have crossed the river behind us.

'Annie!' I shouted. He laughed again and looked up at me, the mist swirling round his legs.

'Just like you to choose today,' he said. 'Go on up to the house and break the news I'm coming, will you? I've got to unlock the boat-house and get this box up the ladder.'

'Can I help you?' I said.

'You'll break your neck, boy,' he grinned. 'I remember the day you joined the mess in *Sunburst*. The house is a hundred yards up the hill, on the left. Remember? And how's your stomach? I'll see you in ten minutes. Oh, and welcome to Port Treloar!'

He hopped out of the boat, balanced on some narrow stone steps, put his hand through an aperture in the top of the door, and drew out a large, flat key. I set off up the hill.

Almost as soon as I'd lifted the iron knocker, the door opened. It was Annie's wife all right. I recognized her at once from the photographs I'd seen. She was a tall girl, with a pale, milk-white face, and red hair. And she showed no surprise at seeing me. Her face didn't move at all, either with pleasure or sorrow. She looked like someone still recovering, slowly, from some long illness. 'You're a friend of Mark's,' she said. 'Come in.'

She led the way into a tiny kitchen. There was a fire burning and a kettle boiling. 'Have a cup of tea,' she said. 'It's a long journey. You're Richard Trethewey, aren't you? Mark used to write about you in his letters from the *Sunburst*. Mark made a lot of friends.'

'Did Annie . . . that is, Mark . . . tell you that he almost saved my life?' I said. She laughed, and her face lit up wonderfully. 'That's right,' she said. 'That's what they used to call him in the navy. Annie. Annie Annear. I've had a lot of visitors since . . . since . . .'

An awful premonition came over me. I suddenly felt as though I might, quite quickly, become desperately ill: even die. I put down my cup of tea and stood up.

'You've had a lot of visitors since what?' I said. There was a little scuffle at the door. She went to it, opened it; brought in a small boy of about four, the image of Annie, and holding an eyeless teddy-bear. The child gazed at me solemnly, smiled faintly, clutched his mother's hand, leaned against her. 'Don't you know?' she said. There was a pause. 'Mark . . . Annie, as you call him . . . was lost at sea two years ago. He was in the *Sunburst*. They were in an anti-submarine patrol covering a convoy in the Barents Sea, somewhere off the North Cape. The ship simply sailed off into the blue and disappeared. No signal. Nothing. I had a letter from the Admiralty, but it didn't tell me much. I thought you knew. Annie's dead.'

My hands began to shake so much that I put them in my pockets. I sat down. My stomach seemed to turn to lead, to roll completely over like a ship in a heavy sea. For a few seconds, I could hardly breathe. I felt as though, for a terrifying moment, I'd been provided with a new inside. Then I said, 'Are you prepared for a shock?'

She looked at me with complete calm. 'Nothing can shock me now,' she said, and adjusted one of the little boy's socks. 'Listen,' I said. 'When I came up from the ferry just now, Mark – your husband – Annie – was tying up his boat down there. He'll be here in a minute. It was misty; raining. I spoke to him.'

I must say that Annie's wife was an amazing girl. She simply looked at me like a mother who has to comfort a feverish child. 'Have another cup of tea,' she said. 'It's the shock. You were very fond of Mark, weren't you? Do you know, for nearly a year, when I was here with the baby, I fancied I could hear him coming up from the river.'

'Are you telling me,' I said, 'that I've seen a ghost?'

'Cornwall's a funny old place,' she said. 'I shouldn't think about what you've seen.'

I stood up and began to shout. 'But I saw him standing up in his boat by the jetty! He had a black box with his name painted on it. He was in uniform and – yes! – a balaclava! *I tell you I saw him!*' And all the time that girl just looked at me and smiled, cool as you like, as if to say: you'll get over it in a moment.

And so I did. And so did she. For the next second, the door opened and in walked Annie, carrying the box. Of the three of us, including the little boy, I don't know who was the most astonished.

You see, I hadn't seen a ghost down at the ferry. It really was Annie. And he really had been posted as missing for two years. The *Sunburst* had been torpedoed off the North Cape, and the German submarine had picked up three survivors: among them, Annie. They had given them a little food and brandy and set them adrift again in one of the leaking ship's boats. Late the following night they had been picked up by some Lapp fishermen and landed on a tiny island north-west of Point Kenahay. Annie's two companions had died, and for over a year he had been unable to speak, from the shock and the cold, and had been nursed by the Lapps. Then they took him by sledge to a Russian hospital on the Kola Peninsula. When he had recovered, and could walk and speak again, he waited for a convoy. In six months, he was back in Belfast. They had flown him to Devonport; then to the nearby Royal Naval Air Station at St Petherwin. Annie had come the last three miles from the air station in a furniture van. 'Look at me!' he cried, embracing us all. 'I'm a blooming Eskimo!'

And that's almost all there is to it. Annie survived the war all right, and is still building boats down at Port Treloar. As for myself, I was completely changed after that jolt to my stomach when I thought I'd seen Annie's ghost. That was in 1944. I spent the last year of the war bouncing about in a corvette: the *Thistle*. And, do you know, I was never sea-sick once. So if you want a really reliable cure for sea-sickness, I suggest that you come down to Cornwall and start looking for Annie.

A. L. Rowse

THE CURSE UPON THE CLAVERTONS

Anyone who knows Cornwall will recognize that Claverton is not, and could not be, a Cornish name. We, in the china-clay district that family came to dominate, were under the vague impression that they had come down upon us from Scotland. All we knew for sure was that they came from somewhere 'up the country'. The probability is that they came from no farther afield than the neighbouring county of Devon; but our horizons were very limited and no one knew for sure.

The original Thomas Claverton came into the district in a humble enough capacity – as clerk to old Cap'n William Slade, who discovered on his farm-holding in the Higher Quarters the rich deposits of best-quality china-clay by which the prosperity of our town latterly came.

'Old' William – the name was endemic in that family and we call him 'old' William to mark him off from son and grandson – had a sharp eye for china-clay and for everything connected with digging it out from the pits with the primitive appliances of those days. No power-driven hoses then to wash the stuff out from 'stopes' and 'glans': it was all dug out with pick and shovel, washed into such little streams as flowed at the bottom of those ever-deepening hollows, quarries lying open to the summer-blue Cornish skies, amid the seas of furze and bracken on the moors.

You know that district, the extraordinary landscape it has become with the vast increase of the pits in size and depth? – A landscape of the moon. There are the gleaming white mountains, perfect cones, visible now from all parts of Cornwall and far out to sea. Those are the china-clay 'burrows', piled high from the sand brought up from the depths below; between them immense and ever-widening gashes; in the depths, where there is clay, white; the sides all shades of grey and blue, granite and glittering quartz; sometimes a sinister black, striped with the rust-colour of tin or copper. At the edges of disused pits the empty shells of ruined engine-houses; the hollows of those pits gradually filling with malevolent green water, or ominous black, where the cliff-sides are black, the desolate cry of sea-gulls echoing in the deserted crevices.

Such is that lunar landscape now, after the best part of a century's working.

It was all on a smaller, more intimate scale in the early days when William Slade and Thomas Claverton worked together. That was how the money was made; this was how the landscape came to look in the course of making it: the source of the Clavertons' immense fortune.

They came into the district with nothing – not a bean. They owned no property; they had no connections or relations. Nothing.

There were only two of them – Thomas Claverton and his unmarried sister – and what they lacked in possessions they soon began to make up in assiduity, shrewdness, and hard work. The sister set up in a little milliner's shop at the end of the town, where she sold ribbons and thread and laces, baby-linen and women's necessities. They soon ceased to be necessities for her; for her brother had, even more than a capacity for hard work, a sharp eye for an opportunity.

Old William Slade may have had a nose for clay, something like second sight as to where it lay – his men all paid him the tribute of respect, ''E d'knaw clay' – but he had no head for figures, could in fact barely read or write.

This was where the newcomer Thomas Claverton made himself very useful to him; and from being useful he became indispensable. None of the fellows in the clay-works had much knowledge of arithmetic in those days. No one in the town, apart from a handful of bank-clerks, had even an elementary knowledge of accounting. And old William wasn't the one to let the townsfolk pry into his affairs.

Thomas Claverton was his man: a young fellow keen as mustard, sharp as a needle, no local connections with their tittle-tattle. William was a close man; so was the young fellow from up the country he took on as his clerk in the tiny office they established over the milliner's shop.

China-clay prospered in slow but steady fashion. The little boats called at the small ports studded around the bay. Teams of horses with their loaded wagons braked creaking down the hillside and through the village on their way to the railway station. Business grew and prospects opened up beyond old William's single resources, though his was the land upon which the best clay lay. He needed capital to develop it.

This was where Thomas Claverton came in handier still. Floating a company offered no mystery to him; suing out papers – no amount of paper-work baffled him. Though he had none of old William's nose for clay, or how to work it, he had a nose for something more important, since it was a scarcer commodity in our town. With the certainty of a somnambulist, he went straight forward.

By this time he knew a number of people in the town – people with whom he had business relations, who would be useful to him.

He had no difficulty in getting the modest amount of capital subscribed or floating the company: 'William Slade and Co.' The 'Co.' referred to two trustworthy townsmen, whom Claverton could answer for better than old William.

William Slade had never been one for knowing people in the town much; nor was he perfectly familiar with the equal voting rights conferred upon co-directors upon the constitution of the company. He saw no reason to object to Claverton being written in as the secretary to the company with a good salary as a fixed claim upon its assets. Claverton was indispensable – more so than ever to the functioning of a company.

For his part, with his salary securely behind him – neither of the Clavertons wasted a penny or spent one superfluously – he became a solider man than ever. A man in whom one could have confidence. Money makes money: confidence creates confidence. No longer was the little milliner's shop, nor the little milliner herself, looked down on: the best people of the town took to patronizing the business. So that, in course of time, Miss Claverton too had something to invest, when china-clay in the eighteen-nineties took a marked upward turn.

It became necessary for William Slade and Co. to increase their modest capital further. There was no difficulty about this – conditions were good, prospects even better – and facts were properly recognized by the company becoming Slade, Claverton and Co.

There was no disposition on Slade's part to resist this addition to the name. Even if there had been, he would have been in no position to object, since there were two votes on the board against his one. It did not altogether escape his observation that there were now three. But what could he do about that?

There was a great deal else that he could do nothing about, as he now shortly found.

Used as he had always been to running his own works – or what he considered to be his own works – he now found that the company regarded it as necessary to support him there with a works-manager. This man was a nominee of Claverton's, and he urged a policy of immediate expansion.

'Take time by the forelock,' he was always preaching. This was Claverton's motto, too, and indeed he was right. It was the obvious policy to buy up the properties surrounding the clay-pit that had proved successful and so well justified William Slade's belief in it. In fact, one might go further – as Claverton did – and hold that the right thing now was to buy up all the options they could on likely properties in that area, before anybody else got a hand on them.

This involved a considerable increase of capital and a new flotation, in the course of which the concern emerged with a new emphasis: Claverton now took open precedence with the change of name to Claverton, Slade and Co.

That sounded altogether better; the name had an easier rhythm, it tripped lightly off the tongue. Facts were more recognizable thus, with Thomas Claverton, whose capacities had grown with the concern, recognized as chairman. And, of course, in the complicated transactions that ensued, it was necessary that the original landholding should be 'amalgamated' with the larger holdings and claims that hemmed it in all round.

Cap'n Slade had no particular objection to this measure, as inevitable as it was progressive. If he had had any such objections, he would have discovered that his original property was so embedded in lands over which all the wayleaves and rights were in the hands of the company, that not a waggon-load of clay could be got out without its permission.

To challenge such an issue did not occur to him. He accepted instead, by way of compensation, a block of shares (without voting rights) in an issue that simultaneously much increased the total capital and much diluted his proportionate holding.

In the years that had passed since Thomas Claverton had come to the town and been given his first leg-up by old William Slade, a certain contrast had indicated itself in the shaping of their respective families.

William Slade's sons had nothing of the old man's one talent – his nose for clay. The family had never uprooted itself from the soil, and though, through their father's lucky strike, they had more money in their pockets, their tastes and capacities in no wise differed from those of the clay-workers their father employed. Whippets, spaniels, ferrets, women, were what mostly engaged their interest; it was only in the order of their interest that they varied.

It stands to reason that Cap'n Slade's sons were of no help to him: friendly and affable, good sorts, they were good-for-nothings.

Thomas Claverton brought up his family on a different plan. His three sons he sent to a cheap, but undeniably, Public School. It was understood that the second was to be trained for a doctor. The youngest of them was too young yet to bother with thoughts of a career. But the eldest, a heavy, coarse, sexy type, who belied his appearance by the meanness of his temperament, was installed in new offices as secretary of the company. And a very competent secretary he made: a tight-fisted, secretive youth, chip off the old block.

Miss Claverton, with her not inconsiderable nest-egg invested in the company, was enabled to wind up her milliner's establishment and take charge of the office-girls, who typed for the greater glory of Claverton, Slade and Co. in the sombre mansion with its magnificent rhododendrons, which they had taken over for offices from the town's oldest family.

Both aunt and nephew were on the pay-roll at good salaries – nothing exorbitant, of course. But when china-clay workers at that date received fifteen shillings a week, the finances of the Claverton family were in a very flourishing state. Their capital went up by leaps and bounds. They saved every scrap to re-invest in clay and clay-bearing lands. They deserved to succeed. And they did.

There followed the china-clay boom of the early 1900s. Clay left our ports in increasing shipments; demand on a large scale from America and from Japan sprang up. The waggon-loads and teams multiplied; as the great waggons with their teams of six and eight tugged and swayed through the villages on their way down to the coast, flanks of the horses sweating and steaming, the waggoners shouting 'Gee-up, Lion! Triumph! Gee-up, Taager' – you should have heard the harness jingle, the brass-plates tinkle amid the clouds of dust that rose along the roads and filtered in through windows, every crevice and crack, until a powdery white film lay upon everything as upon the men's faces.

The little clay-harbours needed deepening. It became the next objective of the company to possess its own dock in the biggest of them. This naturally necessitated a further reconstruction of the company, the biggest yet.

It was marked by a further change of name, a great simplification: it became Claverton and Co. No further mention of William Slade: the name was simply dropped – as indeed he himself was from the board.

No quarrel – at least nothing that came to our ears, though

the change was not lost upon the company's old workers, who had known how things were at the beginning and watched the changes progress brought with it. They were not concerned, however, one way or the other; they were not shareholders, merely the company's employees. Theirs was the part of a Greek chorus: to watch and marvel and comment.

Not that they knew much in detail. The Clavertons were not the people to make confidences. They remained as aloof and secretive as ever a family who held themselves apart. They kept themselves, and their money, to themselves. Never a subscription to the town, never a contribution to any of its public purposes. Not that there was much of that any way: our townspeople had little in the way of public spirit; but for sheer meanness the Clavertons 'beat the band', we all said.

Ignorant as we were of the ins and outs of the story, of the means by which Cap'n Slade had been gradually pushed out of what had originally been his own concern, until he was finally ousted, it was impossible to disguise from us the events that followed.

In the first place, Old William had received a blow from which he did not recover.

He was an ageing man now, long past his best and failing in strength. That did not make his ruthless elimination from what had been his own 'chick and cheel' any the more bearable. Though we might not have much sense of things, we had sense enough to understand that: it was just at such a moment that blows fall hardest.

Then the news ran through the village that the Cap'n had suffered a stroke, and was lying at death's door in the old farmhouse in the midst of the clay-pits.

Day after day during his last illness Mrs Claverton – no bad soul (after all she had not been responsible for what had happened) – would pass through the village with her basket on her arm: fresh fruit, jellies, cold chicken, delicacies of every kind for the sick Cap'n. Always to be rejected at the door.

It was pathetic to see how the poor woman persevered – for

she had taken something on her conscience – and what she endured. Humiliated day after day, she was never once admitted over that threshold, familiar enough in earlier days.

For if the Cap'n had met more than his match in his former clerk, Thomas Claverton's wife was no match for old Mrs Slade.

Elizabeth Slade was born at Trevethow, of yeoman stock in whom the blood of small Cornish gentry had come straight down from medieval times. Uninstructed, she was yet fully aware of her quality: a big, brawny woman of the Higher Quarters, she held herself like a gipsy queen. Straight as a rod, erect in black bombazine, with a little lace cap on her hair neatly parted in the middle to reveal a low broad forehead, with something daunting in the direct stare of dark eyes under querulous brows, there was that about her that betokened, if not refinement, at any rate the mark of her breed.

It was she who ordered Mrs Claverton daily, when she came to inquire for the sick man, to be turned away from the door.

At last one day the two women met face to face on the threshold. There stood the former clerk's wife – to Elizabeth Slade Mrs Claverton, for all her money, remained still the poor clerk's wife she had been at the beginning. For the older woman nothing had changed – and yet all had changed around her: she alone remained unchanged in the landscape, like a monolith on the moor.

Mrs Claverton, her face distraught, and with an absurd propitiatory gesture of uncovering the contents of her unwanted basket, quavered forth something about having 'a thing on her mind'. If only she could see the sick man . . . If there was anything she could do . . . anything in the world?

'Anything *you* can do?' said Elizabeth Slade, screwing up her eyes in the frightening way she had, her face contorted with contempt.

Anyone who saw those two women in the court before the little, shambling farm-house would have thought the tables reversed: that the old lady erect commanded all the clay-pits in the district, while the little woman before her, anxious and afraid, was the dispossessed one.

'Anything *you* can do?' she repeated with scorn. 'There's nothin' *you* can do to undo what's been done.'

And then, in reply to the pathetic gesture of the basket once more held forth:

'No, Mary Claverton. Thanks be, there's nothin' that William Slade do want from the likes of Tom Claverton or any of *his*.'

No one in our district ever spoke of 'Tom' Claverton; whether out of respect, or lack of familiarity, or some more recondite motive, he was always referred to as Thomas Claverton in full. As if he were the company itself: which indeed he was.

Upon Elizabeth Slade's lips 'Tom' Claverton meant condescension, the condescension of a woman of family for an inferior, for a farm-hand.

The door was firmly closed in his wife's face. The poor lady gave up hope and trudged wearily back through the village, basket on arm, all the way home to town.

That evening, when work in the office was over, Thomas Claverton himself came up the familiar hard stony track to the farm. It was he who had something on his mind to deliver to the Master. Stranger that, after all these years and after such a reversal in their positions, he should at this moment think of the old Cap'n as 'the Master'.

He could not but think as he struck his foot against the rocks in the cart-track that the man who had set him on his feet was there in the house before him, dying. He had something to say to him; something to explain, to put things right between them before he died.

The way things had worked out between them was inevitable. After all, it was the way of progress. It had not been his fault if things had grown beyond the Cap'n's capacity to handle them. It was only natural that an older man should hand over to a younger: that was the way things were.

'Hand over?' – he had something else to say to the Cap'n, something for his ear alone, if he could only get to see him.

Things were apt to pray upon that alert organ, Thomas Claverton's mind: something told him that all might not be well if he could not put things right between himself and the Master at the last.

On the threshold, in the dusk, he found himself, sooner than he expected, face to face with the Master's wife.

'So ye've come at last, Tom Claverton, for what's comin' to you.'

It seemed she had been expecting him.

'I've come to see the Master,' he said, with some hesitation in that pliant voice.

'No Master of yours, Tom Claverton.'

'But I *must* see him.'

'There's no *must* about it, Tom Claverton.' The repetition of his name got on his nerves, and he said, almost beseeching:

'I've got something I *must* say to him.'

'There's nothin' ye can say to the Master now: he's past all carin' for what ye can say or do. Can ye give back what you *stole* from him and his children? No. Can ye undo all the evil ye've done to him and his? No. It's past all reckonin' what ye've been responsible for, since ye came into this district with hardly a pair of shoes to your feet, and the Master took ye in and made ye what ye are.'

Drawing herself up to her full height, head touching the lintel, one hand in ritual position on the doorpost, the other with the two end fingers outstretched as in the proper gesture for averting the evil eye, she pointed directly at him and proceeded to lay a solemn curse upon him, his family and offspring, and all his works.

'Take a good look at yerself, Tom Claverton, and see what ye really be: an oppressor of the poor, a robber of dead men's children, the cur that do bite the hand that do feed him, the thief that do come in the night, no man do know whence. But I do know whither ye shall go. The time will come when ye shall be led about the roads, more helpless than William Slade do lie now, for there shall be nobody to pity ye. Ye won't know yer own offspring, nor they know you. Nor shall any good come to they, for the evil ye have wrought upon me and mine. Ye'll be grateful at the last, glad of a grave to give ye rest in. And the day will come when there shall be no more Clavertons in Menagwins, and their name be blotted out from the face of the land.'

Breathless and haggard, like an Old Testament prophetess, she heaved herself within doors and slammed the door in his face.

Claverton felt his nerve giving way, not so much from what he had heard, as from what he had seen. For at the moment she had bidden him take a good look at himself, he had had a strange experience that shook him to the core. That experience that drowning men are said to have, or others at some unaccountable moment – always an omen of death – when a man sees himself as if from the outside; as if the soul leaves the body, and in that split moment a man sees himself as he really is.

What Thomas Claverton saw in that moment made him fly in terror, but without hope, back the way he came.

People in the village had often heard of a solemn curse being laid; but it was always in the past, in their fathers' or grandfathers' time: they had known no instance of it like this. And as time went on they forgot about it.

Elizabeth Slade joined the old Cap'n in the hard, wind-bitten cemetery of Trewarthavean; the Clavertons continued to prosper – everything came into their hands. They were the undisputed masters now, lords of our livelihood, our means of life.

Some few years after these events and before the First World War, there was, for the first time, a strike among the clay-workers in the area. They were still being paid a mere pittance, though it had risen by a fraction to a basic eighteen shillings a week.

The strike depressed the shares of Claverton and Co. The opportunity was taken by all members of the family – the young had grown to maturity now – to buy them cheap. The clay-workers were defeated, and returned to work dispirited and disunited – in true Celtic fashion – for the same pay as before.

China-clay shares were marked up in value, Claverton and Co. by as much as fifty per cent.

Everything that that family touched turned to gold.

Yet Thomas Claverton was not irrefragable, impregnable. The family had its Achilles' heel, after all; there was a weakness somewhere. In fact, there were two.

Claverton had not had that restless agility of mind, perpetually under strain, without paying some penalty for it. In his case a dire one: it was not simply that he had a nervous breakdown, he went stark mad.

I shall never forget the day when, as a boy, I heard my father, coming home from work, say that he had seen Thomas Claverton out for an airing, taken through the village, chained between his two keepers. Not long after this he was taken away and died in the lunatic asylum: a very different end from William Slade's.

Under Claverton's son William – he had been called after the old Cap'n in earlier, happier days – the affairs of the company rose to a new height of prosperity.

The outbreak of the 1914 war contributed only a temporary setback to the industry. The call-up of men into the army, the contraction of manpower, was turned to a positive advantage by the company: it was then that it began to install power-driven machinery into the pits, powerful electric hoses to wash out the clay, to pipe the clap liquid to the ports, to dispense with men.

When men came back from the forces, there were far fewer jobs for them: they had to go elsewhere, emigrate to America, Canada, Australia.

William Claverton, of course, had not gone to the war: far too valuable a man in the industry: in fact indispensable, as his father had been found before him. He did some war-work, however, he was very good at recruiting others.

It was in the course of his war-work that he met his bride: a woman of ample figure and unknown antecendents, equipped with an impoverished but purposeful widowed mother, who made short work of the most eligible bachelor in the district. The mother was lean and hungry: she did very well for herself in marrying her daughter to the largest china-clay fortune in the town. The daughter was as good-hearted as she was stout: she married William Claverton without noticeable reluctance. Then, in giving birth to a son, she shortly died.

After this brief experience of bliss, William Claverton went back to business – to business and the bottle.

Thomas Claverton's widow lived on in their large villa-residence, a martyr to arthritis, immobile in the hands of faithful servants to the number of four – three indoors and one out. When she died, she left everything to the eldest son, William, trusty guardian of the family's interests.

The ageing aunt had her own comfortable establishment in another part of the town, with her own complement of domestics, her own catalogue of complaints. For many years she had entertained a *tendresse* for the family solicitor, whom we knew as Lawyer Treloar, and he for her. But, a confirmed old maid on her part, a confirmed bachelor on his, they made nothing of it. She left everything to her nephew, head of the family – a not inconsiderable fortune of some £45,000. So, oddly enough, did Lawyer Treloar.

Everything came to William Claverton, nursing his surly loneliness, his disappointment in life, his miserliness, along with the bottle.

Hopes had been entertained earlier of the second son, Cyril. They were early disappointed. Though he qualified as a barrister, he never practised. He was the only member of the family not to live in the district that had made their fortune.

But he, too, kept a house in the town he rarely visited. He was the only one of them all to display any aesthetic sense, though it paid tribute to the family spirit by taking an accumulative form. Up amid the laurels of Trenowth Road, surrounded by sombre overgrown shrubberies, he kept a houseful of antiques, but *stuffed* with antique furniture and china. It was a storehouse rather than somewhere to live.

It all came to William Claverton, along with a pretty portfolio of investments, by no means all of them in china-clay. William himself was thinking of dispersing his interests, securing himself more widely.

To what point?

His youngest brother was a regular *memento mori*. Brought up to do nothing in particular, he was already subject to delirium tremens. The family sent him off on long cruises 'for the benefit of his health'; they sent him to South America in the company of his nurse, who married him and took him off their hands.

They came back and settled in a pleasant modern villa they built for him, without much hope, away from the town and its depressing attractions. The best materials from the works went into it – clay cement-blocks, wood, lead, tiles; they had the best workmen working on it, building it solidly and giving it a good finish.

He no sooner moved into it than he died there.

They say his ghost haunts the place. The Slades should know: one of them bought it after his death.

Life was closing in, with its sense of futility and disappointment, for William Claverton.

Futility in every sense, except financial. In this field his hand retained the family touch, his father's cunning.

Shortly before the second war, with the market at its height, he disposed of all his china-clay interests, centred upon old Cap'n Slade's original pit, still gallantly producing, though unrecognizably enlarged. All the landmarks thereabouts had gone, the farm-house disappeared.

Something, however, remained.

William Claverton sold out to an immense national combine: he retained nothing of his personal or family interests, so unscrupulously built up and tenaciously maintained. They brought him well over £300,000 – with what had otherwise fallen in to him, an immense fortune for our small world. He was a man worth well on the way to half a million pounds.

Yet he was a soured and saddened man. It was said amongst us that the dearest ambition of his life was to represent the china-clay area in Parliament. He would give anything to write the letters M.P. after his name: William Claverton M.P.

It seemed a simple enough ambition for a man to cherish, especially for someone with all his money. But no one would dream of asking him and he knew it – perhaps that was the bitterest blow of all. It was not that he could not make a speech, hardly string two sentences together; it was something more undefinable, something hard to explain: no one could conceive of his making even a public appearance. And, in fact, long the most powerful man in our lives, he never did.

An even bitterer source of disappointment lay in his son. The boy, indubitably a Claverton physically, had inherited nothing of the family ability, but only its nervous strain. He was, we all thought, more or less of a moron. The one respect in which he differed from his family inheritance was that he already gave every sign of being recklessly extravagant.

Perhaps this came from his unknown mother's side. Hence also his infatuation with music, or at least noise. The combination in him of the Claverton acquisitiveness with his passion for sound took odd form. The first to have a gramophone in the neighbourhood, and that of the most expensive and powerful type, he used to keep it on from early morning to late at night. Whenever one passed by, there it was blaring forth at full blast all the loudest and vulgarest records, of which he had accumulated a vast repertory.

When the second war came, he served in it no more than his father had in the first. A great effort was made to emphasize the incapacity that normally it was the family line to ignore. A strong push was made to get him exempt from service, and with success. For the time he was got away from home to 'work on the land'.

When the war was over, back he came, a new radio-gramophone, with amplifier, louder and more shattering than ever.

It was at this time that William Claverton suddenly and unexpectedly died – of a heart attack. No one credited him with a heart till that moment, though he had put a strain upon it for long enough.

Nothing became him in life like his leaving it. For, a man only in middle age, he had made no provision against death duties, and he died in the first year of the Labour Government he detested so much, with death duties at their peak and every kind of tax, income-tax and surtax, at its maximum.

It was not long after that his son died in a road accident. Within a couple of years the immense Claverton fortune had two lots of death-duties and estate duties – at a time too of grave financial difficulty, with stock markets precarious to realize upon and shares much below the rates William Claverton's fortune had been calculated at for duty.

Large as it had been, these two successive blows largely dissipated it. As when a meteor plunges down to dissolution, a few fragments split off and went to distant, unrecognized and unrecognizable, connections. Nothing of the Claverton fortune went to charity or to the town and district that had created it. Nothing to show that they had ever been there or walked those roads, the hedges white with the clay-dust from which arose their vanished, confiscated wealth – nobody the better for it. While their name – even as old Elizabeth Slade had prophesied – was blotted out from the land.

Winston Graham

JACKA'S FIGHT

My grandfather was called Jacka Fawle. He used to tell this story, often he would tell this story, and often-times you could not stop him; but it did not matter so much because it was true. He lived into old age, and we children would know if any stranger came by that he would take the first opportunity of telling this story, you could rest assured, so that, hearing it so often, we knew it all by heart and would chime in if he left out a detail. But it was all true.

My grandfather, he was born in Helston in Cornwall in 1853 and went down a mine before he was twelve. At eighteen he married Essie Penrose and in the next twelve years they had eight children, my mother youngest of them all. In 1883, the mining slump came to its worst, and Wheal Marble, where he was working, closed down. So like many of his friends, he thought he would go to America to make his way. There was work there and opportunities there, money to be made. It was a long way and a hard journey, but men wrote home that they were doing well out there. Some even sent home money so that their wives could go out and join them.

Well, it was a hard parting from Jacka and Essie, but there was little chance of her going with him with all the little children crying around her feet. Not that she showed much sign of wishing to go, for, like many women born within sight of the sea, she really feared it and trembled to set foot upon it. So she moved with her young brood of chicks into her father's tiny cottage and bade a tearful farewell to Jacka as he left home. With a Bible in his pocket and a bundle on his shoulder he set off one wet day in March, and they all stood in the doorway in the rain watching while his short sturdy figure grew smaller and smaller trudging down the lane. He walked west on the old coaching road, to Truro, to Mitchell, and thence to Padstow, where he took ship for San Francisco.

It was a terrible voyage – four months it took them around Cape Horn in villainous seas and then all the way up the western seaboard of the New World. Scurvy and sea-sickness and dysentery and bad food. Seven months passed near to the day when my grandmother opened her first letter from him. It was full of good cheer and good heart and he never mentioned the hardships for he still hoped she would join him in a year or two. But in fact he had been little enough time in California, casting around as you might say, before he changed his trade. Mines there might be, but much of it was more like prospecting than what he belonged to do. Chance of riches and chance of nothing at all. While building opportunities were everywhere. Houses, churches, factories, all were going up like mushrooms on a damp evening. And bricklayers were in short supply.

So he became a bricklayer, my grandfather became a bricklayer, and his wages were good and steady.

He too was good and steady because he had been reared in the Primitive Methodist connexion; and many times, he said, in those early years he was thankful for his careful upbringing. San Francisco was a wild and wicked place, where any man could go to hell for the price of a few weeks' wages. Indeed all California was the same: a lost continent where lust and strong drink and greed and vice were raging. So he made few friends and those were strictly of his own kind. There were other Cornishmen in the city and he tended to be drawn to them because of memories of home. And he attended chapel every Sunday.

Each month, on the first of the month, he wrote a letter home, and each month, regular as a clock, he sent home a small sum of money to help support his family. Each letter ended: 'Hopeing that soon dear wife you will be able joyne me your ever loving Husband.'

But the months turned into years and she did not join him. The children were all well and all growing, she wrote, but so slow. And Essie *could not* face the sea . . .

If there had been any work at home Jacka would have returned, given up his regular well-paid work and gone home, for he was a family man, and it fretted him that all his children would be strangers to him. Sometimes too he could not help but cast his eye upon another woman; yet by grace he saw this as a lure of Satan and hurriedly dismissed carnal thoughts from his mind. Even his memories of Essie were fading. She wrote him: oh yes, she wrote him, telling him homely details of life in Helston; but she was no handy one with the pen, far worse than he; and the cost of the post was so high that often she missed a month.

All this time he was saving, was Jacka. He lived quiet and he lived frugal and some he sent home and some he saved. But it was tedious work. First it was $500, then it was $800, then $1,000. By the time he was thirty-seven, he had saved $3,000 and had not seen his wife and family for seven years. Seven long years. It seemed a lifetime. But in all things he was canny, and he kept his money deposited in different banks to lessen the risk. He came to know northern California well, for all his work was not in San Francisco. He worked with Irishmen, Poles, Portuguese, Swedes, Italians, and second generation Americans. But all the time he stayed true to himself and unchangingly Cornish. He would meet with five or six other Cornishmen every Sunday and they'd talk of Pasties and Leekie Pie and Pilchards and the damp beautiful landscapes of home.

One day in the early nineties one of these Cornishmen, called by the name of Sil Polglaze, he came to Jacka and told him that there was this middleweight boxer come to town just fresh come from New Zealand but a true Cornishman as ever was; and he was fighting a man called Abe Congle in the Park next Saturday afternoon and how about them going along? Jacka hesitated about this, wondering if there might be sin in it, but it did not seem so, so he said all right, he'd go. Thus he took his first look at Bob Fitzsimmons.

It was a motley crowd that day, no mistake, and nearly all of them shouting for Congle; but Fitzsimmons stunned Congle unconscious in the second round. So it was that all the patriotism in Jacka, lying underneath and scarce acknowledged, came bubbling out like an adit from a mine, and afterwards he pushed his way sore throated through the crowd and spoke to the Cornish boxer and his wife.

Now Fitzsimmons at this time was twenty-eight, and no figure of a boxer at all. You could laugh, and many did, for already he had a bald patch and had long arms and legs like thin poles quite out of proportion to his great chest and stomach. He weighed scarcely more than 150 lbs, and he had a round red face and his teeth were large and bright like wet tombstones and had stood all the unkindness of the ring. He would have done proud as a comic turn in a circus but it would be foolishness to take him seriously as a boxer. Only Congle did that. Only Congle, still being doused with water like a babe at a christening.

Soon Fitzsimmons was telling Jacka that he too had been born in Helston – in Helston of all places! – and asking all manner of questions about it and whether old so-and-so was still alive, and if the Hal-an-Tow was still danced. I reckon Jacka became his slave for life at that first meeting, and sure enough he was there at the second fight when Fitzsimmons laid low a hard tough Negro called Black Pearl. This time it took him two more rounds, but the outcome was just the same. He went in soaking up the punishment which would have stopped any ordinary man, and then let fly with his long incredible fists and presently there was a black heap on the ground, and Fitzsimmons was standing there, Jacka said, with his long arms dangling and his white teeth glinting like a bone in his raw red face.

Afterwards, after Fitz left San Francisco, Jacka tried to keep track of him by reading the newspapers, but it wasn't that easy. Fitz went all over the States, but his news value was not high and sometimes the San Francisco papers did not bother to mention when he had been in a fight. Only the big ones were reported, and every now and then through the years that followed Jacka would find an item saying that Fitzsimmons had beaten Peter Maker, or Joe Godfrey or Millard Zenda.

Now although Jacka was a rare one for all things Cornish,

he'd made no boast about it living in such a mixed community, and he was content to be called a Limey when talk of nationalities came up. But Fitz's appearance on the scene had fired his local loyalties with a hot new fire, and, while he was not the sort of man to make a show of himself in front of others, he was never above a mention of the wonderful prowess of his friend and fellow townsman Bob Fitzsimmons, and to let it be known what great fighting men Cousin Jacks were when their blood was up. So he became much more vocally Cornish, so to say, and so he found himself sometimes at odds with the Americans and the Swedes and the Irish. Just because he had so much to say for Fitzsimmons they derided Fitzsimmons the more. And so hard words and hard thoughts grew up, half jesting, half serious, and they centred around the name and the figure and the prestige of the scrawny, ungainly, ageing boxer.

When someone brought in the word that Fitzsimmons had put in his challenge for the heavyweight championship of the world everyone except Jacka fairly died with laughter. The great James J. Corbett, Gentleman Jim, six feet one inch in height and 190 lbs in weight, with not an ounce of spare flesh upon him, the best boxer of his age and the idol of the United States, was too superior in every way to be matched with this shambling creature. The challenge was of course refused, and all Jacka's mates told him that this refusal had saved Fitz's life. Quick to defend his idol, out on a limb on his behalf, Jacka shouted that Corbett was afraid and that Ruby Bob was being cheated of the title.

How they laughed! How they lay about and laughed till the tears ran into the bricks and mortar. From then on it was the recognized thing to have Jacka on about it. Any time anyone craved for a quick laugh they had only to mention this challenge and Jacka would be upon his feet and arguing for his friend. I think my grandfather was a good tempered sort of Christian most of his life, but he oftentimes lost his temper over this. It changed him a little, made him morose. He never fought anyone because fighting wasn't his way; but he came near to it more than once.

So more years passed. Jacka was growing grey at the temples and heavier in the girth of neck and stomach. His eldest son was twenty-five, his youngest daughter fourteen, and he was a grandfather four times over. He had not saved so much money in the last seven years as in the first seven, for he had come to live a little cosier himself, to value a good meal and a glass of beer and a pipe of tobacco at the day's end. But he had saved all the same. In another ten years he reckoned he would have enough to go home, to buy a smallholding somewhere around Helford River and live out the rest of his life in quietness and peace. By then all his children would have flown; but some of them with luck would not have flown so far, and he and Essie would be able to play with the grandchildren. It was an ambition as yet too far away to look forward to, but there it stood as a reward for a long life of toil. And patient Essie would be there waiting for him still.

Fitzsimmons too had gone on his way, putting all manner of boxers down and out, growing older too and scrawnier but still not quite finished. He was too hard for the young ones – yet. They just had to bide their time, while age and hard knocks crept up on him. So one day the distinguished Corbett found he could no longer ignore this middleweight that no other middleweight could endure the course with. A match was made, arranged, actually fixed for 17 March next, the contest to be for the heavyweight championship of the world, in Carson City, Nevada, the winner to receive a purse of twelve thousand dollars.

And everyone knew for certain who that would be. In vain Jacka defended his idol. They jeered at Jacka, and the good nature had gone out of it on both sides. One big Irish bricklayer called O'Brien was stronger even than most for Corbett – who was half Irish – and offered five to one in any amount and currency Jacka cared to name – if he dared to back his fancy. Jacka refused. In the years in California he had attended chapel whenever he could, and, although his sternest convictions had worn a little away, he still knew gambling to be sinful and he had never indulged in it.

In the weeks before the fight, however, O'Brien continued to goad him; and at last, hemmed into a corner where refusal spelt cowardice, he bet O'Brien fifty dollars at seven to one that Ruby Robert would win. The money was paid over to the foreman, a big Swede called Lindquist, who was known to be a straight and honest man.

Carson City is only just in the state of Nevada on the other side of Lake Tahoe, and so little more than 160 miles from San Francisco. It was only just off the main railway east, and it was told that the Virginia and Truckee Railroad were laying special tracks so that rich spectators could go all the way on special sleeping coaches, travel overnight and be ready fresh for the contest in the morning. The poorer folk by leaving before it was light could arrive in another special train just the same. Tickets for the fight were $5, and early Jacka bought one. Some of his mates would not pay the money but said they would be able to get in cheaper on the day.

Sitting over his pipe in the evening talking to Sil Polglaze and others of his cronies, Jacka thought much, he said, of the money he had wagered. He stood to lose fifty dollars – but to gain three hundred and fifty. The odds were not excessive, for eight and nine to one were being offered in some quarters. Jacka had the courage of his convictions and so trusted Fitz to win. So *he* stood to win. So he stood to win a considerable sum. It was a sin to gamble; but was this exactly gambling, properly to be so described? He did not feel sinful now he had risked the money. He did not think he would feel sinful if he took O'Brien's stake. He did not think he would feel sinful if he even added to the money at risk.

He would never have done it but for the burning conviction within him that a good Cornishman was better than a good Irish-American. The patriotic resentment he felt towards his mates was as passionate as if he had been called to declare his Faith. And his passion, equally, was not based on judgement or on knowledge. He had not seen Fitzsimmons for six years. He had never seen Corbett in his life. But he was called upon to testify. And the only way he could testify was by risking his money. His hard-earned, laboriously hoarded money. Some of it. Not much, but some. Altogether in the world, if he counted every silver and gold coin he owned and every bank chit, he could muster about $5,600. It was some tidy little nest-egg. How much of it could be put at risk? $300 perhaps? He stood the chance of converting in into $2,000. Such a small investment – less six months' saving – to gain so much.

Where most of the bets were laid was in the pool rooms, and these were places which for long years Jacka had avoided as haunts of the devil. But this last four years he had taken to going into Scherz's Rooms with Silvester Polglaze for a quiet game of pool and a glass of beer. No wagers, mind. Just the play. They played for the pleasure and the relaxation. But this was where the wagers for the fight were placed, and the odds were put up on a blackboard, and Jacka licked his lips and saw them shortening, then lengthening again after Corbett gave an interview, then shortening as the time of the fight drew near. Scherz was a Swiss, a tough, hard, cold man but he'd never cheat you. A lot of working men left their money with him because they trusted him before the banks. So this was the place to risk your money if you wanted to risk your money, where it would be safe if you won. Jacka put on $200 at eight to one, $100 at six to one, another $100 at four to one; then when the odds stretched out again, he put on a further $300 at seven to one.

It was strange, Jacka said, that after he had put the money on, handed over the counter in gold dollars, he felt first a terrible hard nasty sinking sensation of depression, and then after an hour or so a sudden upsurge of hope. No twinges of conscience, that was strange, no feeling that he shouldn't have done it, only an urge to do more. It was like a drug; but it wasn't like the ordinary gambler's drug, when the wins and the losses, the sudden ups and downs of fortune carry a man fluctuating till he loses his stability altogether. There were no losses in this – nor as yet any wins: there was nothing to elate Jacka and nothing to depress him, only a burning conviction that somehow his ungainly hero would come through. A week before the fight he went with two Swedes into the California Athletic Club and, encouraged by them, put on another $500 at twenty to three. Then at work he took a bet with a man called Sullivan for $200. On the Wednesday before the fight, Jacka went like a thief to one of his banks – the one he trusted least – and withdrew $800. From there, with no one to accompany him and no one to egg him on, he went out and laid his bets.

The last days were an age in passing. Jacka lived in a daze, feverishly thumbing through the papers, talking scarcely to no one, refusing even the dangling bait of argument; only stopping in at one bank and then another to draw more money out. Before the fight more than half his total savings had been placed upon Fitzsimmons to win.

On the day all those who were going to the fight had to be up at four a.m. to catch the early morning train. All those leaving off work for the day lost a day's wages and a good conduct mark, but the absenteeism was so great that a whole mass of workers could not be penalized.

It was a long train drawing out of Oakland Station, and a slow one as it wound its way puffing up through the foothills of the Nevadas. Jacka sat with Sil Polglaze and a man called Mark Lothar; Jacka sat in a corner of the hard wooden carriage and spoke to no one. Only his eyes gleamed like one who has seen the light. The train was crowded, and men standing in the compartments shuffled and swayed against each other for four hours until at last it came to rest in the specially built sidings in Carson City.

Here everyone fell out in a swarm: it was as if the train could not have held so many men: they poured from every door and flooded off into the town. The sun was just rising on a brilliant day.

Carson City, the capital city of the State of Nevada, lies in a bowl of the Sierra Nevada at an altitude, so I am told, of nearly 5,000 feet, and is surrounded by mountains. It was then a flourishing township, Jacka said, with a population of about 2,000 people and had several handsome buildings, including the capitol, a mint and an orphans' home, and a good sprinkling of pool rooms. This morning the mountains were glimmering with snow, and an icy breeze loitered through the town. Dust whorls rose in the streets, and the wooden sidewalks were packed five abreast with men strolling through or looking for food or drifting slowly towards the arena to be sure of gaining good seats. In the gutter mendicants and others stood begging alms or selling favours and crying out for attention. Pretty many of the men who had come to see the fight already wore four-leafed clovers in honour of St Patrick's Day and to show they supported Corbett. Some of the badges were six inches across, and some men wore green shirts and green hats and green ribbons on their sleeves. Women were very absent from the scene.

Food was a big problem, for the eating-houses and tents were soon full, and long jostling angry queues formed outside them; but Jacka and his friends had brought meat and potato pasties that Jacka had cooked the night before, and so after a brief walk around the town they tramped off to the arena and got seats. Jacka was much concerned as to which corner the boxers were occupying; Corbett, they found, had been given the south-east corner, so they took seats as near to the north-west corner as they could get. It was a great amphitheatre of a place with the white peaks of the snow-covered mountains all round. You could see the ring from almost anywhere; but although the fight was supposed to start at ten it was scarce dotted with people when they arrived, and they squatted on the grass to break their fasts. After they had eaten they went off in turn, and Jacka, passing a betting booth which had the guarantee of the local bank to support it, could not refrain from slipping in and putting on another $200 as a final token – though here he found the odds had shortened to five to two.

By ten the arena was almost half full, but no sign of the boxers and only one or two officials fussing round the ring. Old pugilists of one sort or another strolled all about, followed by their admirers. Sharkey was there, the only one who had beaten Fitzsimmons – though this, it was generally admitted, was with a foul blow. John L. Sullivan, grey-haired now but as big as ever. And Goddard, and Billy Madden and others. Not far from where Jacka was sitting was a strange contraption on wooden legs which he was told was a kinetoscope. This, they said, would take moving pictures of the fight – or rather many pictures which shown quickly one after the other would give the appearance of movement. It was said this was the first time such an invention had ever been used at a boxing-match.

At ten-thirty the arena was three-quarters full, and the sun beat down and the wind had fallen away. This might be March and high in the Nevadas, but it was more like San Francisco in the summer. Everyone had come wrapped up for a cold day and everyone was now sweating. Coats, jerseys, mufflers, waistcoats came off. They lay in piles on the grass and cluttered up the aisles.

Now the famous boxers each made an appearance in the ring and made speeches, most of them challenging the winner of this fight: and they were greeted with applause or derision according to the wayward fancy of the crowd. Then there was a big cheer as Mrs Fitzsimmons came upon the scene. She looked some pale – though normally she was as rosy-faced as her husband – and went down the east aisle to sit in a box beside Governor Sadler and Senator Ingalls. A man behind Jacka who was a Carson City man and had a stake in the local newspaper said out loud that Fitzsimmons had told him that win or lose, this was his last fight. He would soon be thirty-five, and not many boxers stayed in the game above the age of thirty, except as human punch-balls. And Mrs Fitz was tired of travelling and longed for a quiet home life.

'Thirty-five, damme,' muttered Sil Polglaze, who had put fifty dollars on Fitz. ''Tis old, Jacka. 'Tis a bare five year youngerer than me, and I could no more fight than ride an ass backwards. It makes you think, Jacka.'

'*You*,' said Jacka, contemptuous. 'You could no more fight not when you was twenty. Fitz is differenter. Fitz'll not let us down.' But for the first time for days the veil of self-hypnosis that was upon him was shaken. This ageing man who talked of retiring – was he the man on whom you risked all your own hopes of retirement?

Muldoon, the timekeeper, was up there now, with Dan Stuart the promoter, Physician Guinan, Manager Brady, Billy Jordan the Master of Ceremonies, Referee Siler, and other big pots. The local man behind Jacka was useful, for he knew the names of them all and pointed them out in a loud voice.

Then suddenly there was a great roar from the crowd, which by now was barely short of 12,000 strong. Bob Fitzsimmons was coming down along the side seats. Martin Julian led the way, then came Fitz, and he was followed by his seconds and half a dozen of other men. Fitz was in a bright pink and mauve dressing-gown and looked just the same bald red-faced thin-legged man Jacka had met six years gone. All the fights he had been in since, all the punishment he'd given and accepted, hadn't altered his face except the skin round his eyes was puffier and he walked a little more with his neck thrust forward as if he was wearing a discomfortable collar. As he passed the box where his wife was sitting he stopped and kissed her, then went on to the ring.

Then before ever he had climbed in the great James J. Corbett had appeared from the other side, with his brother Joe at his side and six other men in attendance. The man behind Jacka was giving names to them all, but Jacka paid little attention. His heart was suddenly wanting to fall into his stomach as he saw the difference in physique betwixt the two fighters.

At the roars which went on and on, several thousand more folk outside the ground who had been waiting for a reduction in the price of the tickets concluded that after all they must pay the proper charge and came pushing and thrusting in, filling up the empty spaces. Few women were to be seen, and those few had peroxide hair and you could hazard a lively guess at their business. To all this Jacka was now blind, as he saw the preparations going forward in the ring. Near beside him the man working the kinetoscope came out to take sightings. One after another, men were making speeches in the ring. The time wanted twenty-five minutes of noon. Then Billy

Jordan introduced these two fighters and everyone went mad again. When this was done, the fighters went back to their corners and a silence fell like the day before the Day of Judgement. Overhead was not a cloud, not a wisp, only the brilliant hot sun that made many men drape kerchiefs upon their heads. Fitzsimmons' bald patch shone like a polished saucer. The timekeeper took up his place beside the gong, and behind him stood a guard with a club to strike down anyone who tried to interfere. The referee was in the middle looking at Muldoon. Muldoon nodded, the two boxers stripped off their gowns and came into the centre of the ring, Fitz thin and gangling with his great chest, looking like a hairless ape, Corbett, far taller and heavier, handsome built, in the peak of condition, proudly ready for the fight. The gong sounded and they were off.

Jacka watched the beginning but says he could remember precious little of the first few rounds. Suddenly the veil was cleft altogether from before his self-opinionated eyes and he saw not two men struggling for a crown but his own wicked wanton recklessness in risking three-quarters of his fourteen years' savings on the outcome of a fight. He felt sick, his bowels rumbled, hammers beat in his head, the blows raining on Fitzsimmons might have been raining upon his own body.

And certainly blows were landing upon Fitzsimmons everywhere. He was lighter than Corbett, shorter than Corbett and *slower* than Corbett. He looked smaller even than his eleven stone four pounds. Everyone knew he had a punch like a mule, but he never was given a chance to use it. The crowd were in raptures of pleasure. Nine in every ten backed Corbett; he was from San Francisco, he was Irish-American, he was good-looking, he was quite the gentleman. Fitz was going to receive what was coming to him.

And Fitz does. After the third round it looks like a massacre. Corbett is boxing like a champion, powerful and fast, landing blow upon blow. Some Fitz partly parries, some he takes full strength on his face and his body, yet he scarcely ever seems to wince or cringe away. Every now and then he will snake out that terrible left of his, but it never finds its mark. His face is red, his mouth bleeding, one eye partly closed – already. It is a strange expression he has upon his face, Jacka says; there is sentiment and tragedy in it, and a sort of fixed grin that bears it all while he still keeps closing in, waiting for an opening, his eyes watchful. There is no temper in those eyes, Jacka says, no resentment, just watchfulness and utter determination that he must not be beat.

In the fourth round there is a lot of in-fighting, with Corbett landing three punches to Fitzsimmons' one. 'Good old Jim!' the crowd screams. 'Good old boy, good old Jim!' while Jacka sits there too paralysed even to shout for his man. Unmarked, Corbett steps away from Fitz, thumping in half arm blows the while, to the face, to the nose, to the ribs, to the jaw. Sometimes Fitz looks like a turtle, his head, red and damaged, half sunk between his great shoulders for protection from the storm.

In the fifth round it appears as if Fitz is done. His lips are swollen, the eye half closed, his nose bleeding, his body crimson all over, part with the blows it has received, part from the blood on Corbett's gloves. He begins to lie on Corbett's shoulder, trying to get a breather, trying to smother Corbett's blows to his ribs. 'Knock his head off, Jim!' they shout. 'Punch his 'ead!' 'Lay 'im out, boy!' It seems endless, that round. At the bell Corbett walks smiling to his corner. Fitz turns and plods slowly back to his. They are betting again around Jacka, or offering bets: no one is taking them. Eight to one it is again now. Back to the first odds. Now ten to one. Ten to one, a loud-mouthed check-shirted miner is shouting. Jacka gets up, near sick, fumbles in his pocket, takes out his purse and from it a hundred dollars in gold, offers it to Check-shirt. Everyone stares – there is a wild cackle of laughter. Check-shirt thumps Jacka on the back. 'Right, pard, right, it's a deal: settle after the fight.'

In the sixth round it is all Corbett, and he lands a tremendous smash in the second minute that forces Fitzsimmons to his knees and sends more blood spurting from his nose. Fitz climbs slowly up, patient, his great teeth still showing white in a face that no one any longer can recognize. Corbett's body is smeared with blood now, but it is not his own. The seventh round is much the same, Fitz crouching to avoid the worst punishment, and every now and then darting out his terrible blows that still have not lost all their strength.

In the eighth round Corbett has clearly decided to finish it off. Dropping his own skill, he steps in and lands almost as he likes, blows to the neck and the chest and the ribs and the heart. Men round Jacka shout: 'Why don't Fitz give up? Why don't he quit?' In the ninth Fitzsimmons is down again after a right upper-cut that would have put an ordinary man out for ten minutes. He is up on the count of nine, leaning on Corbett, hitting back, weakly but enough to prevent another knock-down before the bell. Corbett is smiling again as he walks back to his corner. So far as you can tell he is unmarked. The check-shirted miner offers Jacka another hundred dollars at fifteen to one. Jacka just stares and shakes his head.

The minute rest has given the seconds a chance again to sponge the blood off Fitz's face, and he comes up looking no different from what he looked six rounds ago. Corbett will need an axe to finish the job, nothing less will do. They fight toe to toe through the first half, and Fitzsimmons seems no weaker for all his terrible punishment. Now he suddenly lands hard and high and often on Corbett, and though Corbett is not hurt, it is blow for blow for the first time in all the contest, and a significant change. He goes back to his corner with a more thoughtful look on his handsome face, and you even hear one or two men in the crowd shout: 'Game boy, Fitz!' The eleventh round is much the same, and much whispering after it in Corbett's corner. Divided counsels. There is no doubt Corbett can outbox this indestructible land crab but can he outlive him? Can he by boxing ever tire him out? It is a fight to a finish, and somehow Fitzsimmons must be put down for a count of ten. In the twelfth round Corbett is getting tired and he takes a breather. He boxes comfortably, leading Ruby Robert about the bloodstained ring, landing when he wants but avoiding a fight, while Fitzsimmons patiently pursues him. Suddenly at the end of the round, Fitz manoeuvres Corbett into a corner and lands some violent vicious punches to the body.

The bell goes and Corbett's face has changed. You can now see no expression on Fitz's at all; it is too badly cut and battered. So to the thirteenth and Corbett comes out with a last intent to finish it. Incredibly it is the fastest hardest round of all the whole bout. Now Fitzsimmons is giving as good as he gets, and the crowd stand up and shriek and bawl its head off. Toe to toe they fight, and Corbett again gets the best of it. A great blow to Fitz's ribs causes him to drop his hands and for a moment it looks all over. Corbett swings to the jaw, and by a split second Fitz takes the step back that saves him. Then they are at it hammer and tongs again to the last moment of the round.

So to the fourteenth and Jacka is standing up all through it, jaw slack, eyes staring, like a revivalist who has seen the light. For Fitzsimmons is growing confident, those long thin terrible arms after all his punishment are shooting out like pistons, driving Corbett before them. The crowd are mad with the noise and the excitement. Fitz's blows knock aside the champion's defence, a half dozen take their toll, and then a withering deadly left just below the ribs and Corbett sags. Fitz's right comes up to the point of the jaw and Gentleman Jim Corbett topples and slides and kneels and falls, and is down and out.

Then all hell breaks loose. Within moments the ring is invaded, officials swept away. Men shout and scream, seconds fight to protect their man. In the middle of it Corbett comes round, dazed and shaken, and thinks the fight is still in progress – he lays out a newspaper man cold with one swing and rushes across to Fitzsimmons and gives him a tremendous punch in the face, which Fitz shakes bloodily off like all the rest. The men pull Corbett away and minutes pass in a maelstrom of fighting and shouting. Somewhere amidst it Referee Siler holds Fitzsimmons' shaking glove aloft, and somewhere amidst it Corbett, still protesting, accepts defeat.

Jacka is trembling from head to foot and his shirt is like it has been dropped in the river. He fights his way towards the ring and near him is Mrs Fitzsimmons fighting her own way, and he catches up with her and kisses her hand, mumbling meaningless expressions of joy. Others are fighting and falling over the chairs, and it is an age before anything like order and sanity is restored. Then the biggest surprise of all for Jacka is that he finds big-mouth Check-shirt waiting beside him shaking his shoulder and wanting to pay him a thousand dollars.

So my grandfather, as a result of a single fight for the heavyweight championship of the world, because of his reckless pig-headed belief in a fellow countryman and a fellow townsman (who was no more than a middleweight, and an ageing middleweight at that) and the insane risk he took in backing that belief – made $24,000. So with this and the little extra he had not put at risk, he came overland to New York and thence by sea to Falmouth, and from there by coach to Helston. And there he arrived in triumph and was met by Essie, grown grey and portly, and his five sons, all taller than he, and his three daughters, of whom my mother was the youngest, and his four daughters-in-law and his one son-in-law and his five grandchildren, all waiting for him, all nineteen of them, who with Essie's mother made a round score, and they partook of a splendid tea together at the Angel in Helston and then went out their several ways all over the country, and all twenty of them never met together at the same time ever again.

But Grandfather Jacka, a rich man by the standards of the county and the time, bought a handsome little farm with land running down to the Helford River, and there I was born, and there he lived out a pleasant, useful, quiet and agreeable life for another thirty-six years. And never a stranger would pass the door but what Jacka must tell of how he came to be there and how he had risked so much over a fight in Carson City, Nevada, at the turn of the century.

And when it came to my turn, from that fight, thirty-six years later, I inherited three hundred pounds.

David Watmough

ASHES

In the March vigour of a Cornish spring I stared contentedly past flimsy muslin curtains to the rockery awash in the morning sun. Years before I had built that rockery: staggered with the granite stones from the car trunk to that site below the stone wall.

Helped by my brothers Tom and Joe I had piled and patted the mound of earth on which the boulders were to finally sit. Then the casting around for special plants and flowers to splash color between the silvery grey stones. The wild daffodils that swayed there now were from the orchard of Polgarrow Farm – their small white bulbs easily uprooted from the loose black loam beneath the apple trees. Joe had gone with me for them. They were still in bloom, I remembered. It must've been about the same time of year.

Joe had still been in Dental School. Now fiftyish, fat and raising a second brood of children and quarreling with a third wife, I doubted whether he could lift one of those boulders that had sunk to deceptive size in the earth, through the years.

Then, though, he had been lean, fresh-faced and full of energy: challenging me at every point over the proportions of the rockery, the disposition of the granite stones, the kinds of rockery plants. I shrugged. Joe had changed . . . So had I . . . So had the rockery . . . I stared out a clump of sea-drift which Tom and I had collected from the clifftop near Pentire Head. Change? Well who hadn't changed in the twenty years or more since the rockery'd been built?

Playing in the rooms of that house, pushing our way laughing through the tamarisk hedge, chopping firewood in the linney, mowing lawns, squabbling over toys . . . my brothers had been my best friends. Now we were all three complete strangers. You can't change more than that, I thought. And sighed, my nose to the cold glass of the window, as mother walked in with a cup of coffee.

'Here you are, Davey. There's a biscuit in the saucer: You like the chocolate ones, don't you? It's funny, Tom always went for the gingerbreads. And Joe . . . Joe would stick to my cake – provided the top was burnt enough, that is, and I hadn't used candied peel. Remember that, Davey?'

'And we'd all scream if you put in any marzipan! 'Course I remember! As a matter of fact I was just standing here remembering building that rockery out there. We all three did it – a Saturday morning. It was about this time of year because the daffs were out then, too.'

'Davey?' There was something about her voice which made me turn fully around, away from the living room window.

'Yes mother?'

'There's – there's something I had in mind for you to do when you came home.'

'You mean you waited for me to come all the way from Vancouver? My goodness! Must be special!' I spoke lightly but I knew she was having difficulty in getting something out – something that was important, maybe even painful. My mother, diminutive, in her mid-seventies, never had hesitations in speaking frankly. Her shyness never frustrated her candour. 'It's – it's to do with your daddy.'

I knew it was. She'd been a widow for little over a year. Once, when 'phoning from British Columbia, I had heard her sob a little: the first time her voice had caught in my hearing since childhood. My presence there, at that moment, was largely to do with finding out how she was coping with widowhood, with the new loneliness . . . She busied herself rearranging some African figurines that she and my father had brought home on successive visits to my brother in Nairobi.

'It's something I'd rather you not bother the others with – I mean there's no need for you to tell either Tom or Joe.' I just waited.

'It's his ashes, Davey. I've got them here.'

'You mean – in the house? Here at Tregildern?'

'I brought them back after the funeral – from the crematorium. He wouldn't have wanted them left in London, you know that.'

'No. He'd want them in Cornwall all right.'

'Over the parish was what he always used to say.'

'Where? Where've you –'

'Got them? In the bureau over there. I didn't really know what to do, you see. I mean I can't get out in the fields any more, Davey. Not with my legs acting up. Then there's no one round I'd like to ask – I mean not on something as personal as that. Then – when you wrote to say you were coming . . .'

'Well of course I will. It's just the thought –'

'Your daddy was the last one to be sentimental about death, you know. When he wasn't saying he'd like his remains scattered, he was telling me to fling them in the dustbin!'

'I tell you what, I'll take them this morning. It's Sunday and there'll be less people about. I want to take the car to get the newspapers anyway.'

'Will you then, dear? I'd be very grateful. It's been on my mind a bit – you know . . .'

I got up and kissed her. 'Don't be daft – thanking me! I'd love to do it for daddy, you know that.'

When she turned from stooping and handed me the package in extremely stiff brown paper, I was surprised at its weight. An official-looking label was stuck on one side, and I held the parcel up towards the light from the window in the dim room, and read the inscription. Name – Joseph Trebland Bryant. Deceased's remains cremated June 21st, 1968. The city Crematorium, Isleworth Cemetery, etc.

'You know what, Davey?'

'No. What?'

'It's Easter Day, isn't it? Couldn't be a nicer time.'

I clutched the package under my arm. 'No, it couldn't,' I agreed and made for the door.

Driving the rented Ford Cortina into Wadebridge (for some

reason I had decided to get the Sunday newspapers first) the parcel would not stand on its base but kept falling over in front of the bucket seat next to mine. It bothered me vaguely lying there, the white label with its funeral lettering staring up from the black rubber mat on the car floor.

Just before I reached the man who sold his newspapers on the deserted Sabbath sidewalk I pulled over to the kerb of Wadebridge's main street. Taking off my jacket, I draped it as casual-looking as possible over the carton of ashes. It looked decidedly suspicious to me, but I couldn't think of anything else I could do.

When I eventually lowered the window and asked for the two newspapers the vendor, thank God, looked right into my face. 'Observer and Sunday Toimes,' he repeated; 'Brave bit of reading there, boy, for a sunny day. Should be out walking, you, gettin' a bit o' air in your lungs – not stuck over the ole papers.'

I handed him the money and made sympathetic grunts in my throat. That kind of inane remark always confounded me.

'Bit windy, though, without your jacket on,' he added suddenly, nodding towards my coat on the floor. 'Need that on if you'm walking the cliffs, you. 'Twill be bravun fresh up there on a day loike this.'

I revved the motor, sweating in nervousness. If he hadn't stuck his fool head halfway into the window I'd have slammed the car into gear and departed in a swirl of dust. But even manslaughter added to the illicit disposal of mortal remains, was something I could certainly do without.

'Down here for the Easter holidays, then?'

'Garrulous shit,' I thought. 'Yes,' I said. 'Yes, I'm here on holiday.'

'Will 'ee want they two papers next Sunday then? Shall I put 'em aside for 'ee?'

'For the next month,' I breathed, edging the car slowly forward. 'I've got to go now. Got to meet someone,' I lied.

He was still standing there on the kerb, I saw through my rear mirror, as I moved towards the railway crossing. I hoped he was thinking of the few shillings he would make over the upcoming Sundays rather than of that mysteriously draped sports coat on the car floor.

Twenty minutes later found me parking the car in the gateway of Polgarrow Farm. I'd be in no one's way I realized, as I switched off the ignition, for that track led only to that empty farmhouse where my dad had first discovered the world – and where he'd subsequently brought his wife and sired the three of us.

I had always thought it was the most beautiful farm in all of Cornwall, but for the past fifteen years that once child-teeming farmhouse had been silent. All the farmers in my family, you see, had died off.

Even five years of unhabitation can be fatal to a domicile in that moist and fecund Cornish climate. I wasn't surprised, then, to note a daintier version of a jungle sprawl had been at work. Ivy and periwinkle swarmed over the windows, tiny saplings sprouted amid the mossy hillocks of a perpetually damp roof, tongue ferns flourished in clogged gutters – and, imprisoned in unheated rooms behind dank cob walls, I could imagine the Cornish mustiness, smelling like yeast and stale cheese.

With my bulky package clutched under my coat I tiptoed carefully over the moist ground. Though Polgarrow stood empty a neighbouring farmer had use of the land. It was his scarring tractor treads that had churned up the soft grass approach.

If it hadn't been for the sunny brilliance of the morning, the rich mosaic of greens in the freshness of spring growth, then the dilapidated farmhouse with its caved-in roof, which for centuries had housed the yeoman history of my father's family, would have certainly depressed me. But now I experienced a not unpleasant melancholy over the relation of Polgarrow, at this stage of its dissolution, to the parcel I clutched tightly out of sight and which I was about to open.

Where the granite outcropping created an island in the surrounding mud I stopped and carefully opened the paper at the neck. As the covering came free to flap in one hand, I found I was clutching in the other what looked like an outsize milk carton. First, though, what to do with the wrapping? It was so stiff it wouldn't bunch easily in the hand.

I finally got it, if not exactly a neat ball, at least crumpled up enough to stuff in my jacket pocket.

When I had fiddled for a few minutes I got the carton lid open – only to find a folded document lying on top of the ashes themselves. This turned out to be a rough duplicate of the paper attached to the outside and proclaimed my father's full name, the place of his incineration and – somewhat superfluously – the fact he was deceased.

Conscious that the document was dusty with the contents in which it had been partly embedded, I could only fight my distaste and stuff that paper too in my pocket. The pressing business was the emptying of that brimming container and I looked about me at bushes and trees to see by their swaying which way the wind was blowing. Briskly, it seemed to me, from the ocean in an inland direction.

I took a few steps westwards, towards the Atlantic that is, opened the lid fully and lifted the package preparatory to letting the wind waft my dad's dust across his ancestral acres.

I paused. Perhaps a prayer was called for. Some little religious articulation that was in harmony with what I was about to do? My father had always loved Evensong among the church's services – what better, then, than the Nunc Dimittus which all five of us used to sing together in that ancient oak pew of St Kew Church. 'Lord, now lettest thou Thy servant depart in peace / according to Thy Word / For mine eyes have seen / Thy salvation / which Thou hast prepared . . .' I stopped, for one thing I wasn't sure whether I could remember it all. For another, I had an uneasy feeling that what I was singing was redundant. He had already been sent from this world with the benisons of Holy Church. I was surely confusing the ministrations of the priest with that of a sexton. Action was required here – not words. With that I lifted the cardboard container to shoulder height and jerked it forward so that the ashes would spill out. They did. Some of them even got lifted by the wind and a small grey cloud floated towards the grass-sprouted hedge that bordered the farmyard from an adjacent field.

But then I happened to look down towards the ground. What I saw made me wince. Apart from the fact my brown suede shoes had themselves taken on the pallor of death, the churned clay through which I'd just picked my way, now had a narrow grey swath of my father's death dust clearly delineated across it.

Nervous, upset, I tried again – lifting the carton head-right and jerking its contents out even more fiercely. Again a misty grey patch drifted away from me – but this time the quantity falling immediately to the ground, to make stark dry patterns, was even greater.

To make things worse, I either stepped forward too quickly or the wind veered slightly. At any rate I felt the gritty particles from the package brush against my face, sensed their rubbing against my hair line. I panicked a little. I tried for a second to scatter the ashes on the ground with my toe – to mix them with the mud, that is. It didn't work. Apart from a yet more scruffy toecap, the only result was the conviction in me that if anyone walked in from that lane and I looked about where I was standing he would say at once that someone had been there recently scattering human remains about the mud and dung of a farmyard.

Jamming the lid folds closer together, I fled from that hummock of granite back to the car to try somewhere else.

Inside the Ford, after re-combing my hair and wiping my face with a handkerchief, I looked once more at the contents of the container. With a sense of gloom I discovered that scarcely a quarter of my father's remains had been yet disposed of.

Tight mouthed, I moved the car forward, thinking furiously of the time of an alternative site to finish the task I had promised my mother I'd perform.

The place I finally came up with was a small granite quarry which my family owned and had once worked. It provided, I recalled, a superbly panoramic view of St Kew church and the village nestled about it.

'You never beat that, son,' my dad used to say, standing there by Uncle Petherick's quarry and gazing out on Cornwall. 'Most beautiful sight in the world, boy – and I seen the sphinx and Gallipoli too in the Great War, don't forget. Ancient human roots in an ancient land – that's the secret, Davy. 'Tis a proper old job, yon, isn't it?' Then he'd grin. 'Better than that old Canada of yours, I reckon!'

With a quick glance about me as I got out of the car, to make sure I was alone up there, I grabbed the carton and walked hurriedly away from the massive wall of slate and granite which formed the quarry's face. By climbing up on the eastern edge of what formed a rough amphitheatre I found myself in the brightness of a momentarily uninterrupted sun.

A large spread of the Cornish peninsula seduced my eyes until, when I tilted my chin and I searched the horizon of clay pit slag heaps over towards St Austell, their white pyramids merged with the dazzling whiteness of a sun-shot haze.

Just as I stood there, growing contentedly aware that I had come to the spot that surely my father himself would've chosen, there came, caught on the brisk wind playing about my head which brimmed my eyes with tears, the abrupt clash of bells proclaiming Eastertide. Louder and louder (or so it seemed to me), the sound swept up from that gorgonzola'd tower which in a matter of weeks would be entirely screened by the foliage of the surrounding elms.

Once more I was constrained to join my voice with that of the church now pealing from tower to tower at eleven o'clock across the valleys and hills of Cornwall.

'Hail thee, Festival day / blest day thou art hallowed forever' – and with that I opened full the neck of the carton and flung the final dust of my father to join the earth, the wind and the sky, which had initially served in his shaping.

With a wonderful, an exhilarating sense of completion, I saw those grey particles hover, just for a second, in the hand of the breeze – then vanish into the broader realms of the parish below.

Some dust went on me I suppose. But now I no longer cared.

What was I, after all, than a later echo of that earthen womb down there?

Then, not the wind, but some inner sadness squeezed my eyes. 'Goodbye, daddy,' I said. And then because afraid of the daftness of sentimentality from extempore words, I said the line, the opening line of his favourite hymn: 'The day Thou gavest Lord, is ended.' I would have said more except my chest was filled with emotions that allowed no space for air. As the bells pealed and pealed, rooks cawed and other birds sang. Distantly, lambs bleated. I wanted it to go on and on – forever . . .

Feeling the sun as a faint warmth on my closed lids, I gave the carton a final jerk – like old time sowing of wheat being broadcast across a ploughed field. At the same time I found breath to conclude with another handful of churchy words . . . 'Glory be to the Father, and to the Son, and to the Holy Ghost. As it was in the beginning, is now and ever shall be . . . World without end . . . Amen.'

I opened my eyes. The bells had stopped. A large cloud was trespassing on the blue space the sun occupied. In a moment, I realized, the land would be in shadow. I looked at my hand still stretched out and at the carton held in it. I gave the thing a jerk, it rattled. There were a few bits left in the bottom. For some reason they gave me the creeps in a way the ashes in my hair and on my face had not. Perhaps it was some fragment of bone that didn't incinerate? Anyway, something unpleasant. I wasn't going to peer in to find out.

Now, of course, I had to dispose of the carton itself. That, and the brown paper covering stuffed in my coat pocket – oh yes, and also the label with its formal description of the contents.

Away to my right the land veered sharply, almost precipitately, down towards the lush valley of the ambling Amble river. But there, at the top, the vegetation was thick thorn scrub before opening on to a bleak outcrop of heather, gorse and bracken – moorland, in fact.

As a sturdy thirteen-year-old, a member of the St Kew Scout Troop, I had tried unsuccessfully to push through that mass of blackthorn, now just beginning to foam with blossom. With all my strength I flung the carton into the impenetrable midst of it. By the time those branches were bare again, the sun, the wind and the rain would have dissolved that cardboard composition.

Satisfied that it had entirely disappeared, I crumpled the brown paper covering once more, and hurled that in the carton's wake.

Brushing my hands on my jacket lapels, I turned back towards the car in the shadow of the cliff-face. I felt a paper in one of my pockets. It was the document I'd discovered in the neck of the parcel on first opening it. Carefully I folded it small, stuck it in my wallet.

Then I turned for home and my mother: able now to tell her the thing was accomplished. The cycle wholly completed.

Only months and months later, walking a Vancouver beach with my dog, staring out from Kitsilano at a westering sun across the Pacific, did I bring to light that piece of folded paper from the recesses of my wallet. I rolled it into a tight ball with the palms of my hands. Then I flipped it lightly with forefinger and thumb, out across the water. My bassett hound, Wendy, saw it, and made as if to retrieve it. But the rippling tide put her off. She never has been that keen on water, nor even with retrieving, come to that.

To divert her I ran quickly along the flat sand of the beach, calling to her. Soon she was baying at my heels and we ran till we were both puffing.

I never did look back to see whether that scrap of paper had finally sunk below the small waves.

Howard Spring

CORPORAL STRIKE

The long white gate hung askew between the brick gate-posts. One of the hinges was broken; and the paint of the gates was cracked and blistered where it wasn't gone altogether. But the gate-posts were lovely: rich red brick that had stood there for a hundred years or more, and now were patterned over with lichen, green and orange and sulphur-yellow. On each post was a great eagle in white stone, wings outspread. They, too were weather-stained; they had the loveliness of things with which the seasons have for long had their way. One was headless.

The gravel path upon which the gate opened was grown thick with weeds, and the rhododendrons and kerrias and hollies that made the shrubbery intruded upon it. They had not been pruned for years. I could not see the house – only its chimneys. They were lovely Elizabethan chimneys, each a separate work of art; and they stood smokeless against the autumn sky of milky blue.

The notice which said that the house was for sale had itself decayed. Someone had propped it against one of the gate-posts, and I saw it had fallen because time had rotted its foot.

I had walked for a long time and seen no one. There was no one to be seen now. The lane from which the gate opened stretched before me, bordered with little trees that were all bearded with moss. They must have had a hard life through many winters with the wind roaring among them from the sea that could now be glimpsed in the distance, spread out and as unruffled as a blue silk coverlet.

The whole scene had the melancholy beauty of decay. I should have turned from the gates had not a thin plume of smoke caught my eye – smoke of so pale a blue that it was almost invisible once it had risen above the dull evergreens and taken the sky for background. It was such a little trembling wisp of smoke that it seemed to come from the ghost of a fire; and when I had put irresolution aside and crunched over the gravel, and come to the lawn before the house, it was, indeed, a poor sort of fire that was burning there.

It was lit at the edge of the lawn, and an old, bent man, with a besom of twigs, was feebly brushing towards it the beech leaves that even now loosened themselves and spun down through the still air.

After a moment of surprise at seeing me there where, clearly, a visitor did not often come, he straightened his old back, leaned his besom against a lovely stone urn, and asked, with a pathetic pretence of being businesslike and brisk, if I wished to see over the house. He was, he explained, the caretaker. He and his wife, and nobody else, had lived in the house for years. He had a look at once so eager and so wistful that it was with regret I told him that nothing but curiosity had brought me inside the gates. Ah, well, he said, for all that, I would perhaps like to see the house and drink a cup of tea.

And so I found myself in the drawing-room from which so much had been taken but which, nevertheless, was gracious still. It was on the sunless side of the house, and a scrap of fire tinkled in the grate. Before it sat an old, shawled woman. Her face, cut like a cameo against the white panelling, reminded me of Whistler's paainting of his mother. She was as calm as that, and seemed as far beyond the possibility of turmoil. On the mantelpiece was a photograph of Karen, full-length, poised so lightly that it seemed as though she were about to fly off the earth.

I didn't know, of course, then, that it was Karen; but I learned about her that night. They were so out of the world, that old couple, that they listened to my talk as to travellers' tales; and, sitting there, with my rucksack at my feet, I let the hours go by, a willing captive in that pensive, lovely room. And then they said that I must not go, that I must stay the night; and so it came about that I heard of Karen.

It was nearly midnight when the old man preceded me with a candle up the wide oak stair. When he was gone, I leaned from the window, and saw how all the house was set about with great trees; I felt how deeply one might come to know there the sense of imprisonment. I could imagine that, perhaps from this very window, with owls calling as they were calling now, Karen had leaned out into the night and shuddered as she heard the voice of Corporal Strike howling in the darkness.

' 'E was very 'andsom, midear,' the old man said. He was as fair as that to Corporal Strike, though he had killed him. Very handsome and muscular, swarthy as a Spaniard. I had come that afternoon across the ferry, so I knew the setting in which Karen and Strike had first come face to face. From the fields on the other side of the tidal river you slithered down a path through a wood and there you were at water's edge with that steep wooded bluff rising behind you. The ferryman's cottage lay across the water, a little white huddle under a crown of thatch, and you yelled to call his attention. On a still summer day you needed full lungs to get that call across; and the night when John Tregaskis brought Karen home was a March night of raving wind and surging water.

Karen, you may be sure, didn't mind that. It was an appropriate end to the mad adventure of loving Jack Tregaskis. They had met in Munich, the Danish governess with the blue eyes and the corn-gold hair, and the Englishman with nothing on earth to do but wander the world and spend his father's money. You would have thought they had little enough in common, but you don't want much in common to fall in love. One thing at least they loved besides one another, and that was music. They were both exalted when they met. They were walking from a concert hall and the great harmonies of a Bach fugue were crashing in their heads. You can imagine anything in a moment like that. To Jack Tregaskis Karen's eager figure, hurrying along under the lime trees, seemed to embody all the music's poise and elegance, and to her he seemed the epitome of its strength and depth.

For he did not take long to know her; and there they were, sitting at a little tin table under the trees, drinking coffee, and feeling at ease, each in a strange land, but each at once merry and comfortable with the other.

Then Karen said that she must go, for the baroness, her employer, did not permit her to be out too late. So Jack Tregaskis learned of her dependent position, but it was not of that he thought as he lingered there, but of her eyes that were the colour of chicory flowers, and of her hair that was the colour of ripe corn, and of her body that swayed away from him under the light of the street lamps as gaily as corn sways when the wind is in it.

It was inevitable that he should think like that, for all his background was of country scenes. He was born in the house with the eagled gate-posts, as his forebears had been for generations. Beauty and solitude were his birthright, and with them he inherited the headstrong blood of all the Tregaskis men. You can see their tablets still – as I did the next day when I walked out of that house – in the nearby church: captains and admirals, many of whom had died in battle or shipwreck, few in their beds. An old rogue who had sailed with Drake was the first of them – Sir Harry Tregaskis, who built the lonely house that so many centuries had left still uncompanioned.

One letter to his father was enough to convince Jack Tregaskis that never would the old man's blessing light upon Karen. A nobody, picked up in a foreign town. A fly-by-night, no doubt, out for such wandering fools as Jack, who had better come home while yet he had a pound in his pocket. So the old admiral flamed his thoughts upon paper, and Jack could picture him, stumping furiously upon his wooden leg up and down the gravel paths of the house he never left: the house where now he was alone, his wife long dead, his daughter married, his son abroad.

But Jack did not come home. To be in Munich, and to be young and in love with Karen: what could an old man's anger weigh against that? So he took the way Tregaskis men had always taken: he did as he pleased, and it pleased him to marry Karen and damn the consequences. And then, because breed was strong in him, he must hurry home, convinced that, seeing Karen, the old man would be conquered.

Karen was a gay and merry soul. She had never seen England before, and she spoke English badly, but all was joy to her as they journeyed through the drear March day. The wind rose as they went west. The train swayed across great viaducts, plunged through forlorn valleys drenched with rain, and the windows streamed. A high wind was raging through the little town to which they came in the dark of the evening, and out in the harbour which they must cross on a ferry the sea was noisy and turbulent. On the ferry they did not go below. They stood side by side in the bows with the seas hissing about them, and the darkness over them, and the wind howling.

When they came to the village across the harbour Jack announced simply, 'Now we must walk,' and Karen as simply said, 'Come on, then.' So they slipped and slithered in pitchy darkness up through some fields; then downwards towards the little wood at whose foot was the wide river. There Jack went first, holding with one hand to a rail, and Karen kept a hand upon his shoulder. She could not see. She could only feel him stumbling before her into the darkness.

The tide was running in, with a great wind pushing it into confusion. Across the welter, seemingly the only thing alive in the world, was the tranquil light in the ferryman's cottage.

'We are at the end of the world,' said Karen.

Jack put an arm around her, taut in a rain-polished white mackintosh, and kissed her wet face and blown hair. 'Not yet,' he said.

Then he let out a great bellow which the wind caught and tore to tatters so that it died upon the water. He yelled again and again, and at last in the darkness a slit of light suddenly came and went alongside the window as the door was opened and shut. Then they saw a lantern bobbing down the cottage path, and it seemed miraculous, with the wind reverberating through the river valley, that it could live for a moment.

But it did; and soon it seemed to be of its own accord, leaping across the tumult of the water. It was a long time, so inky black the night was, before they could make out the boat or the rower.

'Come on, Strike,' Jack Tregaskis shouted. 'I'll give you a hand with her.'

'Good evening, zur,' Strike yelled through the wind. 'It's a long time since I heard your voice. I suppose the bad news 'ave brought you home.'

'What news?' Jack threw into the teeth of the wind. 'I've heard no news.'

'The Admiral, zur. They say he be dying.'

'What!'

'Ay, zur. So I 'ear. Taken very sudden to-day.'

Poor Karen stood stricken at the water's edge, all the gaiety gone from her, lonely as she had never felt lonely before. What share did she have in all this? – in this wild winter country which now, swiftly, seemed inimical and forlorn; in this tragedy of the sudden death of a man she had never seen. Strike held aloft the lantern, and the light fell on Jack's face, gone grey and anguished. Silently he helped her into the bucking boat. He took an oar at the bows, and Strike with the lantern on the thwart beside him, sat amidships. He was a wild figure, in the fullness of his youth, bare to the waist, with his smooth brown hairless skin glistening in the rain. They pulled out into the tug of the current and the lash of the wind; and as the man bent to his oar Karen was repulsed by the pride of him. He grinned, exulting in his strength, his white teeth flashing in the lantern-light, his muscles strong as steel cables, his whole body a grand machine that seemed as oblivious of the slapping waves and drenching rain as if it had been inanimate.

'It be no good wearing clo'es a night like this, zur,' he shouted over his shoulder. 'If I'm to be wet to the skin, let's wet the skin and nothing else.'

'Pull, man,' Jack snarled; and Strike fell silent, grinning at Karen.

When they were across, Jack leapt ashore and held the

heaving bows. Karen stood up, and Strike without ceremony or question took her round the waist and stepped overboard. In the darkness of the howling night he pressed her tight to his naked body and murmured: 'You be light, midear – light as a li'l bird.'

She strained away from him and did not answer. He waded through the edge of the hissing water and put her down high and dry.

In a fainting voice she said to Jack: 'Is it far?' For the first time, it seemed to her that they had come a long way.

'Three miles,' he said, almost harshly. And when they had panted three miles through the wet windy dark and come to the great gates with the eagles poised proudly upon them, Jack knowing every step of the way, Karen stumbling blindly at his side, she said tragically: 'Now we are at the end of the world,' and Jack answered: 'Yes, now we are.'

What must she have felt, standing there in the blustering dark, with the great trees weeping all round her, and listening to the sudden alarm that shrilled through the house when Jack hauled at the bell-pull?

'She came in out of the dark like a ghost.' (This is how the old man told me the story.) 'You never saw such a pale little thing, her hair clinging to her face and her shoes wet through.

' "God 'a mercy, Mr Jack," I said, "we didn't know you were in the country."

' "How is my father?" he asked, very short.

' "Very bad," I said, "but still alive."

'Then he threw off his hat and his overcoat – just threw them down to the floor – and rushed upstairs. "Look after my wife," he shouted.

'And that was the first we heard about any wife. So we brought her in here – into this very room where you're sitting now. I was the butler in those days, you know, sir – twenty years ago – and my wife was the housekeeper. And a fine, bustling house it was. A staff of fifteen indoors and out. My wife put her in the chair here by the fire, and took off her mackintosh, and pulled off her shoes and stockings, and rubbed her feet. When I came in with a bit of food and a hot drink on a tray, she was lying back with her eyes closed. She didn't eat anything.'

The old man died that night. He never saw Karen, never heard of her; and she never saw him. She saw the relatives, who came and stared, and attended the funeral, and went away after the will was read. Everything that mattered was Jack's; and perhaps they wondered whether things would have been like that had the old man known of the marriage to Karen.

The storm in which she had arrived sobbed and moaned about the country for days. It faded out the day the old man was buried: a wet, troubled March day, full of fits and starts of the tired tempest; and the next day it was spring.

Then Karen was happy. Everyone was gone; the house was hers and Jack's; and though he was moody and preoccupied with affairs of the estate, all the country about was hers to walk in: a country whose corners sheltered violets and primroses and whose hedges were fledged with the early green of hawthorn.

She didn't mourn. What was there to mourn about? Jack was hers, and this wonderful country was hers; and in a yellow skirt and green jumper, looking as fresh as the daffodils themselves, she wandered alone under the blue sky.

She met George Strike. He was whistling down a lane, swinging his stick at the grasses. He raised a finger in half salute, as she went by, head in air. Strike's eyes darkened, and he shouted after her: 'Don't 'ee know me?'

She stopped then, and he took a step which brought them again face to face. He looked her gay clothes up and down, and said: 'Bain't 'ee in mourning? Bain't 'ee one of the family?' and laughed insolently.

The implication of the words did not strike her. She merely turned the cold light blue of her eyes upon the violet-blue of his, and said: 'I do not like you. You holt me too tight.'

With that she went, and Strike went too, his handsome

face twisted with anger, but with a loud laugh on his lips. And in the pub he told how she had said, 'You holt me too tight.' 'I did, too,' he boasted. 'The foreign piece.'

He met Karen often that summer. They did not exchange another word, but when she came up from the beach where she bathed, she would find him lying among the whins on the cliff path, and she knew that he had been gloating upon her, and that he placed himself just there on her return so that she might know she had been watched.

That secret, sardonic surveillance might have become too much for her. She might have complained to Jack, though she would have felt it a thrust at her pride had she been compelled to do so. But it seemed to her then so little a thing. How could it weigh against the great felicity that was hers, against Jack himself, and her joy in the lovely land that all through the summer belied the tragic promise of her first acquaintance?

And then, suddenly, it became a great thing, for that was 1914. It was incredible, there, where nothing violent seemed thinkable, to feel the swift rain of blow on blow. War! Jack gone! And before the year was out, Jack missing. Then, with the year's end, silence. No word from Jack. No word about Jack. And Corporal Strike muttering in the pub about the foreign piece. ' "You holt me too tight." That's what she said. The foreign piece. 'I'd like to "holt" her again, the foreign piece!'

The boys went swinging up the road with a fife and drum band. Karen ran down to the gate to see them pass, and Corporal Strike, in charge of the route march, shouted, 'There she is – the German piece! And is she married to him? I wonder.' Then as the head of his little column drew level with the gate, he commanded: 'Eyes left!' And every head swung away from Karen, went by averted, as though she were something too unclean to be looked upon.

He was indispensable, was Corporal Strike. Others came and went, shipped overseas and died; but Strike remained at the camp, so physically beautiful, so superb a trainer, that for long they would not let him go. And every day he marched his men by the gates. 'Look at the eagles!' he shouted. 'German! German eagles!' And they took up the mud of the road and bespattered the spreading wings; and not only the soldiers but the villagers spat out 'German eagles' when they went that way. Some threw mud and some threw stones, and the wings were chipped and scarred.

Karen did not go down to the road again. She remained in the great house, a prisoner, and her garrison, one by one, deserted. Men and maids alike, they went as the weeks drew on. Some were driven to the colours, some would not remain with a German, some would not serve a woman who, after all, had arrived in queer fashion. There had been no wedding among the Tregaskis tombs and effigies, and that was how a woman should come to the Tregaskis family. There was something all wrong about the woman who had appeared in a night, and was dancing round the country like a rainbow the moment old Admiral Tregaskis was dead.

And so they went; and soon no one was left but the old man and woman who told me the story; and a boy who saw the gardens run to decay under his hands, and the weeds grow up in the paths; and a little maid whose relatives lived far away.

It became difficult to get food. Karen was the last to be served from the village shops. She loved the evening. Throughout the day the bugle calls rang from the camp. She would listen for 'Lights out' and the 'Last Post'; and then she would clap her hands and say, 'Now we can be quiet!' Then she and the old people would sit together in the drawing-room. They at least had plenty of fire: there was no lack of wood. 'You must call me Karen,' she would say. 'We are friends.' And, difficult as they found it, those stiff English folk, bred in the tradition of deferential service, they called her Karen, and they were, at first, her friends. Then they loved her.

They loved the gaiety that now and then came back to her, making her a woodland thing of light and happiness; and they loved her the more for the ache that came when her sorrows were too many, and she would sit at the piano, white and tragical, beating out great harmonies that stirred their marrow. They came to love her like their own child.

The first time she cried was on one of her nights of gaiety. She talked of Denmark and her happy childhood there. She told them how she had left the country because she had no longer a relative – not a soul in the world. She was gay about the pompous old baroness she had worked for, and she talked of Munich and Jack, and how, soon, they must hear from him.

It was then that they heard a banging at the door and the voice of Corporal Strike, drunk and obscene, howling in the darkness. Karen knelt on the hearthrug and covered her ears with her hands, and the tears rolled down her face. 'Oh,' she sobbed, 'our nights – our beautiful nights! Now he will spoil our nights. We can no more forget.'

And then Corporal Strike disappeared. He went the way of all the others, overseas; but though he was gone, his handiwork remained. Each new draft of recruits learned of the German woman, the recluse behind the stone eagles; and to bedaub the eagles became a traditional joke. So Karen remained a pale prisoner behind the spattered gate-way, and when the lush spring drew on, she became more deeply captive. The weeds in the paths, and the stretching arms of untended trees, and the flower-beds unthinned and riotous, made a green prison, and in it she languished.

When the sun grew strong again she said one day that she would go and bathe. The old people were glad of that. They hoped that it was a sign of reviving life and interest; but when Karen came back, pale and panting up the weedy paths, they saw at once that something was wrong. She threw herself into a chair and stared stonily at the fireplace. This time she did not cry. She said in a shaking voice: 'Even the sea – the clean sea – is denied to me.' She never cried after that.

She had gone to the beach and swam out and out. She was a glorious swimmer, and she must have rejoiced, after all those months of captivity, in the clean exhilaration of sun and solitude and salt water. She swam for a long time, and rested, floating with the blue beneath her, gazing up at the blue above where the gulls glided with heavenly beauty. Perhaps she had begun again to find something to live for; and then she swam ashore.

She had begun to dress when a file of soldiers scrambled down the steep pathway that gave the only access to the cove.

'Hi!' one of them shouted. 'This is reserved for the troups.'

Then someone recognised her. 'It's the Bosche!'

They closed in, warily, inquisitively, and Karen stood there, half-dressed, clutching her clothes, shivering and speechless. A lout picked up a handful of sand, but someone shouted: 'Drop that!' He added: 'But keep out of this, miss.'

Then Karen started to run, her heart pounding. The cliff path was steep, and she slipped, falling face-downwards and cutting her cheek on the shaly scree. She lay there for some time, pressed to the ground, her fingers digging into the earth. Then she climbed into the fields, wounded to the soul, and finished dressing.

'You must not go alone next time, Karen,' the old man said. 'I shall come with you.'

She did not answer for a while; then she said: 'No, you shall not. Next time I shall go again alone.'

What could they do? They could not lock her up. They had written to Jack's sister, hinting that things were not well with Karen. But Mrs Charwood had troubles of her own, as who had not in those days; and it was a long way to the north of Scotland where she lived. She wrote a sympathetic letter, and was sure that there would soon be news of Jack, and that things would straighten themselves out in God's good time.

So there was nothing to do except wait with growing anguish for the day, which they were sure would come, when they would find Karen's bed empty and Karen gone. They had not long to wait. It had been a night of glorious moonlight; and Karen was a splendid swimmer. She must have swum on and on under the sky where now there were no gulls flying, nothing at all but the empty and unregarding glory of the moon.

'And so,' the old man said, 'I had to kill Corporal Strike.'

The old woman sitting there calm and austere as a Quaker in meeting, nodded her head: and, when I look back on that moment, I recall that to me, too, the old man's remark seemed unsurprising, a logical and necessary continuation of his story.

Karen was never seen again, nor was Jack Tregaskis. Mrs Charwood, the nearest relative, instructed the old people to remain in the house in order that it might be kept in good condition. So there they stayed, and the war ended, some men came back and some did not. Corporal Strike came back. The job at the ferry had passed into other hands, and Strike, in any case, seemed disinclined for work. He was more handsome than ever, but devilish in his disposition. He poached and fished and boozed, running on gaily with the war's momentum of ferocity and violence till, like many another, he ran himself out and came against the hard fact of poverty. Then, with great adaptability, he began to turn his hand to any job about the countryside. He did bits of carpentering and bricklaying, white-washing and paperhanging.

'And so,' said the old man, 'the time came for which I had been waiting.' It was on an autumn evening in 1919 that Strike passed by the gates and found the old man standing there, looking up and down the lane. The eagles were still bespattered, and that was the fact which drew Strike into conversation. 'Many a handful o' that muck I threw myself,' he boasted, and went on to speak of Karen's disappearance. 'I s'pose she'd finished her spying job,' he said, 'and went back where she belonged.'

Perhaps that was it, the old man agreed; but that was all dead and done with now, and the sooner they got back to their old ways the better. There was plenty to be done, and if Strike cared to do it, there was work waiting for him. The brick pillars of the gate needed pointing, and the eagles themselves were so loose on their bases that a high wind, catching their outspread wings, might bring them down. And he persuaded

Strike to climb to the top of a pillar and feel for himself how the eagle rocked on its base.

Strike agreed to do the work; and in his loud-mouthed way told everyone about it at the pub. 'There were Strikes here as long as there were Tregaskises, and maybe longer, and I dare say we'll be here when there bain't no more Tregaskises above ground. But I'll put the old eagles straight for 'un. Fair rockin' they be, not safe to touch.'

'You see,' the old man explained to me patiently, 'I had been loosening them for a long time, so that a touch would send them over.'

And so, when Corporal Strike arrived the next day with all that he needed for the work, he did not get far with it. He died instantly, and never knew that the sudden agony that flamed through him, coming upon him as he knelt at the base of the pillar, was the eagle's beak smashing through his skull.

'I had a mallet,' said the old man, 'so that if he were not killed at once I could finish him. But it wasn't necessary. I left him there for some passer-by to find. It was fortunate that he had told everybody how loose the eagles were. You may have noticed, sir, that one of them has no head? This is it. It smashed when it fell on Corporal Strike. I filed the base smooth and keep it here.'

He took from the mantelpiece the head with the hooded eyes and the curved cruel beak that Strike had so often affronted.

'We like to see it there.' And the old woman nodded placidly as though it were a memento of a visit to Scarborough.

It was only in the morning that the whole thing seemed to me fantastic, incredible. Were these dreams, on which those two old people, cloistered from the world, nourished the emptiness of their days? Or was it all true, and had the necessity of confession welled up, not to be denied?

I do not know. I took the trouble to discover that in 1919 an inquest had been held on George Strike, who died in the circumstances that had been described to me. I took the trouble to look at the Tregaskis tombs and at the memorial tablet which reported that John Tregaskis had been reported wounded and missing in the Great War, and that his death had been presumed.

But of Karen there was not a word. Yet who, after all, would bother to put her on record, and what manner of record could there be concerning one who came so swiftly, stayed so briefly, and so strangely went away? It could not with certainty be said whether she was living or dead. She was, by then, a wraith, a nothing, like the lovely but insubstantial radiance into which she had gone.

J. C. Trewin

CARRIAGES TEN-THIRTY

I

It was there, close to the Green, when the village had begun to wake and a smoky morning haze that had drifted in from sea dispersed itself in the strengthening light. Though the tent was clumsy enough, stuffy and cramped, St John Randolph reflected moodily that it would hold all the villagers anxious to see their play. He still proposed to give them *Hamlet* – by no means an easy thing to do with eight players – but he knew very well that they would prefer the after-piece, *Bertha's Baby*, good easy fun and followed by a series of songs and recitations. Ventriloquism, perhaps, even if Sedley Walters was losing the knack. Then why *Hamlet* anyway? Nothing, Randolph mused, would stop him from doing it. He was probably too old at forty-nine – yet who cared? In a sense it would be his gift to the village (one it would probably appreciate later) for having made no fuss on the night before, when the company arrived. The thought cheered him. He felt benevolent.

Far from any fuss, their arrival had been almost unnoticed. Randolph surveyed the pitch. They were on a broad strip of rough grass – locally, a flappet – just outside the churchyard wall: the road ran between them and the Green. The church itself, beyond a range of tombstones, looked small and withdrawn except for its granite tower and four pinnacles that were strong now against the eastern light. It had been simply a shadow among other shadows when they had run up their tent late in the evening after that exhausting drag, ten miles down the southern road across the emphatic plateau from Polruth. Most of the dusty day they had plodded with their three burdened handcarts, one much unwieldier than the others. It had been a relief to find a pitch so soon, to finish most of the bread and cheese, and to put down their bedding where later, if needed, the stage would be. The only specks of light in the village had soon faded; and two or three loiterers had given no more than a surprised but amiable good-night.

Certainly the place was quiet: the church, a fair-sized Green, a shuffle of slated whitewashed cottages, a chapel with two round-headed windows in front, a tiny general shop not open yet, and curving by it a road, or rutted track, that must lead soon to the cove and the open sea. That would be possibly a quarter of a mile off. Pralla village was at the end of everything except a splatter of little fields and what might be a farm. After this the sea that, on a morning of late October, was a white-streaked, dull blue crescent beyond the cliffs.

Cornwall was a strange country, thought Randolph, choosing the most tactful epithet and asking himself for the fiftieth time, without finding an answer, why he had crossed the Tamar from Plymouth and pressed down so steadily across the peninsula. They had made just enough to keep going. Two Feast, or fair, days had helped; but no one had been particularly cordial. No one had recognized what he was getting in the Randolph company: players who, in spite of the handcarts and the empty tent, were not merely strollers, but artists who before now had had their stock seasons at Knaresborough and Trowbridge and Ottery St Mary.

Outside the gleaming, whitewashed chapel a two-horse waggonette had drawn up. Quietly, about a dozen burly men, self-conscious in hard hats and broadcloth, clambered aboard; and presently the sound of the trotting hooves dwindled up the Polruth road. Better than three handcarts, Randolph said enviously. Pulling his coat round him, he walked across the now empty Green, an incongruous figure in a worn maroon velvet jacket and trousers, and peered in at a chapel window. The building was demurely simple and bare, only five years old according to its foundation stone, which had been laid by Albert Tregenza, Esquire, of St Venn, in September 1869.

Randolph moved back towards his tent and the church. He

was aware that a tall, craggy, morose man in a torn blue guernsey was watching him. 'Good morning to you, sir,' he said swoopingly: Hamlet addressing an improbable Osric.

The man, without speaking, studied the tent and the florid figure before him. Then: 'Circus?' he asked.

'Circus! My dear sir, we are the legitimate.'

'Please?' The word was clearly unknown.

'The legitimate. The St John Randolph company ... Shakespeare, of course. The newest comedies from the West End of London ... A strong supporting cast, Morris Tapping, Lucy Clayton, Sedley Walters – '

'Peter Curnow,' said the man, introducing himself. 'You'm pompin' folk.'

'Players, sir.'

'Pompin' folk!' Curnow repeated meditatively and without heat. 'Like apes, I say. 'Tain't in the nature of a man ...' He nodded towards a still laden handcart. 'Been walkin', I reckon.'

At all costs, thought Randolph, I must not lose my temper. 'Ten miles, sir,' he answered. 'From Polruth Fair. We represented *Hamlet* – '

'And who might he have been?'

Randolph could not resist the flourish: 'This is I, Hamlet the Dane.'

'Furrin as well, I see. No life for a man, whatever his nation. Treadin' the high road, speakin' out po'try.' He glanced past Randolph: 'These your people?'

They were: yawning, untidy; Lucy, with her hair half-braided, Morris Tapping shivering in a plaid greatcoat, Cora Clementi less like Queen Gertrude than a disturbed bird's-nest. Slowly the others emerged upon the Green, gathering behind Randolph in an uncomfortable, unlikely huddle.

'The members of my company, sir.'

'An' 'tis sad,' said Peter Curnow as his considered view, 'to find so many short of salvation. Outside a church at that.'

Cora Clementi shuddered. 'Must we talk of salvation at this hour? At breakfast time. Milk, bread – where can we get them in this – this field?'

'For milk,' Peter Curnow said, 'you go to the farm, though I don't swear they'll serve 'ee. Bread in Reynolds' shop at eight . . . You'll be takin' the road again?'

'Take the road!' Randolph was affronted. 'Tonight, Mr Curnow, we perform here – at Pralla. Morris, kindly hand me a bill.' He held out the crumpled paper. 'See there. The St John Randolph company, direct from the principal London and provincial theatres, in the plays of Shakespeare, Sheridan Knowles, Wilkins Tomlin, Hubert Crabb, and many other eminent authors. Sumptuous effects. Songs introduced. Six-thirty o'clock nightly. Prices ninepence, sixpence, threepence. Carriages ten-thirty sharp.'

'Carriages!' Curnow muttered. 'My dear life! . . . You'd best be gettin' along.'

'Why, pray?' exclaimed Morris Tapping.

Curnow glanced westward. 'See they clouds out to Pentillie. Rain by noon, and you'll need to be well on the road.'

'We have come here to perform,' said Randolph firmly, 'and perform we will.' Even as he spoke, he was beginning gloomily to weigh the chances. There seemed to be no village hall, not even a Reading Room. That would mean playing in the tent; and if there were no chairs to borrow, not even a few handy benches, the audience would have to sit on mats and rugs, or on the old blue cloth that was usually one of the sumptuous effects. And what about the lighting? Naturally, they travelled with their own lanterns, four of them. Doubtless they could borrow others. Or could they? Well, if he must, he would have to lower the prices: sixpence in front, threepence behind. While he thought of these things he observed that Peter Curnow had shredded the playbill into small pieces and was scattering them histrionically to left and right. The man could have been a good actor, Randolph agreed grudgingly, though what he was saying appeared to be irrelevant.

'Babylon the great is fallen, is fallen, and has become the inhabitation of devils,' intoned Peter; and he made an admirably timed exit across the road.

'Meaning us, I suppose,' snapped Cora.

Randolph was grieved and laconic. 'Let the man be. There'll be friendlier folk.'

But were there? They could get no milk at the farm. After making the journey over what they described as a marsh smelling of camomile, Cora, Sedley, and little Annie Mack met only a severe elderly woman with a broom. Having ascertained their business, she said sourly that she saw three unclean spirits, like frogs, come out of the mouth of the dragon, and out of the mouth of the beast, and out of the mouth of the false prophet. This being unanswerable, she closed the door. However, there was water up at the clanking pump, beside the shop; the shopkeeper herself – a passable First Witch, said Morris – sold them, without enthusiasm, a loaf. They had still a rind or so of cheese; but they were hungrier than usual when they set out on the morning's task of coaxing an audience, stubbing playbills under cottage doors, and walking out as much as two miles on top of a broad hedge that appeared to be a local highway. Their object was to woo the occupants of two outlying farms. No one was at home, so they left the bills behind them and came back painfully to the Green in a steadily thickening drizzle.

By the time they had reassembled in the tent it was pelting. Clearly there was not a spare bench or superfluous chair in the whole of Pralla. 'Lay out the mats,' instructed Randolph. 'If we play to a dozen tonight we shall be lucky.'

'Then why play?' asked Cora, who had her own brand of logic. Randolph was about to tell her that the profession had a duty to its public, when a mild, bearded face looked round the tent-flap. Its owner wriggled in, shaking himself and adding to the general damp. 'Samuel Bosworthick,' he said informatively. 'Clerk to the parish. If, sir, there is any assistance I can render – ?' Theoretically, it seemed, there was much; practically, nothing. Mr Bosworthick regretted the absence of chairs and benches: the Methodys would have them in stacks, but it was no business of his. Lanterns? Not one, but Mrs Reynolds, up shop, would sell a pound of candles. Food? A poor man himself, he had no means of entertaining them. An audience? He, and maybe his wife, would attend, but no one could bring in the Methodys. Too late for the childurn. Too early for the doctor. And most of the Pralla men were out for the day: a meeting of fishermen's interests at Falmouth. Had they seen the waggonette? Altogether, a sad outlook; yet Mr Bosworthick was affable in his negative way. Thirty years ago his granny, over to Halsetown, had known little Johnnie Brodribb. Irving he called himself now: 'A dark and masterful man, so they do tell me.' Randolph was relieved to hear that, even in Pralla, ignorance was not total. 'I am myself a Hamlet,' he informed Mr Bosworthick. 'Irving plays the part next week.' But the rain had lulled a trifle by then, and the village's potential playgoer was slipping off to his presumably seatless, lightless, foodless, but not entirely uncultured home.

2

At six-thirty the rain was teeming again and a searching wind had begun to blow from the south-east. It hammered against the side of the tent where the pomping folk had prepared hopelessly for the evening, Randolph himself in fringed black doublet and frayed tights, Cora in the Queen's sole orange robe, Morris clamped into the crown that the King wore at all times. Since they lacked any planks that could serve for a stage, they marked out an acting space between two of the handcarts which each held a pair of lanterns. Not a soul had come at six-thirty. Sternly Randolph waited, and at last, after ten minutes, a powerful gust seemed to toss in Sam Bosworthick with a diminutive, iron-spectacled wife. 'Pay later, friends,' cried Sam, as they shook themselves like spaniels on a dry mat. No sooner had they settled than Peter Curnow, of all people, stamped in, thrusting his threepence in halfpennies at Lucy who, in white muslin, doubled Ophelia and the doorkeeper.

'Peter Curnow!' said Sam Bosworthick. 'There's a facer, my dear. When did 'ee last go to a play?'

'It is a man's duty,' said Peter conversationally, 'to bear witness against the idolators. Upon them shall fall a great hail out of heaven, and the night shall destroy them.'

'Go 'long, you teasy toad!' shrilled Mrs Bosworthick. And between the handcarts the play began, leaping at once in a violent cut from 'What, has this thing appeared again tonight?' to Hamlet's 'O, that this too, too solid flesh would melt!' Randolph had no need to simulate his passion: 'How weary, stale, flat, and unprofitable seem to me all the uses of this world!'

'The man's soft,' said Peter Curnow audibly. As he spoke, the wind gathered itself into a harsh stampeding gale that blotted out Hamlet's mouthing and even the voice of Peter Curnow insisting that there were lightnings and thunderings and a great storm. In an immediate sharp lull a thin cry rose outside, 'Wreck! Wre-e-eck!' The tent-flap flew open. A pair of dim forms blundered in, snatched up the lanterns, and disappeared. Blindly, the pomping folk and their audience stumbled into the sheeting rain, and Morris flung over Lucy's already soaked muslin the only cloak, apart from his plaid, that the company possessed. By habit he reached up to straighten his crown.

Southward they could just discern a blur of light in the black cloud. As it flickered out, a brighter streak flashed through the sky to explode briefly in a falling star.

'That's a rocket,' announced Sam Bosworthick to the world at large. 'Ship out beyond the Frigate reef.'

Somebody at the end of the Green had lifted a flaming torch that spluttered into oblivion. Randolph's arm was seized. 'You'll come in the boat,' cried Peter Curnow. 'Soft 'ee may be, an' furrin, I'll not deny it, but 'tis no time to choose. Every man to his oar.'

'His oar?'

'Where else? Richards an' Pascoe are sick an' abed; others away to Falmouth. We'm short of a crew ... So smart now! Along with 'ee and worship Him that made the sea and the fountains of waters.'

Randolph, in Hamlet's doublet and thin slippers, the foolish brass locket rattling about his chest, felt himself pulled and hurtled over the soggy grass, into the mud of track and ditch, and then, at the roughest speed, down the slimy, stony chute of a lane, narrow and high-banked, where the brambles spiked them as they rushed by, a freezing rivulet swirled round their ankles, and the long rain lashed. They had been out of the wind, but in a minute or so it struck like a sabre-cut. Now they were on the exposed and crumbling cliff down which Peter Curnow tugged his bewildered Hamlet to a ledge a few feet over the beach. 'Jump!' Randolph was ordered, and he crashed down through the dark on a bed of cobbles. Instantly he was dragged up again and hauled into a boat heaving at the very rim of the tide. Then they had pushed off, and, with half a dozen others invisible in the drenched blanket of the dark, he was pumping away at an oar, Hamlet's locket jumping absurdly on his breast, and Peter Curnow working through the Book of Revelation behind him. The boat bucketed out towards a solid wall of blackness. Then they penetrated it, through some channel in the Man o' War Rock, and were thrashing desperately in the general direction of a glimmer, vaguely seen, that might have been on the farthest horizon. No rockets now; the end must be near.

'That's she,' bellowed the man in front of Randolph. 'Spaniard, they say. Tight on the Frigate, and she'm holdin' still.'

' 'Tedn' true, boy. This shud scat her to flinders.'

Wave upon wave climbed, curled, crashed inboard. Randolph thought of being sick, abandoned the notion, and clutched at his oar. What good he was doing, if any, he had no idea, but by and by a towering comber bore them close to the dim lantern-light and to a few seamen crouched upon the slanting deck of a barque that had lost her masts and broken her back on the ridge of the Frigate reef. Somehow a rope was tossed aboard; somehow four spent seamen dropped to the boat; and perilously overcharged, half waterlogged, it began its battling return to the cobbles, the draped weed, and the crumble of cliff.

Randolph remembered little else: the smeech of oily rags burning by the cove as a signal-torch, a lessening of the storm, a struggle up the lane with the four survivors who struck him as more alive than he was, a cottage door banging, an immense and crackling salt-blue fire, the steady flinking of a towel, strong, sweet tea, and Peter Curnow's voice intoning some sonorous passage from Revelation about the sixth angel that poured out his vial upon the great river Euphrates. Then, after a long blank gap, the Green and an effort to crawl into the dripping bundle of a tent. The pomping folk lay there beneath wads of sodden cloth. Annie, Cora, and Lucy were asleep, and two of the men. Only Morris was relating to Sedley his interminable yarn of the graveyard scene at Wantage.

3

Morning dawned as if the gale had never been. With the others, Randolph – changed from soaked doublet and tights into damp coat and breeches – struggled to work the tent into some feasible shape.

'Surely we don't stay?' wailed Cora.

Randolph was as stern as his chattering teeth would let him. 'We have not yet acted here. Tonight is *Hamlet*.'

'And what, may I inquire, will Hamlet be wearing?' asked Cora in her wardrobe-mistress voice.

They had not noticed a shadow on the grass. 'Mornin',' said Peter Curnow. 'Straight from the dog's mouth, the lot of 'ee.'

'And where are the Spanish sailors?' said Randolph stiffly.

'Ah, they'm survivin'. We'll look to they ... Packin', I note.'

'Indeed, we are not,' exclaimed Randolph. 'We shall be performing tonight at six-thirty.' When, he wondered, had he said that before?

Peter Curnow gazed at him earnestly. 'You'm as obstinate as a badger, but you'll not be playin' tonight. That's for the chapel – Penny Readin' at six. Stay for 'n, if 'ee wish – but, mind, no furriners or graven images, the kings and the princes, their wives and their concubines.' He moved off in the midst of Revelation, with a last word over his shoulder: 'Carriages at ten.'

Randolph opened his mouth and shut it again. Behind him Morris and Sedley, with Annie Mack, were loading the three handcarts. Already Peter Curnow was striding away into the morning. Sun glittered on a gentle sea. The muddy road led towards Polruth. He sighed and picked up Hamlet's doublet.

'Leavin' then?' Now it was Sam Bosworthick's voice. The little man pushed a paper at Randolph: 'Will 'ee be settlin' up now?' Randolph looked at the paper, bemused. It said, in copperplate: 'St Nicholas Church, Pralla, 26th October, 1874. To hire of Church Green for one night, 10s. S. Bosworthick, Parish Clerk.'

Randolph turned on him like Macbeth on the cream-faced loon. 'What foolery is this?'

'No foolery,' said Bosworthick. 'Law's on our side, an' Passon'll write to 'ee when he gets home . . . Now, now, don't tear 'n.'

Beaten, Randolph stuffed the paper in his pocket.

'Tonight,' Bosworthick went on, 'you'd go whistlin' in the air. Everyone in Pralla'll be over to chapel, Jane and me excluded, though I'm not sayin' they Methodys don't make a brave night of it. Every pew taken an' half a score benches.'

He stared at the battered doublet on Randolph's arm. 'That *Hamlet* now . . . Wisht piece, I reckon, even if Johnnie Brodribb gets his penny from it. I'd recommend a change . . . Good day to 'ee all.' Suddenly he turned back, the bearer of news. 'That was a wreck last night. Did 'ee knaw?'

'We were informed of it,' said Randolph. He dropped the doublet into the third cart and took his place between the shafts. Slowly, very slowly, the pomping folk trudged northward from Pralla in the strengthening sun.

Denys Val Baker

THE DISCOVERY

I can remember the clay pool now as vividly as the first morning when Luke and I climbed through the ruins of an old Cornish mine house and followed a path up the steep, moss-covered slope – and there, falling away from us into vast, silent space, lay the shimmering blue, unbelievably bright blue surface.

We were staying with our parents at a cottage just outside Nancledra, in the Penwith Hills above St Ives. Everywhere around the hills rose up bleak and austere, more often than not crowned by some forlorn finger of a mine chimney, rearing impotently against the ageless sky. The mines were long since silent, the shafts filled with water, and the crumbling ruins of their machine heads merely served to emphasize the strange atmosphere of past.

It was a country ripe for exploration by two youngsters glad to escape from London smog for a while, and most mornings Luke and I slipped away, adventure bound. Luke was my elder brother, nearly fifteen, three years older than I, with an air of native authority to which I was glad to succumb. He was tall and fair, with a boyish charm that was just beginning to set with a touch of manliness: beside him I felt an inadequate, uncouth schoolboy. And needless to say I worshipped him with the peculiarly concentrated devotion that younger brothers have at that tender age.

It was Luke, naturally, who took the lead on our expeditions. Luke who said, 'Let's see if we can find that old Roman village at Chyauster.' Or, 'What's Castle-en-Dinas? Let's go and find out.' And we'd set off on the trail, Luke remembering to be a very grown-up fifteen frowning on too much horseplay – myself, at least secretly, imagining us as some scouting party of ancient Britons, or maybe the current equivalent of Davy Crockett.

But whatever our attitudes, I think both of us were always impressed, and often awed, by the magnificent solitude and mystery of those Cornish moors, so impregnated with weird memories and suggestions of the past. It was not difficult to feel, as I have since read that George Meredith wrote, that in Cornwall the past was always at your elbow. We always felt that at any moment something strange, perhaps supernatural, could happen.

It was rather like that with our discovery of the blue clay pool. We had heard one or two of the farmers talk about it, but only casually. Somehow it did not seem altogether real. For us it was part of the general mythology, a place that existed – somewhere.

And then, suddenly, there it was spread out before our astonished eyes in all its delicate and transparent beauty. Anyone who has walked among mountains and come upon a lake will know the strange excitement of seeing enclosed water high up, many miles away from its natural home of the sea. But lake water is usually a rather dull grey or green: this was quite different, this was a huge dazzling splash of glistening blue – indeed, it might have been the sea itself. What's more, all around the edge there were sloping white sands, just as if there was a real beach.

I can remember how Luke and I just stood at the top for quite a time, staring. Perhaps neither of us had ever seen anything quite so beautiful, and we wanted to savour it to the full.

Then we awoke to reality, and with wild cries of delight we charged down the slope, and across the wide white sands, to the very edge of this secret and mysterious blue sea.

'Look, Luke,' I cried, pointing in wonder. 'You can see right to the bottom!'

And indeed, the water was crystal clear, pure and innocent. How long had it lain silently there? How many hundreds of years ago had this pool begun as a tiny trickle, rising higher and higher as the nearby clay pit deepened, gradually enveloping more and more of the land? We could not know: the blue pool stared blandly up at us, and we knew we could never know all its secrets.

But at least it gave us a new, marvellous playground. For at least half the way round we could follow the sandy edge before it became lost in a mass of tangled undergrowth. There were several bends in the 'coast' and round each one we found new excitements. At one point a small red stream trickled out of the hillside, forming a tiny tributary running into the pool: we spent hours damming it up with broken pieces of rock. In another part a tree had, weirdly, grown out over the water. We climbed catlike along the swaying branch, until we could lie there staring down into a depth of water that seemed unfathomable.

'Ugh! I wouldn't like to fall down there,' said Luke.

But there was no real fear behind his remark. Somehow the blue pool wasn't like that. It was strange, it was even ghostly at times, and it certainly seemed a world of its own – but it was never sinister or evil, like some parts of Cornwall can be. It was always, for us both, a magical kingdom of its own, our blue heaven.

By tacit consent, Luke and I said very little about the pool. It was our own secret, we wanted to keep it for ourselves, and so we did – from our parents, anyway. We weren't able to get there every day, of course, but usually we did – sometimes quite early in the morning, and on one or two occasions in the evening, when the fading sunlight gave the pool an added charm.

I suppose in the uncomplicated way of children we came to look on the pool as our own. After all, hadn't we discovered it like explorers of old, that morning when we breasted the hill? I really think we must have felt rather like that, possessive and proud.

And so we were quite upset one afternoon when we found our kingdom invaded by intruders. We watched angrily, sheltered by a tree. There they were as bold as brass, rambling along the far side – a tall, thickset man with a walking stick, and a young girl.

We glared suspiciously, willing them to go away and leave us in peace. But they did nothing of the kind; indeed after a while the man with the stick sat down on a boulder and began unpacking a packet of sandwiches, and the little girl went and sat by him and they settled down to a meal.

Somewhat self-consciously, Luke and I came down on the beach. Usually we would gambol about or chase each other, or climb up and down the rocky parts. Somehow, now it was impossible. We felt conscious all the time of the strangers. Their sharing of our secret took away its pleasure.

It was only when they got up to go, and came along past where we were seated, rather disconsolately throwing stones into the pool, that we felt our depression lifting. As they came along, out of curiosity we could not help looking. The man, to us, looked quite old. He had frizzy grey hair and a lined face, and leaned heavily on his stick, walking with a limp. As he came abreast of us, he paused and eyed us keenly from under bushy eyebrows.

'Ha!' he said, in a booming voice. 'Captain Morgan and Captain Kidd, I presume?' He turned and stabbed his stick out across the pool. 'Better look out, there's a Government frigate on the horizon.'

And then, with another 'Ha!' and a 'Ho!' he went on. And as he did so, just behind him, we were both conscious of the little girl. She wore a dress of almost the same colour as the pool, and against it she shone with a delicate radiance of her own. She had dark hair done up in pigtails, hanging over her back, and I can remember that her blue eyes were large and solemn, as they looked at us. I didn't feel there was anything special about her. She was just a girl, older than I, maybe about Luke's age.

But Luke, I knew, felt different. It wasn't anything he said, just something in the way he looked at the girl, and the way, once or twice, after she had walked on, clinging to her father's hand, that she cast a backward glance. Just something – something in the air as you might say.

'Well, I'm glad they're gone,' I said, irritable from my awareness of Luke's interest.

He watched them go, up the hill and out of sight. His face looked vacant, as if his thoughts were far away.

'Yes,' he said. He picked up a large stone and threw it far out into the lake, watching the ripples travel all the way back to the shore.

'I wonder who they are?' said Luke.

We found out soon enough. Somehow, whether by some accident or design I never knew, they were there again the next day. This time, in the way these things happen, we began talking. The man with the stick and the booming voice probably began it, with his jokes about pirates. I rather liked him. With his frizzy hair and broad shoulders he reminded me of a great bear, and he had about him that warmth and friendliness which, rightly or wrongly, I have always associated with bears.

Mind you, he was a very talkative bear. He enjoyed the act of talking itself. His voice seemed to well up from deep down and fairly boom out, echoing and re-echoing over the pool. He had a curious way of talking in fantasy, too. Just as he had immediately labelled us as pirates, so he had a way of referring to ordinary things and events, and making them sound quite extraordinary.

'That's why I like living in Cornwall, boy,' he said to me once. 'Feel at home here, you see. Ha!'

His daughter, Elizabeth, was far less forthcoming. At first she stayed very close to her father, staring at us with those round, wondering eyes. Indeed it was he, with his bluff laugh and a careless wave of his walking stick, who first encouraged her out of her shyness.

'C'mmun, girl. You needn't be afraid. They're only children like yourself. Why don't you go and play?'

It wasn't as easy as that. Elizabeth, rather like her name suggested, was one of the serious, quiet types. And I guess Mr Slater, that was her father's name, understood her well enough, for he led her along very slowly into our company, not forcing or bullying. He was very fond of his daughter, we could see that. We learned later that his wife had recently died, and he was bringing Elizabeth up on his own.

I suppose I was antagonistic to her from the beginning. Or suspicious, maybe. I suspected that faintly ethereal appearance. I suspected those round, innocent eyes. I distrusted that shyness, that gentle withdrawal. In my bones I knew, withal, she was of the stuff that women are made.

Gradually, we began playing together, the three of us. Most afternoons we would come up and find Mr Slater and Elizabeth already there, waiting, and then we would go off and play, leaving Mr Slater leaning against a rock, staring out upon the water.

We played – but it wasn't the same as before, not for me. We still went exploring, and climbed out on the tree, and made up adventures. But none of them were quite the same. Upon them all, even if she was not aware of it, Elizabeth imposed a curious, soft feminine restraint. Once or twice I saw Luke helping her, across a stream, over the tree branch – grinning quickly, an arm holding her elbow. Girls, I thought. Girls . . .

Sometimes, in that mood, I would wander away on my own, perhaps down to where Mr Slater sat. I suppose I went for the entertainment. I liked the way he brought out startling images and created fantastic situations. He was an author, apparently, and though that meant very little to me, I gathered from the way in which Elizabeth breathed the word that it was something distinguished.

'He sits in his room every morning, writing. He's written *eight* books,' said Elizabeth importantly.

Luke whistled.

'He must be very clever.'

But I looked at them both irritably, for I knew they were just saying words – they didn't really *feel* Mr Slater's cleverness deep down, like I did. I didn't care how many books he'd written, but I knew he was somebody special.

'Look at that seagull, boy,' he'd say, poking his stick. 'More beautiful than all your airplanes. And not factory made, eh?'

'Sky's like a painting today, boy. Can't you just see some

fellow stick on the paints – all crimson and orange and indigo. There, dab-dab-dab!'

And somehow, under Mr Slater's wandering gaze, my own eyes began to open upon the world proper, upon all the topsy turvy inexplicable wonderful things that went on in the world.

But all the time, Luke and Elizabeth would be playing, down by the beach, maybe making up games on their own.

And then one afternoon we were surprised to see Elizabeth come on her own. She said her father had decided to lie down for a rest. He might come along later.

I can remember that afternoon. She wore a bright green blouse and a red skirt; somehow she looked much older than usual, much more grown up.

And, yes, it was odd, but she seemed different from other times. There was no doubt about it. It was as if the absence of her father had produced a liberating effect. Perhaps, secretly, she had always wanted to be free of that guiding hand – had really not wanted the familiar figure to shelter behind.

I don't know. I couldn't fathom it then and I don't suppose I would now. I only knew that this was a different girl and that Luke felt the same, too, because he kept staring at her puzzledly. That is, until she turned round eyes upon him and stared back. Then he did something I couldn't ever remember seeing before. He blushed. Luke, my elder brother, blushed.

We all went along the white sandy beach. It was a perfect afternoon: the sun scorching down, the sands hot on our feet. It was the sort of afternoon when you could think of nothing really except how wonderful it would be to dive deep down into some cold clear water.

'I know,' said Elizabeth suddenly. 'Why don't we bathe?'

Luke and I both looked at her remembering that on past occasions any such suggestions had been vetoed. But we didn't need to see the unfamiliar glint in her eyes to realize that the obstacle to the suggestion, Mr Slater, was for the first time missing.

'You never know,' he would have said, shaking his great head gravely, 'Quick sands in the middle ... very deep ... mustn't take chances at your age.'

But though we would have obeyed him, we knew in our hearts that the dangers weren't important. We were young and healthy. We could manage. It had always been a great tantalization.

'All right,' said Luke suddenly. 'I'm game.'

'Me, too,' I said, liking the idea at least, even if it was Elizabeth's.

Luke hesitated. 'We haven't any costumes.'

Elizabeth hardly seemed to hear him. Already she had turned away and was stepping over the rocks towards a patch of grass.

'We'll go in without.' She half-turned and looked back, and it seemed to me there was a secret mischief in her eyes, all for Luke. 'Promise you won't look until I'm in the water?'

We promised, and resolutely turned our backs. Once I essayed a quick peep, and Luke smacked me on the shoulder, quite hard. I looked at him in surprise, and saw that his face was curiously set.

'You mustn't do that,' he said. 'You *mustn't*.'

Suddenly there was a whirl of air and noise and then a frothing sound, and then a final splash, and a moment later Elizabeth called out, from a long way away.

'All right – come on in. It's lovely, really lovely.'

We undressed quickly, and ran into the waters of our familiar magical blue pool. How cool and refreshing they were, how soft and gentle to the touch – what rapture to plunge out of the sun's heat into such exquisite coolness.

We splashed around for a while, and then began swimming around. So far we had not gone out of our depth, but now Luke proposed swimming across to a rock jutting out on the opposite side. It wasn't far, but I knew I couldn't do it.

Luke knew, too, and gave me stern admonishments not to try. Then he and Elizabeth, who were both good swimmers, set off side by side.

I stood and watched them going, their bodies white, and to me almost transparent in the clear water. Suddenly I felt as if

I were watching two strangers, perhaps creatures of the pool. Their white limbs, so much longer than mine, seemed to merge into the eternal blueness of the pool. Soon I could only see their two heads bobbing from side to side – and hear from afar the laughter of their voices as they shouted to one another.

Then, suddenly, I felt unutterably lonely. I felt I did not want to stay in the water any longer, indeed I felt rather foolish. Quickly I turned and ran back to the bank, and put on some clothes. Then, almost casually, I turned, and saw Mr Slater.

He had just arrived, and was standing by the rock where he usually sat, leaning on his stick, and staring across the water. Following his gaze, I saw that he was watching his daughter Elizabeth and Luke. They had reached the rock and were clinging on, and lazily splashing one another. It was too far away to see their faces, but we could hear quite clearly their laughter. It seemed to rise up out of the blue pool, as clear and definite, as positive of meaning as the sunshine itself. There was no mistaking the tone of their laughter – no mistaking the sound of their happiness.

As I watched it seemed to me that Mr Slater, the great bear, almost crumpled up. I saw his shoulders sag, and his whole body seemed to lean with almost unbearable weight upon his walking stick. I felt the utter poignancy of the moment. And then, slowly, he turned and began walking away, back the way he had come.

'Mr Slater!' I called. 'Mr Slater!'

He didn't stop, but I ran after him and caught him up along the path lined with brambles and blackberry bushes. He didn't say anything, because I realize now he was too full of emotion. For that matter, so was I. We walked along in silence all the way back to his cottage, and it wasn't till we reached the broad stone porchway that he turned and put a hand on my head.

'Ah, well, boy, don't worry – you'll grow up one day, too.'

I didn't know what he meant really then, but I do now. I went back to the blue pool the other day. It lay cool and shimmering in the midday heat, and as I lay and feasted my eyes on its quiet beauty, I couldn't help remembering. I guess Mr

Slater and I were both mourning the same thing. Something to do with the magic of a blue pool on a summer's day, of youth growing up, of love blossoming. But I guess if I'm honest there was something else too – something to do with a girl with dark pigtails and round, questioning eyes – and how for the rest of my life a part of me would always wish it had been me, and not Luke, who swam with her across the unknown, virginal waters of the blue pool.

C. C. Vyvyan

THE WITCH OF TREGONEBRIS

Sophia Crowgey was, undoubtedly, a witch. The boys would always stone her when she crossed the village green to go 'down shop', or when she took her pitcher to the village pump. Parson went to call on her once, but never again. The Wesleyan minister, a man with eyes and heart turned only to the things of good repute around him, would always shake his head if anyone named Sophia Crowgey, and he would murmur in regretful tones, 'She's a hard case.' And Farmer Golly swore by all his pigs and mangolds – for he deemed it wrong to swear by all that's holy – that more than once she had laid a spell upon his cows.

However, none of these things, not even Farmer Golly's oath, are evidence that Sophia Crowgey of Tregonebris rode a broomstick or wore a pointed hat or peered into the secret places of her neighbours' lives. Evidence indeed! What has evidence to do with wizardry? No; those things, taken alone, were little more than the chittering of sparrows or the swaying of some reed-bed in an idle wind. And yet there was something in the glance of Sophia Crowgey, something looked out behind her eyes, but never more than half revealed, that would surely turn the devil in his path and shatter any human enterprise or human resolution.

Yes, in the spirit of that dirty old woman, a creature so near the margin of poverty that one step lower would lead her inevitably to the workhouse, some occult power had surely found a home, a home whence, looking out on the little world of men and women, it could play havoc with their desires, hopes and fears.

And what a home! The cottage where Sophia Crowgey lived

alone, or with whatever evil spirits bore her company, was thatched and whitewashed; but the whitewash had turned green with damp and slime of ages trickling down the walls, to find a breeding-ground in every crevice of the building. As for the thatch, it had no longer any affinity with clean straw, but was more like some rotting lair where animals had turned and slept and turned again, some lair that now lies open to the world, displaying dank putridity and foulness.

The garden gate was broken; it had only half a hinge and now was tied to the granite post by a piece of twisted wire; inside the gate there was a path of cobblestones and a sour patch of ground where half a dozen hens picked hopelessly beneath some gooseberry bushes that bore neither leaf nor fruit. On the window-sill, below the broken panes stuffed up with rags, sat a very large black cat, emaciated, furtive, watchful; and below that window-sill, pushing up through the cobblestones, there grew a plant of honesty and two of the strongly scented feverfew.

The cottage was a single one, set back in the lane some hundred yards or two above the village green where the Rose and Crown, the smithy, the little shop and the other dwellings clustered in comfortable fashion, looking across at one another as if to say: 'We all stick to each other in Tregonebris.'

So homely and self-sufficient was the little hamlet that, when a son or daughter married and settled in some cottage, it might be five, it might be ten minutes' walk away, the older folk would always tell you; 'Mary-Jane she've gone away to live.' Or: 'My William-Herbert gone away to Tregoverras 'e 'ave, iss, gone away for good'n all.' Tregoverras being the sister hamlet some four hundred yards higher up the hill.

From ancient times the Tregoverras people had looked down on Tregonebris as 'no more than a whisht li'l oal duck pond buried down in a hollow'; while Tregonebris had hugged the thought of its own shelter when, on wintry nights, Tregoverras was swept by every wind that blew.

Thus it was natural that Sophia should be regarded by the cosy Tregonebris people as an outsider, for her windows looked into no other windows, the smoke from her chimney mingled with no other smoke, and her wall adjoined no other wall. But the isolation of her cottage in the lane was nothing compared with the strangeness of her mind, her ways and her appearance.

She was spare and shrunken, rapid in her movements like a bird, and like a bird she had eyes that were never still; but there was about her shrunkenness something unnatural, as if it had happened to her in a very short space of time and left her with the habits and gestures of something larger than herself. The upper part of her body was encased in a black coat shaped like an hour-glass and drawn together firmly at the waist by a single button. A heavy silver brooch, as large as the cover of a jam-pot, adorned her very dirty blouse, and a rusty, steel watch-chain did duty for a necklace. Her skirts or petticoats were an indescribable blend of moss-green and faded brown.

Perched on her grey and straggling locks was a hat shaped like a saucer, guiltless of a brim; it was trimmed with strangely assorted odds and ends. Were they souvenirs, or symbols, or some impious relics of her calling, or a collection of talismans by which she wove her spells? First of all, there were a couple of blown-glass beads, one green, the other filmy-white. Then there was a purple velvet pansy, edges turned towards the centre as if, aware that its day had come and gone, it were making one frantic effort to curl up and die. There were also faded flowers, blue and pink and yellow, and one unfaded brilliant scarlet petal detached for ever from its fellows; and many another object of metal, bone or woven stuff. The foundation of these relics which, in variety and number, would have put Louis XI in the shade, was rusty black, and over her forehead, in fact from one ear to the other, there ran a triple entanglement of beads, all black, some keeping line and others hanging on loose threads.

But the eyes below the hat were the strangest things about Sophia Crowgey, for they held – yes, you had only to look at them once again and you could swear it – two expressions in one single space of time. They were set wide apart and, like the eyes of a child, they were filled with wonder, with expectation, containing more of hope than fear of what the next hour or the next turning was about to bring. But in those eyes you could see also a gleam of evil stabbing their innocence as with a pin-point; not merely one wrong thought, one wrong impulse or another, but the very spirit of evil, reinforced by all that envy, hate and cunning, cruel spite and hoarded malice could throw into the balance.

What depths of evil lurked in Sophia's soul no one ever knew, for only fragments floated to the surface, in the baleful influence she cast upon her neighbours' fortunes and in the scraps of conversation she would shout at every passer-by.

Some folk could remember Tregonebris before the Crowgeys left their home in the sister hamlet and came to live in the cottage in the lane, but they were few and far between, for old Richard, Sophia's father, had died in that cottage, and that was more than a score of years ago. Nothing more than a 'dung-dabber' up to Mitchell's was Richard Crowgey all his days, and he left his only daughter little but his name. And now, for five or six years, it seemed as if a blight had fallen on Tregonebris, and one and all agreed that Sophia was the author of their troubles.

Often they would discuss the matter, drawing water, as they talked and listened, from the village pump. 'A proper oal witch she be,' said one. And another: 'John Tobias 'e told me that 'is sister's husband's uncle went for to mend her chimbley, years agone it wore, an' as 'e was pitchin' to 'is job, all ter waunce 'e saw two stramming gurt toads a-setting under the obben they was, both together so 'omelike as never was. Who ever heerd tell 'pon such hathen craitures in a body's house?'

'An' they do say,' added Mrs Treloar, who always reserved her contribution until the group round the pump had reached its full dimension, 'they do say that Sophia Crowgey be holdin' unnatural conversations, an' I tell 'ee what's aav ut, the devil hisself is in ut an' no person else. My Thomas 'ave 'eerd things when 'e be comin' 'ome from keepin' a heye to them birds in Squire's wood. Times 'e d'come be the lane, an' times 'e d'come over the road, 'tes all accordin'. Be 'e sez comin' down that theare lane waun night 'e 'eerd voices comin' right out o' the chimbley, scritchin' an' hollerin' they was, not natural human voices like. I axe 'ee,' and Mrs Treloar made her peroration with an arm on each ample hip, 'es ut right an' es ut fitty, an' she a lone woman too? My Thomas d'say, "Mark my words, Liza," 'e sez, "the devil 'isself is in ut."'

Nor were the tales in circulation round the pump without continual reinforcement. One year Farmer Golly's herd was decimated and the following spring a black shadow fell on the vicarage family. For many months that shadow brooded there, and even the tongues around the pump were hushed in sympathy, or horror, at the 'goings-on' reported by the vicar's little maid who was cook, housemaid, messenger and confidante in one. Before the winter came the vicar's wife was 'putt away' to the asylum. That cloud had at last 'outwept its rain'.

Hardly had the vicar returned from his melanchonly expedition to Bodmin, when the little maid slipped upon the planchen of the parlour and broke her leg. And they were not only private persons who suffered from the spells cast by that solitary old woman who, since her father's death, had not exchanged one friendly word with any human soul. For first of all the village pump went dry in the middle of the summer, and even Widow Hockin who was nearly ninety-two could remember no such calamity. Next spring there came a blight on the potatoes and after that the belfry church was struck by lightning.

And then there was young Squire up to Chyandour, Squire who was in truth more like an institution than a private person, since he was universal landlord and justice of the peace; since, like his father and grandfather before him, he belonged to hand the bag in church, and subscribe to both the chapels, Billy Bray and United Free, and to play providence to any whom sober age or illness should bring low. Perhaps young Squire never had been quite like the Honourable George. He was a proper man was the Honourable: gruff as gruff he was, his 'yes' was always 'yes' and his 'no' was like a growl of thunder. He would never stand any skylarking among the old nor yet among the young, but he held his rent dinner when he was rising eighty-nine and he died that very evening in his chair, with his pipe and his empty glass beside him. Yes, he was a proper man and a proper squire, was the Honourable George Calenick of Chyandour.

Perhaps it was the times, or these new-fangled ways of education, or maybe too much travel in foreign parts had done it. However that may be, young Squire always was one for skylarking, and later he fell into evil ways. His wife ran away after a while, through no fault of her own, and thereafter he lived alone in godless contentment with a young housekeeper, and she 'weth her hair so gold as a brand new sovereign'. This was nothing less than a public calamity, for it was among the things that don't belong to be.

At first, amid these many troubles, one misfortune would wipe out the memory of the other; but as the years went on suspicions centred on Sophia, and at last there was never a man nor woman nor child in the parish who ignored the fact that Sophia Crowgey was in league with the devil. Her own conversation was another proof if proof were needed now.

No friendly greeting ever passed her lips; her business in the little shop was done by sign and mumbled words. But when the urchins baited her, or sometimes when a body merely passed her in the road, she would turn and utter such a torrent of broken phrases, where evil thoughts and evil words were half submerged in raving nonsense, that no reply was possible. The only course was to hurry on out of earshot, to hurry away from those piercing eyes which surely had the power of drawing down Heaven's anger on luckless men and women.

'Walkin' 'pon their noses,' she would shriek, 'iss, walkin' right 'pon their noses 'e was, an' they wudden knaw nuthin' aav ut ... Three nights in the bed, I sez to un, an' then you'd want three more ... garn!' And here would follow an evil chuckle and some words of unknown origin and indescribable sound. 'Transported for life 'e was ... an' 'is flesh was nuthin' but worms – worms – worms ... I sez three nights more, I sez, an' be hanged to you ... an' fowls runnin' up the rope ladder ... an' married men an' all ... 'tes vipers an' emmets suckin' of the chillern's blood an' darkness comin' on so thick; vipers with gurt yaller eyes lookin' out from the holes an' winders . . . aw! but 'tes them cruel vipers . . . take me home – home – home . . . 'tes witches I tell 'ee,' and her voice would rise to a piercing shriek, ' 'tes witches tearin' at me 'eart like as it 'twas loosened from me ribs, an' rotten stinken fly-be-nights every waun o' them!'

And then she would utter a stream of curses and invective from which sometimes the very boldest urchin would turn in flight.

And so the years rolled by and as Tregonebris people lived their daily lives they watched and wondered, unable to oppose or even to detect Sophia, but laying every trouble at her door. And like slime spreading over a duck pond the sense of evil grew and grew. Lunacy and crime and sickness, blight among the fruit trees, disease and infection on the farm, all were undoubtedly due to the witch, and everywhere there was now a sense of lethargy and hopelessness that killed all enterprise. The very slates upon the dwelling were covered with green mould, and the spirit of decay and evil seemed to reign without a foe.

Of all the people living in the parish, the sister's husband's uncle of Tobias-John was the only one who had crossed the threshold of Sophia's dwelling. Every straw upon her roof, every feather of her half a dozen fowls, might be familiar to her neighbour's searching eyes, but never a one could tell you how Sophia's home was furnished, or what manner of cloam was standing on her kitchen dresser. So far as they could tell, her cottage might be empty, save for the presence of those stramming great toads which sat, as rumour would have them believe, year in, year out, below the oven door.

Thus it came as a thunderclap presaging great events when Mrs Treloar, without preamble or warning, placed her hands upon her hips and addressed a half-formed group at the pump with these words:

' 'Ave 'ee 'eard the news? My Thomas 'e bin seein' Squire's lawyer up to Chyandour an' 'e toald un how they've bin an' gone an' served a notice on Sophia Crowgey. Out she d'go come next Michaelmas as ever is. Out she d'go, toads an' fowls an' all. Iss, fowls I tell 'ee.' And her voice rose here to a crescendo of tone and fervour. 'That's the mischief on ut. Roostin' in the kitchen!' The last words were given forth on the highest notes her vocal chords could compass. 'An' the place more like a pigsty than a kitchen the rent man d'say.'

'Where ever be she gwain to?' asked one of the neighbours as Mrs Treloar drew breath and gazed about her to watch the effect of her news. There was by this time a complete circle round the pump, two deep in some places – heads stretching over the next one's shoulders, anxious faces peering, each one afraid of missing a syllable.

'Where she be gwain ded 'ee say? Axe oald Nick, for no person else caan't tell 'ee that. But I can tell 'ee there bain't no empty houses in Tregonebris, no, nor in Tregoverras neether. I reckon she's gwain acrosst the water this time.'

But Michaelmas came and Sophia made no move across the water, nor indeed did she make any movement at all, except her usual ones to the pump and the village shop; and when they saw her on these little journeys folk noticed that her eyes were bent on the ground and that she moved more slowly than before. Moreover, instead of turning on the lads and shrieking evil words at them, she would mutter with an absent air, as if reminding herself of something that she had nearly forgotten, and then she would scold herself for some unknown delinquency.

' 'Tes my belief the woman's maazed,' said Thomas Treloar to his wife one evening. 'You mind oald Dicky Crowgey always was a bit short,' and he tapped his head with a look full of meaning. ' 'Tes in the family like, an' now Sophia've gone so bad as he; gone whimsical she 'ave. You mark my words, Liza.'

But Liza only replied: 'Passel o' nonsense, Thomas, you be talkin' a passel o' nonsense.'

Nevertheless she stored his remarks in her memory and spread them abroad next morning at the accustomed trysting-place. But they did not secure the usual hushed attention that was wont to say more plainly than words can speak: 'Well, we caan't beat that bit o' news, Liza Treloar, an' we ain't gwain to try, not nohow.'

On the contrary they raised a chorus of dissent.

'Whimsical? Naw, naw, I tell 'ee Sophia Crowgey she've got all her wits about her.'

'She be a black witch shure nuff an' I'd rayther fer to do weth Willie Pickle than weth she,' chimed in another.

'Who was Willie Pickle?' asked a third.

'I dunnaw,' replied the other speaker, 'but my old grandma whenever any trouble comed along she ded use ter say: "Theare's Willie Pickle's horse faalled down again." '

' 'E was a teasy oald bachelor, I reckon,' said Mrs Golly, 'but Sophia Crowgey she ain't so plum as you'm thinkin', Liza. She d'naw all what goes on inside every person's house. You caan't hide nawthen from her I tell 'ee; those eyes can see through walls, iss, walls of wood and stone.'

'Iss fay, she d'naw what a body's thinkin' too an' what a 'as for Sunday dinner an' all.'

By this time Mrs Treloar, seeing that the discussion had slipped from her control, was returning home across the village green with a pitcher full of water and her faith in the wisdom of Thomas considerably shaken.

From that moment the gossips at the pump were broken into two opposing parties; those, and they were by far the greater number, who declared that Sophia's faculty for brewing evil was unimpaired, and the few who supported Liza's Thomas in his contention that the old woman had gone whimsical. 'She be failin',' these would say, 'she wean't be weth us long.'

However, one quarter-day followed another and Sophia and her fowls remained in undisturbed possession of their home. Punctually the writ was served and punctually reported on by Liza's Thomas, who served as link for any news between Chyandour and Tregonebris; but the notice never took effect. It seemed as if no human writ nor any earthly power could wield an influence on that solitary old creature.

After a while her visits to the shop became less frequent, and though folks did not fail to notice and discuss the fact, they never troubled to discover how she lived and what she lived on. When she did appear she would cross the village green like one bereft of purpose, with her shoulders hunched forward and one leg dragging after the other; it seemed as if she were searching for something she had dropped. Even the urchins ceased to follow her when they found they could get no response in word nor look; there was no sport in baiting a thing that never turned on one.

Then, late in one of the autumn months, her visits to the shop stopped altogether, and the smoke from her chimney was the only sign of life about her dwelling. One morning, someone drawing water looked towards the lane; 'I b'lieve Sophia Crowgey's ill in the bed. When ded 'ee see the smoke arisin', neighbours?'

Each one looked at the other and no one could say for certain. Jacholiah Moyle, a pleasant-spoken lass, but soft from her teens, was heard to murmur: 'Aw, but 'tes whisht for an oald woman like she alone in the bed an' no person anyst for to tend her.'

'Tedden whisht at all,' said another, ' 'tes her spells 'ave brought 'er to ut.'

'She wean't die no Christian death in the bed, never fear,' chimed in Farmer Golly's wife. 'Witches don't never die like decent folk.'

But when the second day came, and the third, and still no smoke was seen rising from the chimney, then Liza's Thomas was approached. It was surely time to make enquiry and who but Thomas Treloar was the man to go and investigate? Supported in the enterprise by a sense of his own dignity, but dreading unknown things in that unknown kitchen, Thomas Treloar advanced across the green and up the lane; he lingered for a moment looking at the chimney, as if he half expected that smoke would issue in response to his upward glance, then he undid the twisted wire, and as he did so the gate fell in pieces across the cobblestones.

A crowd of neighbours in support were gathered in the lane,

hushed, expectant; only Mrs Treloar once broke the silence by murmuring: 'My Thomas, he's the man.'

He knocked at the door, once, twice and again; once, twice, three times. Not a sound came from within. Again he knocked, a double postman's knock, then, turning to the crowd as if he sought to gain their support for an act of courage: 'Neighbours,' he said, 'this ain't time for shilly-shally. I'm gwain right in.'

He opened the door and disappeared. Suspense and silence mingled with curiosity were nearly stifling each one of that expectant crowd, and Mrs Treloar stepped forward at last, impelled by several hands. 'Where my Thomas goes I go too,' she said, and she also disappeared over the threshold. It was useless for the others to peer in through the window, for wherever a rag had not replaced the panes of glass, cobwebs now concealed them. There was nothing for it but to enter the cottage and see for themselves whatever might be seen.

There was neither jostling nor hurry as the neighbours followed Thomas and Liza into that little kitchen so long unused to company. It may have been the silence within, or it may have been some instinctive reverence for death that held the crowd outside while, one at a time, each passed in with never a word thrown back across the shoulder to those who were expecting news behind. Thus, without pomp and ceremony or any preparation, nearly every inhabitant of the village attended the lying in state of Sophia Crowgey.

She lay there as she had lain for heaven knows how many hours, shrunken past recognition, her head propped on an ancient soap-box filled with sticks for kindling; she lay there cold and uncomforted on the old stone floor of the kitchen, her feet stretched towards the ashes of the hearth. Underneath the table the black cat crouched, glaring at an empty saucer, with every rib showing through his skin. Cobwebs hung from the ceiling, dust lay on the walls and dresser, the atmosphere could never, in long ages, have felt a breath of wind or a ray of sunshine.

And the fowls? One was caught in the chimney, the others, mere skeletons in feathers, were dead in different corners of the room. There was no crumb of food in the cottage, no vessel with any drop of water; only a Mazawattee tea-tin on the table with a spoonful or two of tea; only dirt and cobwebs, broken cloam and one dilapidated chair and table, strips of paper hanging from the wall, and on the floor the corpse of a grey old shrunken woman.

Sophia's many-coloured hat, like a bird-of-paradise skin in a charnel-house, lay on the three-legged chair, and a tattered piece of sacking stretched across the firewood was the only pillow she had found in death.

All the people who entered that airless kitchen one by one looked about them with a sense of wonder near akin to pity. They had little thought for the woman's life and for all those years of isolation in the midst, but solitary death, with never a friendly hand to raise her head or close her eyes, could hardly fail to touch a chord of something like regret.

' 'Twas whisht an' no mistake.'

This was the only comment heard on the threshold of the cottage among that silent, wondering crowd, and it was only later in the day that Mrs Golly, remembering her prophecy, declared:

'Shure nuff I toald 'ee so. I toald 'ee one an' all that Sophia Crowgey wudden never die in the bed.'

There were neither clothes nor furniture nor bedding in the cottage to warrant any sale, but in a rusty tea-tin on the mantelpiece there was a pile of silver coins, sixpences and shillings, enough to pay the cost of burial. Seeing she was a Tregoverras woman born and bred, the people of the sister hamlet could do no less than turn out, one and all, for the funeral; Tregonebris and Tregoverras would always sink their rivalry to share each other's funerals. Thomas Treloar was first among the bearers, and Liza, in the absence of all friends and relatives, took the place of chief mourner in the procession and beside the grave.

Young Squire put the cottage up to auction, but no one made a bid. Finally he pulled it down and then the ground was let to Farmer Golly who teeled potatoes there.

The years rolled by in Tregonebris. Good harvests followed

one another in turn with moderate ones and bad; death claimed accustomed toll and lunacy secured her few, while every now and then some unforeseen misfortune would set those tongues in motion round the village pump. All these things had happened before, and the cycle of fortune, good and bad, was in no way changed. But, now that Sophia Crowgey was no longer living, there was not a soul they could blame for casting spells and brewing all their troubles, and so they grew accustomed to regard these troubles far more lightly, taking ups and downs alike without surprise or any sense of injury.

Only now and then the older folks would shake their heads and say:

'Times is changin' faast since I was young, me dearr, an' we ain't so quiet like, nor near so comfortable. 'Tes all ridin' forth an' back to the towns now, an' runnin' aafter pleasure. An' the people now! They'm soft, the men an' women both, you don't see nary one like there was in my young days. I can mind the Honourable George, I can, a proper man an' tough as leather. An' oald Sophia Crowgey, too, a proper witch she was. I can mind the times when Sophia Crowgey would cast a spell so easy like as winkin'. Aw but they oald days was proper times, me dearr. There bain't no witches now in Tregonebris, nor in no place else. Iss, times is changin' faast.'

Frank Baker

TYME TRYETH TROTH

The field was very wide and the path twisted across it towards a tall stone hedge. Above the hedge the man could see the chimneys and the two top windows of a cottage, and as from one of the chimneys there was smoke, he assumed that the place was occupied. The path seemed to lead to some flat stone jutting out like steps from the hedge, and it would only bring him, he reflected, into the garden of the cottage. But peasant people would not mind him passing through; and he could ask them the nearest way back to the village.

The evening was October and the rose colours of sunset were dawning in the sky. He could smell wood-smoke as he drew nearer to the stone hedge, and looking to the window of one of the upper rooms he saw the face of a small child pressed against the pane.

He smiled, pleased by the picture. He was reminded of those old glass paintings which he liked to collect; and he had a momentary sensation that he was seeing the picture the wrong way round, not looking at the reverse side of the design which was meant to be seen but at the crude blobs on the back of the glass which were not meant to be seen – except by the craftsman himself. Then the child moved, and at the same time the sun burnt in the window and the image was dissolved into a shivering chord of fire.

His foot was on the lowest stone jutting from the hedge. And now his other foot touched the second step and he pulled himself up with an effort, feeling suddenly very tired although he had walked only a couple of miles from the sea. Tired and curiously anguished; burdened with matters he could not understand; an uphappy man searching for home, and hardly able to drag his body up to the hedge top.

He realized in those few seconds while he was climbing how intensely unhappy and desperate he had become, how much his soul longed for peace, how weary he was of being alone, and how futile his efforts to make happiness his child had become. A scruff of beard made this man look much older than he was; and the hand, rather yellow and wrinkled, that now touched the patch of grass on the hedge was more like the hand of an old man than a young one.

And all these hopeless feelings were centralized in a point of bitter envy for the inmates of the cottage on the other side who, he guessed, were happier than he was. For there was a child; there was smoke in the autumn sky; and (he noticed this suddenly as he drew himself up to the top) there was a woman in one of the downstair rooms, sitting before a small table, writing, her hair as gold as the leaves that now began to drift from the trees, hanging loosely and obscuring her features. A wood fire was alive in the grate near her.

He watched her, deeply fascinated. Her attitude was so full of unconscious beauty, she was so completely wrapped up in whatever she was writing (perhaps a letter to her mother, he thought); she was so living and natural a part of her surroundings, he could not imagine her anywhere else but in that room, with the generous autumn fire always burning yet never consuming its fuel.

And then, with a sudden shock, he realized he was not the only person watching her. Some way back from the window stood a man, a saw in his hand. There were many sawn logs of wood by the open cottage door, an old wicker basket twined with a green decoration; and on one of the logs a small white kitten played with its tail. This man, too, was watching the woman, very intently, with a happy reflective smile; a young man, clean-shaven, wearing only an open shirt and corduroy trousers, and looking full of that natural and beautiful tiredness which comes of physical labour.

The trespasser felt suddenly that he had committed an unforgivable sin. It was not possible to talk to this man and thus to break in upon what was so obviously a touching family reverie. The wife busy with her letter; the child, supposed to be in bed upstairs, who had climbed to the window-seat to watch his father sawing wood and to see the sun slide the day away; the husband pausing in his work to survey his treasure and to wonder at the beauty of his wife – all this had a significance that meant much to the traveller. He was a very sensitive man and he dared not break in upon their peace; for he feared that his own unhappiness would infect them and leave a mark of disquietude in the air.

And the man had not seen him. It was still possible to retreat before he should turn round. Perhaps the child might have seen him; but he would be too young to relate it. The picture of this visitor who had paused on the hedge top would drift deep down into the child's memory and one day, perhaps many years hence, float up to the surface like a rising tendril of weed in spring water.

Quickly he jumped back into the field, extremely anxious now not to be observed. Right back across that long field he hurried, the day hurrying with him and night calling a full moon up from the fir trees across the downs. Presently he was on the main road and walking back towards the Trevelyan Arms, where he lodged.

After he had had supper and was in the bar, drinking with one or two local people whom he knew slightly, it occurred to him to ask who lived in the cottage. But being bad at describing places he could make no one understand exactly where it stood. There were so many cob-and-plaster cottages like that. 'A mass of tree lupins in the garden,' he explained, 'and a young family, with a small boy – at least, I think it was a boy.' But there were many families with small boys. Where was this cottage, he was again asked. He could offer no precise guide to it and so the subject was dropped.

Thinking of that happy family, he sat till the bar closed, drinking beer, and looking, without noticing it, at an account of the Trevelyans, extracted from some old antiquarian journal and framed above the bar. It was a Trevelyan who had escaped on his white horse from the devouring wave that had lost Lyonesse under the sea. A glove was in their arms. And the family motto was printed in large gothic lettering at the end of the article: Tyme Tryeth Troth.

Tyme Tryeth Troth ... the words rang the bells of memory in his mind, and he repeated them lazily to himself as he sat there in the quiet bar. It had turned two, and the landlord, with whom he had become very friendly in the past few weeks, wanted to close the house. The bar was empty but for him, and he, in a happy and thoughtful mood, had fallen half asleep over his midday pint of beer. And in his dreaming he had retraced his steps across that field ten years ago, a walk that had ended in the bar where he now sat, though there had then been a different landlord and the house had not been in so smart a condition as it was now. But the outline of the fortunes of the Trevelyan family had still hung on the wall, in the same corner, below a faded photograph of the village football eleven taken in 1913; and as he looked at it now he realized how deeply the words had become engraved on the tablet of his mind ... engraved like lovers' names in an old tree-trunk, obscured by the weather of many years, yet never lost.

He read a modern version of the motto: Time Testeth the Truth. And considering the wisdom of this statement – of the human and the universal meaning contained in both – he said goodbye to his friend the landlord and wandered out into the October sunshine. He was a composer and, wanting to think out the form of a new work, he had told his wife he would go for a long walk that afternoon. She would expect him back towards sunset.

But instead of the actual shape and colour of his music he found himself alive only to thoughts concerning himself, the woman he had married four years ago, and the son that had been born to them. Soon there would be another child and his life would grow more complicated. It was hard to keep his mind clear and faithful to the work he knew lay within him to do, when the demands of others, now dependent upon him, had, above everything else, to be met. He was certain that he was happier now than he had ever been; but to live firmly upon that knowledge was no easier.

He walked to the sea, and then along the coast, and rested by a fringe of tamarisks over feather waves that brushed the quiet shore. He watched shag and cormorant over the grey-gold sea where the sun enriched the water as it fell; they flew so close to the surface that it seemed as though they were chained to a submarine self who floated beneath them.

He thought how strange it was, though not in one sense at all strange, that he should have come to live for a time in that same cottage which had so much attracted him years ago; not strange, because the unknown family he had that evening for a moment studied had fixed his mind upon a destiny which for him, he had then realized, was meant to be his. And strange, because at a time when he had brought his wife and child to the West in search of somewhere to live, that particular cottage should have been empty.

Yet this all fitted into a pattern and had never surprised him; for on that first evening when he had walked to the cottage and had so hurriedly jumped back again into the field for fear of breaking in upon another's peace he had known instinctively that he would come to live here; and that he would find and bring the one true lover whose troth would be plighted with his: whose truth, united with his, would resist the tricks of time. And, after all these years, he had come: the troth was plighted eternally; time had, and certainly would again and again, test this indisputable union of flesh and spirit whose validity lay open for all to see in a son; and he was – he knew it – happy.

Yet – 'Again and again,' he murmured as the sun toured slowly across the sky. Again and again time would test them. This very evening, perhaps. One had to be for ever on guard. However firm the link united them, there was, just precisely because of that link, a constant tug to snap it. Cruel and sharp and saddled with resentment these divisions had been, some too terrible to be remembered. It must happen no more, he told himself; never again. She was too beautiful, too secure in her universe, too serene in her inner detachment ever again to be submitted to the bitter misery of his own rebel self.

And now he had walked again across that field and was climbing the hedge, and only realized how tired and hungry he was, with no conclusions reached regarding the music he wished to write, and the sun setting in the clear autumn sky. She had lit a fire. He could see her through the window of the sitting-room, sitting by the small table with the remains of tea scattered round her, writing a letter. Probably to her mother, he said to himself. Then he jumped down into the garden in a curiously excited way. Near the open door were logs of wood, and a basket with green twine circling its rim.

On the ground was his saw, left where he had thrown it down that morning. He stooped to pick it up, then stood with it in his hand, staring at the window where the red firelight leapt in the lower room. For a moment it seemed to him that he was struggling to remember something, to recall an instantaneous image which had flashed in and out of his mind. He felt tormented by a question, and he did not know precisely what the question was.

Suddenly he turned his head to the hedge, thinking he had heard somebody there. He climbed to the top and looked across the field; but it was empty, very long and broad, with the greenhouses at one end shivering in the vivid colour of the sun. Then he turned back to look at the cottage and saw a white kitten, their own, sitting on a bit of wood by the open door and playing with its tail.

Upstairs, from one of the windows, came a tapping sound. He looked up and saw the little boy standing in the window-seat, trying to attract his attention with a cotton-reel he was tapping on the glass. For some reason he could not respond; he even felt irritated by the sound which had broken in upon the strange confusion of time in which he found himself. And he felt it was impossible to go into the cottage and interrupt his wife, though he knew she would be glad he had returned to her. But he could not go in. He had the most certain foreknowledge that if he did go in now he would quarrel violently with her. He would invent some excuse to anger him. For he was at war with himself; and intense battle was taking place inside him, and if he met her now he would only drag her into the conflict.

Crossing the field very quickly, his hand shading his eyes against the brilliant light, a burning impatient feeling sending him on, as though he were in pursuit of some enemy, he returned to the village and sat in the bar of the Trevelyan Arms, talking in an absent way to friends there, knowing his wife would be wondering where he was, reluctant to return home till something had been answered.

And now one question clarified itself from the muddle of his thoughts: what had he seen on the occasion of his first walk across that field, ten years ago? A child's face painted on glass? (But *had* there been? Wasn't he confusing the scenes?) A white kitten and a basket with green twine? (Again, was this *certain*?) A woman with golden hair writing by a wood fire? (Yes – surely he had seen her?) A man standing with a saw in his hand, watching the woman through the window – a man intensely happy and proud and full of peace in his soul whose vitality leapt towards the vitality in the woman and the children, born and unborn, as the wild flames of the first autumn fire leapt into the soot-encrusted chimney of the old cottage?

Oh – but had he seen that – *had* he?

Suddenly, from his seat in the now crowded bar, he rose to his feet. The words 'Tyme Tryeth Troth' stared him in the face. 'The illusion we have made of time', he muttered, 'mocks at and challenges the truth of eternal instant which is at the very heart of all of us.' And then again he thought: a troth is plighted, two hands clasp in the eternal truth; this is not just something that once happened. Like the hands plighted upon the cross of man's intolerable misery, this happened, was happening now. And the false fruit that man had eaten in the garden – was this the fruit of the great illusion? That self-wounding half-knowledge of existence and essence which had crucified man to the unfolding of seasons and the toll of the bell of midnight?

A strange desperate feeling seized him. He wished his lover were here now. For it was dark, it would take him half an hour to walk home, and in that time the urgency of what he wanted to say to her would be lost. Yet to hurry away from here when he had found no solution to his problem seemed impossible. Already he hesitated. Somebody was offering him a drink. He smiled, accepted it, began to chat. And then the question that he had asked once before in this bar came from him.

'You know where we live, up by Kitto's field – Lupin Cottage – tell me, do you remember who was living up there ten years ago, this time of year?'

The answer was unequivocal. 'Why, old Miss Trewhella. She had that place for years before you took it over a month or so back.'

'You're dead sure about that? There was never a young married couple living there, with a baby?'

'No. The old woman lived there nigh on twenty years.'

And now he was hurrying back, bursting with the excitement of new knowledge, desperately anxious to impart his news to his wife and convey its full meaning to her.

Its full meaning? In the lane, looking up to the moon where clouds soared in massive sinister shapes, he felt baffled and cheated. What was the meaning? He would never properly know. Never now be able to swear that on that first walk across the field he had indeed seen that family who was himself, his wife and his son. And all that would now happen – he would find his wife tired and irritable, angry with him for being out so long, the food she had cooked spoilt, her spirit wounded by his thoughtlessness (as she would naturally interpret it). It was something he knew he would not be able to defeat unless she herself came out with willing arms to meet him.

The lane was full of ghosts; the damp earth pressed into the air the mists of the sorrows and joys of many men and women; the sycamore leaves drifted willingly from their naked stems to join the trampled leaves of older years, and a straight pillar of thin smoke rose from the cottage chimney. Against the back wall which faced the lane the little ash tree stretched its long branches.

A window above the stairs showed a small light through a thin curtain. Who was in this house? His love, or emptiness? He felt that he did not know, that he might open the gate upon nothing more than memory. There was the long trunk of the apple tree waiting to be sawn. But it might remain there many years, the cottage empty and falling to decay, and nobody would touch that piece of wood. Was he approaching a place where he had once lived with his wife and child? Had all this beauty gone, and was he left alone to remember it?

But there, in the long bright rays of the moon, leaning against the stone lintel of the door, was the woman who loved him.

He did not like to go near her: he could not say anything. And she smiled and stretched out her hands.

'What a lovely night!' she said.

'Yes. You look so beautiful standing there. This evening I saw you writing at the table. And I couldn't come in.'

'Couldn't you, love? Why?'

She smiled, and he came nearer to her, unwilling to touch her, to break the austere beauty of this moment. He almost prayed that she would not move for a long time, not ask him any questions. So he replied, in an indifferent tone, 'Oh, I don't know; just a mood.' And he stood very near her, still not touching her, and thinking again, 'A day will come when this cottage will be empty and the weeds will grow up in the path.'

Then her arms were round him, his head lay on her shoulder and she was stroking his hair. There was nothing, he suddenly realized, to tell her. For she was a person who had reached a strange unconscious union with the mystery of time, and his own doubts would only infect her with bewilderment.

No – there was nothing to say. It was only necessary to remember that his happiness, even though it might be assaulted by the weight of past and future sadness, stood eternally graven upon the tablets of time. In their quiet room where the fire still burnt and the candles were alight he ate the food she brought him and listened to her as she talked of the day's events. They were both very happy. And presently, as they lay in their bed, he took her right hand in his and clasped it, and fell, with her, into sleep. While they slept the West wind rose and the small rain scudded to the window-panes. Autumn was blown away and winter came and in their sleep many seasons passed and came again. The day came when they had to leave this cottage, and that day too passed, becoming one amongst their many shared memories.

Once, in another autumn, this man walked alone across that wide field to a cottage that he knew was empty. And climbing in through one of the windows he stood in the pitch darkness of the large bedroom where ivy trailed down through holes in the roof. He was neither sad nor happy; yet contented; and he knew that he had entered the cottage for the last time.

When his son was a young man his father told him much about their earlier days and quoted the words of the Trevelyan motto. 'There's a very great deal of wisdom in those three words,' he said, 'and I'd like you to remember them.'

The son did not forget them – for who could? And one day with a girl he loved, he found himself in that part of the West country where he had lived for a short while as a child. They walked across a cornfield on a September evening when the sun went slow and red and large down the sky; and climbing a wall lost in brambles and thorns they looked at the crumbling ruins of the cottage. Masses of yellow lupins had spread over the ground.

'This is the place,' said the boy. 'And this is my first memory – do you want me to tell you? It's not really interesting.'

The girl, being in love with him, was interested in everything about him. So he told her.

'I don't really remember the cottage at all. I can't have been more than three and it's all gone from me. But I know we lived here for a time. It was called Lupin Cottage – and there are the lupins – see?'

He stood on the hedge, suddenly growing excited, and taking her hand helped her down to the other side. 'There's something I'm trying to remember,' he said. 'But from here – no, I can't.'

He paused and battered his fist impatiently against his forehead. 'We must go inside,' he told her. 'Come on. I shall remember then.'

The padlocked door was choked by a mass of willowherb and nettles. But the glass in the windows was broken and it was easy enough to climb in. Smashing a way through the nettles, he encouraged her to one of the windows. She was not happy about it.

'It doesn't look safe. Need we go in?'

'Yes, we must. Come on.'

Now he was through the window and leaning over to help her inside.

'I don't want to come,' she cried. 'It's horrible in there – dark and smelly and full of spiders.'

'Please – please come. I'm here, aren't I? You can't come to any harm. It's important to us. You must come.'

Suddenly she realized that if she wanted to retain his love for her she would have to follow him wherever he went. Shivering and trembling with fear, she climbed over the sill and joined him inside.

They went upstairs, all the time the boy filled with an excitement she could not properly understand. Then they went into a room where some of the boards were rotted away and the sky showed through the fallen roof. Taking her hand, he led her carefully to the window-seat where great chunks of plaster and slates and laths of worm-dried wood had fallen. He looked through the window to the wide field where the sun shimmered in the corn. And then he gave a great sigh and tears were in his eyes as he clutched her hand tighter.

'Yes, this must have been my room,' he said. 'This is the view I've always wanted of that field. The first thing I can remember, seeing that field from here one evening, about this time, when the sun was setting. Something odd happened, which probably hasn't got any significance; but it's very clear in my memory. I must have got out of bed and stood on this window-seat. I had something in my hand and was tapping the window and looking at the field. It seemed immense – like the whole world. I could see my father in the garden, standing down there with a saw in his hand. And I tried to attract his attention, but he wouldn't look up. I called, I think; but he didn't hear me. Then something happened – what was it?'

He rubbed his left fingers across his eyes and with his right hand still held hers. 'Yes, I remember. It was only this. A man suddenly appeared on the top of the hedge. He was a very old man, or so I remember him; with a grey beard. And he looked terribly tired and miserable. But suddenly he looked up to this window and smiled at me. I remember that smile – it was very sweet and trustful; the sort of way a child would smile. But I was very angry. I wanted my father to look up and smile at me and he wouldn't do so. Then the old man turned and jumped back again into the field; and suddenly my father dropped his saw, climbed over the wall, and started to follow the old man right across the field. I watched them both. The old man was hurrying as though he was scared; and my father was chasing him. I believe he was running. You see right across the field – by those fir trees?'

The girl followed his pointing finger.

'Over there, I could hardly see them, the sun was so bright – my father caught the old man by the shoulders and swung him round and stared at him. Then they disappeared together. That's all I can remember. Doesn't it sound silly?'

The girl looked at him. 'No, it doesn't. Nothing that you tell me about yourself seems silly.'

By the window, overlooking the broad field, these two plighted their troth.

Ruth Manning-Sanders

JOHN PETTIGREW'S MIRROR

This is a story my grandmother told me; nobody need believe it unless they wish, but everybody may believe it who will.

Well then, long ago there lived in a small seaside town an honest basket-maker, called John Pettigrew. He lived alone, for he had neither wife nor child, only an old shrew of a married cousin, Sarah Polgraine, who came in to cook and clean for him. John was as accustomed to Sarah's grumblings and scoldings as he was to the voice of the sea, and he did not notice them unless he was obliged to. He was grateful to her for looking after him and, being thoroughly good-natured himself, and inclined to think well of his fellows, he had a conviction that, underneath all, Sarah was a good sort.

Underneath all, *everyone* was a good sort, so it seemed to John; but, when he tried to tell Sarah this, she would sniff and say, 'That's all *you* know!' And then she would point out everyone's faults and failings, and tell John to 'just look' at this, that, and the other one of their acquaintance! And John would shake his head, and say, 'That's a squint-eyed way of looking, cousin Sarah!' And Sarah would sniff again, and say *her* eyes saw plainly enough, and if some old fools would learn to face facts it would be more satisfactory for all concerned. But then John would chuckle, 'You're better than your words, Sarah, *I* know!' And with that he would leave her, and go out to the yard where he worked, and where the sound of her scolding voice reached him but faintly.

This yard of John's was built against the sea wall; there was a shed in it for wet weather, and plenty of sunshine when the skies were clear; and there he would spend his days, among the ozier bundles and the big and little baskets, that were some of them severely practical, and some cunningly decorated, according to his mood and fancy. A leisurely yet useful life was John's, with plenty of time for contemplation, and for an occasional tune on his mouth-organ when his fingers grew tired, or his mind felt the need of refreshment.

One stormy afternoon in late summer, John took a sack and went down to the sea shore in search of wreck-wood. The shore was littered with shining brown ribbons of seaweed, and the wood that he gathered was all tangled up with sand and shells. Great waves staggered and broke along the shore, and the run of them swirled up around John's feet, so that sometimes he was ankle-deep, and sometimes high and dry. From the tops of the breakers an off-sea wind flung foam into his eyes. The low and watery sun, shooting its rays from amidst rapidly moving storm clouds, brightened the foam, and flung wide mirrors of light across the backs and amongst the hollows of the mountainous waves that rose and fell beyond the breakers. And in these waves two seals, an old one and a young one, were merrily playing. Up they floated like things of cork, and down they dived swift as birds flying; and when they dived John saw the shadow of their bodies through the waves, and when they floated up he saw their big eyes shining.

'Blessed creatures!' thought John. 'No need to ask if you are happy! And they do say that all the wisdom of the deep unsearchable flows through your oily noddles!'

A powerful gust of wind set him stumbling backwards. The sun vanished in the gathering storm; between two close-packed clouds a wan fork of lightning flashed through the grey air; thunder rolled echoing among the rocks; a deluge of rain dropped its murky curtains between John and all else; and through this curtain came the roar of the unsearchable deep where the seals played.

'Time this old man was safe indoors!' thought John. And he slung his sack over his shoulder and made for home.

What a night to be sure! In all his long life John could not remember such another one. The wind boomed in the chimney, and the smoke blew down it; the light in the lamp jumped and flared and sooted the lamp-glass. The windows shook and clattered as the rain lashed them. The wind flung itself against the door like a wild beast determined to get in; and, at every thud the door gave, all the crooks on the dresser set up a protesting rattle. From every crack and hole came shrieks, whistles, hootings, flutings and trumpetings; and behind all sounded the steady roar of the sea, crazed and billowing, dementedly leaping the wall beyond John's yard, and washing in among his ozier bundles and piles of baskets – even volleying under the kitchen door in a series of mad chuckles and lunatic snickerings, that added their small frenzy to the general hubbub.

John set a sandbag against the door, and hung up a blower in front of the fire. The storm seized the house in its fists and shook it, like a man rattling a dice-box.

'But the house is builded upon a rock,' thought John; and, offering up a prayer for those 'that do business in deep waters', he put on his spectacles and took down his Bible.

'They mount up to the heaven, they go down again to the deeps ... They reel to and fro, and stagger like a drunken man, and are at their wits' end. Then they cry ...'

Bang! Crash! A wave hit the kitchen door with the roar of a cannon. And – heark'ee! – out there, a strange cry, that was neither bleat, nor bark, nor the groan of a man. One cry, and then no more. 'If 'twere a fiend from hell,' thought John, 'on such a night a man must ope his door to 't.' And, laying his spectacles between the leaves of his Bible, he kicked the sandbag aside, and pulled back the door.

The wind came into the kitchen with a whoop and a gallop; the lamp flared and went out; the fire roared, and the blower clattered on to the hearthstone. A wave leaped ghostly at the yard wall. John stooped in a pool of water, felt a fur-coated bundle lying there, dragged it over the threshold, slammed the door, and relit the lamp.

Then he stared at the fur-coated bundle. It was a young seal; its eyes were glazed, its hinder feet curled up, and its foreflippers sprawling. 'Dead and gone!' thought John. 'And a while back so prettily playing! I guarantee your mammy told you to keep clear of the breakers. But youth is headstrong – and see what comes of it!' He shook his head and stooped to run his head over the grey, sodden body.

Hullo, hullo! What was this? The body gave a hump and a wriggle under John's caressing hand; a flipper waggled, the lack-lustre eyes kindled. The young seal was looking up at John Pettigrew with eyes of unutterable wisdom.

'Oh, well, come on then, if that's the case, little fellow!' A delighted John lifted the seal in his arms and laid it carefully in front of the fire.

It was a merry evening they spent after that, John and his new companion. The little seal drank milk from a bottle, and ate the fish that was meant for John's supper. And John, remembering that seals are fond of music, played it a tune on his mouth-organ, and the little fellow clapped with his flappers, and bleated for more. More milk, or more fish, or more tunes? John couldn't be sure; so he plied it with all three.

And then they both fell asleep, the seal on the hearthrug, and John on the settle; for this was the first house-companion he had ever possessed, and he didn't feel like going upstairs and leaving it lonesome.

But, in his dreams, an old seal came to him, and the tears were flowing from her eyes in silver streams; and it seemed to John that if he didn't stop the flow of those tears they would presently drown the whole world. So, in the morning, when the wind had dropped, and the sea heaved grey and sullen, as if in sulky apology for the havoc it had caused, John carried his new friend through the wreckage in his yard, and over the bricks of fallen chimneys and the slates of torn roofs out in the street, and among piles of blown sand and great heaps of stones and seaweed, down to the shore, and there he pushed the little fellow out into the sea.

The little fellow spun round and round like a rudderless boat, as if it had forgotten which way to steer itself. And then it struggled out of the water and bleated after John; and when John turned for home, the little fellow came flipping and humping up the sand so fast that it reached the yard gate as soon as John did. So then John borrowed a boat, and rowed a long way out to sea, and dropped the little fellow gently overboard – and there was the little fellow spinning round and round once more, and crying out so loud that half the town could hear it. And so pitiful was its cry that John was obliged to take it into the boat again.

It came into John's mind, then, that perhaps the young seal was still suffering in some way from the bang the breakers had given it, and that it didn't feel able to fend for itself. 'If only I could catch a glimpse of your mammy,' he said, 'I should know what to do.' He looked this way and that over the sparkling water, but all he saw was a couple of gulls, circling and mewing. 'Seal, mammy seal!' he called. But there was no answer.

'I don't know what may be in her mind – exactly,' said John. 'But I do think I'll have to care for you a while longer.' And with that he pulled for home; whilst the young seal lay contentedly in the bottom of the boat, and watched him with its wise eyes.

'Now,' said Sarah Polgraine, 'you can shoot the creature; and I'll make me a fur tippet for Sundays.'

'I've never handled a gun in my life,' said John with a chuckle. 'And I don't intend to handle one now.'

So then Sarah, who coveted the sealskin, carried on alarmingly; and said that John couldn't keep an outlandish creature like that about the place, and that if he was afraid to handle a gun he could use a sharp knife. And it came into John's mind, then, that though both he and Sarah were looking at the little seal, yet they were seeing different things. *She* was seeing a fur tippet, and *he* was seeing a dearly loved child. So he told her his dream about the tears that might presently drown the whole world, and Sarah said 'Stuff and nonsense!' But it seemed to John that the young seal understood, and nodded its head in approval. He went into the yard, cleared up the mess that the storm had made, and set to work again; and the little seal watched him with its shining eyes. And when John crossed the yard, it crossed the yard; and when John sat at his trade, it lay at his feet; and when John played on his mouth-organ, it made happy sounds and clapped with its flippers; and when John threw a ball, it caught the ball on its nose, and spun it up and caught it again, which was very pretty to watch; and in the evenings it lay on the hearthrug and gazed at the fire; and so things went on for some days.

But John, much as he joyed in the company of his little friend, couldn't get the dream of an old seal with tear-streaming eyes out of his mind; and every day, when his work was done, he went down to the shore and looked into the grey, or the green, or the blue water for sight of the one who had shed those tears. And the little seal went with him, but it looked at John, and not at the water.

And then, one day, through a wave green and clear as glass John saw the shape of a swimmer; and up came a round, glistening head, turning this way and that, as if in search of something. 'There's your mammy at last,' said John; 'and it's into the water you go, my beauty, and no-nonsense this time!'

And, so saying, he picked the little fellow up, and waded out as far as he could, and flung his playmate from him. Then he made a run for dry ground, and hid behind a rock, with just his head poked out to watch what would happen. And first there was the young seal spinning round and round like a rudderless boat, and crying after John; and then, out to sea, there was the old seal reared upright through a green wave and calling after the young one; and then there was the young one swimming out towards the green wave; and then there was nothing but the tossing water; and then a lifting wave bore the shapes of two swimmers in its bosom, and, as they floated up on the wave's crest, John saw their big eyes shining.

And now there was John going home, rejoicing that he had done right, but with a lonely feeling in his heart.

And is that the end of the story? No, indeed! Though it has taken some time in the telling, it is only the beginnning; and what follows is what you may believe or not believe, as you will.

Next Sunday, John took a walk by the sea-shore. He wasn't

exactly looking for the seals, you understand, but he was thinking about them – picturing to himself what life would be like in the deep places of ocean, and of the things to be seen there, which no man has ever seen. And, all of a sudden, the thought came to him that man knew but little, and thought less, of the strangeness and power and glory of creation, and he took his mouth-organ out of his pocket and began to play a hymn. Well, he hadn't played more than a bar of that hymn when, down in the bright water just beneath him, he saw the old seal swimming, and balancing something on her nose. It wasn't a ball; but what it was John could not tell, for as she tossed it up and caught it again, it spun so quickly, and flashed so magnificently, that it made John's eyes water to look at it. And then – whizz! – it was flying through the air towards John, and he caught it in his two hands.

It was a small round mirror – and such a mirror! The frame was fashioned like a garland of flowers, and the heart of each flower was a great pearl, the petals were rubies and sapphires, and the leaves emeralds. John turned it this way and that in admiration, till it chanced that he turned it so that its glass reflected the sea, and there beneath him he saw, not a seal, but a beautiful woman with a child in her arms. The child wore a little crown of gold, and he stretched out his arms and waved to John, and the woman smiled at John very sweetly, and then they both disappeared under the water. And John stood staring into the mirror as if he couldn't believe his eyes.

He slanted the mirror to the sky, and saw the clouds; they *were* clouds, you understand, and yet they were also palaces and towers, and great white swans, and majestic old men in snowy garments. He slanted the mirror to the earth, and saw the flowers and the bushes; they *were* flowers and bushes, but stems of the flowers were birds, and the leaves were wings, and every branch was a king with a jewelled crown. 'Oh,' thought John, as he made for home, 'I shall never be tired of looking in *this* mirror!' And, looking into it once again, he chanced to see his own face reflected; and he tucked the mirror hastily into his pocket, for he was almost ashamed to look at the glory and brightness, the majesty and beauty, of the lordly one who gazed kindly back at him.

Over against the sea wall he passed a group of old men, in their Sunday clothes, lounging to watch the water; some of them were squinny, some pot-bellied and bandy, some sad, some foolish. 'I wonder now', thought John, 'what the mirror will make of this lot!' So he took it out of his pocket and slanted it upon them. And there they were – lords of the earth, every one of them: strong and straight, and handsome and brave, and dressed fit for the Kingdom of Heaven.

'If that's the way it is,' said John to himself, 'not only I, but the whole of the town, would be better for a peep into the mirror.' And he got a strong nail and hung the mirror on his front door, which was always shut, because he never went in that way.

You may be sure there soon a crowd round the door, everyone jostling and pushing to have a look at themselves. Nobody knew quite what to make of what they saw: giddy girls came up, and looked and went away hushed and awestruck; old men and women looked, and walked down the street holding their heads high and smiling to themselves; young men looked, and walked off proud and solemn as priests at a sacrifice. And in the dawn, when the street was empty, a thief came by, and coveted the frame for its precious stones; but, as he reached to unhook the mirror from its nail, he saw his face reflected, and it was the face of an angel. So he left the mirror where it was, and tiptoed away; because, of course, angels are not thieves.

It would take too long to tell of all the people who looked into John Pettigrew's mirror, and of what they saw there; but be sure that whoever looked saw nothing but beauty and goodness, because there was nothing else to see. And it wasn't long before there wasn't an evil, or a selfish, or a sick, or an angry person left in the town; because everyone remembered what they were really like, and behaved accordingly. The prison was empty, the law courts were turned into a dancing school, and the policemen, after yawning for a while at street corners, got tired of doing nothing, and took to growing strawberries. The mayor, by common consent, was left in authority; and if any citizen for a moment forgot himself and behaved foolishly, the mayor had but to order that he take a peep into John Pettigrew's mirror, and after that there was no more trouble with him.

There was only one person in the town who wasn't quite happy, and that was Sarah Polgraine. She was so used to grumbling and complaining, scolding and finding fault, that now, when everything was perfect and there was nobody left to find fault with, she felt like a pricked bubble. For what was the use of her having lived such an exemplary life, and worked herself to skin and bone, and done so much for John Pettigrew and a host of others, if it didn't give her the satisfaction of knowing herself to be more virtuous than anybody else in the town? All this nonsense about reflections in a mirror! *She* knew what people were like, and she knew what she was like, without any lying mirror to tell her! And so, every time she passed John Pettigrew's front door, Sarah Polgraine shut her eyes. For it seemed to her that the mirror had robbed her of her one pleasure in life.

That was an unhappy feeling to live with; and the unhappy feeling grew and grew, until there was no putting up with it. So one winter morning, when the wind was blowing half a hurricane, and the sea was grey and angry, she rose with the first streak of daylight, and ran to John Pettigrew's house; and, shutting her eyes, unhooked the mirror, tucked it under her shawl, and went and stood on a rock by the sea-shore, to throw the tiresome thing back to the deep places where it had come from. The wind was blowing so hard that she nearly lost her balance, but she raised her arm and threw; and there was the mirror now, flashing out over the water with its myriad-coloured jewels agleam in the rising sun. But, just as it left her hand, it happened that Sarah Polgraine for the first time saw her face reflected in it; and though it was but for a spinning second that she saw that face, certainly it was not the face of a woman who could do such an evil thing, and she began to weep bitterly, and cried out in a loud voice: 'Oh, what have I done? Give it back! Give it back!'

Then the round, glistening head of the old seal appeared on the top of a wave, balancing the mirror on her nose; and first she spun the mirror up and caught it, and then she gave it a toss and sent it flying back over the water to Sarah Polgraine.

Sarah Polgraine stretched out her hands; but what with the tears that were streaming from her eyes, and the wind was blowing her hair across them, she couldn't see anything clearly, and, instead of catching the mirror, she let it slip through her fingers. It was dashed against the rock, and broke into a hundred pieces.

Sarah Polgraine scrambled off the rock and set up such a loud wailing that soon half the town was on the sea-shore. Some began to gather up the splinters, and they were the sensible ones, for in the fragments that they picked up they could still see, though cracked and piecemeal, the image of their glory reflected. Others began to blame Sarah Polgraine; and, as soon as they did that, she began to justify herself, and clean forgot the face she had seen for one spinning second in the mirror. And soon the place was echoing with angry voices and hot words, such as had not been heard in the town for many a long day. One man picked up the jewelled frame and said he would have that, anyway; but another tried to wrench it from him, and then there were blows, as well as angry words. Hitting and snarling, the two of them fell off the rock into the sea, and there might have been murder done, had not a policeman, peacefully at work on the strawberry bed in his back garden, heard the racket and come running to take up his official duties once again.

And so, it wasn't very long before the townspeople went back to their old ways, as if no such thing as a mirror from the unsearchable deep had ever hung outside John Pettigrew's door to show them a different image of themselves: the quarrelsome quarrelled, the drunkards drank, the giglots giggled, and the thieves stole; the law courts were reopened, and the policemen put on their helmets and stood at the street corners. In fact, as Sarah Polgraine said, it was shameful the way people went on, and what the world was coming to she *couldn't* think!

Only the sensible ones, John Pettigrew amongst them, cherished each his piece of broken mirror and, by taking a peep into it now and then, carried the image of a lordly one in their minds, and in their hearts.

Yes, that's the end of the story; except that whenever, as a young girl, things went criss-crossed with me and life seemed all awry, my grandmother, who was a wise and peace-loving old body, would smile and shake her head over my glum face, and say, 'Ah, child, you'd think differently if you could take a peep into John Pettigrew's mirror.'

Ronald Duncan

WHEN WE DEAD AWAKEN

I do not think I am more avaricious than most men; but the chance of obtaining something for nothing has always appealed to me. Especially when I could pick it with my own hands; blackberries, for these I will tear my clothes to pieces, nettle my face and hands, all for the pleasure of reaching the inaccessible something for nothing, and the pleasure of holding the plump fruit in my fingers. So, too, with mushrooms; as a child I began the search; and as a man, with less energy but the same incentive, I continue it. I will walk my friends' feet off to find a few more of those will-o'-the-wisp delicacies; and always there is a hope at the back of my mind that I will again find a complete mushroom ring, enough for a feast and to sell the rest as sheer profit. Such frail chances are strong ropes tethering many of us to pursuits and hobbies which, were we to consider the time we devote to them, would prove to us that it is impossible to obtain anything for nothing. And, as my wife has often reminded me, there is little profit in obtaining three pounds of wild fruit at the cost of a torn shirt and a large cleaning bill.

As the spring came round, I looked greedily across the beach to the great gaunt Cornish rocks where I knew the gulls would soon nest and lay their clutches of mottled blue and black eggs; to my taste a gull's egg is a delicacy, whereas a fowl's egg is just an egg.

And so, with my wife's blessing and a pair of old rubber shoes on, I set off with the privileged loan of her precious basket to the rock.

I knew every inch of the way and was soon scaling the precipitous surface which, being dry, seemed safe even to my nervous eye. Gulls scissored the air and sliced the sky and then would stay poised, and then fall and then rise. I kept my eyes to the rock and felt like a wood louse invading their pinnacle of a home. The top of the rock was relatively flat. I climbed on to my feet and eyed the ground for the precious eggs. To my disappointment I found only three where I had expected at least three dozen, though I saw scores of clumsily built, empty nests littered with the husks of my own seed corn. I could not allow myself to return with only three eggs; for there would be six of us to luncheon and I promised my wife that I could provide the *pièce de résistance* for that meal. On descending the rock I noticed that a great number of gulls circled a ledge of the main cliff some hundred feet above me. It was there, I supposed, that a friend of mine went for his eggs; for he always returned with a full basket and sold them for sixty pence a dozen, something for nothing. The cliff looked easy, that is, as easy as the rock I had already climbed. So, with my basket in my teeth, I began the ascent. Within ten minutes I was at the top, my basket full, it had been easy. I smoked a cigarette and admired the view, meditating on the pleasure the eggs would give my wife and wondering whether she would be able to preserve some for the winter. I had two pounds' worth of eggs; something for nothing, I was happy. I picked up my basket and then looked for my way down. But I could not see how I had managed to climb to where I now stood. I stood on a ledge of cliff four feet wide; at the back of me was an overhanging precipitous cliff which I knew it was impossible to scale. And each side of me a sheer drop of one hundred feet with the rocks and the sea's snarl at the bottom. In front, the ledge narrowed till it was a foot wide – no more than a plank – and on each side a sheer drop with nothing to hold on to.

Instantly, as though pricked by a hypodermic syringe, sharp panic spread over me and the sick fear of what lay before me settled in my throat as I realized what I had done. I had walked this narrow ledge, this one-foot plank, without noticing it, with my eyes searching for something for nothing; I had managed to keep my balance over nothing. But now it was a different matter. My nerve had gone. I could not even stand where the ledge was comparatively wide. So I crawled inch by inch to where it narrowed and peered over. Each side was a sheer descent of slate-smooth rock. The ledge was less than a foot wide and more than five yards long. I must have crossed this without noticing it.

I knew I could not do it again.

I knew that I must do it again.

There was no other way, no other alternative. If only I could regain my nerve. I lit another cigarette and lay flat out, my hand holding a crack in the rock. My only chance was to make a run for it, with my eyes on some distant point, some imagined gull's nest. It could soon be over and, when it was, I swore in my panic to keep so many resolutions. I thought of my wife waiting for the eggs, and our laughing over my present predicament. Standing up, I threw my cigarette away and, with my eyes on a fixed point the other side, began to run towards the ledge, the sea almost meeting underneath it, the gulls swooping over it. I was on the ledge, my eyes still fixed on the point beyond it. In two seconds I would be across. A gull swooped towards me, my eyes lost their fixed objective, I hesitated . . .

Then later I found myself sitting on the beach; I do not know how long I had sat there. I cannot tell; I may have dozed, I may have slept. The tide may have turned or the year turned. I do not know. I picked up my basket and walked up the path from the beach to the cottage. I thought of my wife waiting, the table laid, the guests' inconsequential chatter.

I put my basket behind my back and opened the door. The room was empty, there was no table laid. I went upstairs still carrying the basket of eggs. My wife lay on the bed. She was sobbing. I asked her what was wrong, she made no reply. Sobbing, she looked away from me. I begged her to tell me why she was crying. She made no answer. I put out my hand and touched her smooth, hot forehead. Instantly she screamed, rose from the bed and ran down the stairs out into the night. I followed, but could not find her. I returned to the empty house and went to my study and lay there, miserable and bewildered.

How long I slept there I do not know. The day may have drunk the night a dozen times for all I know; but when I awoke the stream still ran by the cottage. And I listened. My study is next to the sitting-room. Through the door I could hear voices and a fire crackling. It could not be the luncheon party, for we seldom light fires during May. I listened. My sister was there, she was serving coffee. My wife was there and there were two men with them; one was my neighbour, the other a friend of the family. Both people who would often drop in for an evening. I listened; my wife was no longer crying, the wireless was on. I opened the door slowly and went in; my neighbour sat in my chair, so I went over to the divan.

Nobody looked at me, nobody spoke to me and nobody passed me any coffee. They went on talking with the music playing.

My wife looked pretty; she went on knitting. What had I done to be left unnoticed?

I stood up and went to my wife's chair and on her lap placed the basket of gulls' eggs. Her eyes rose slowly from her knitting and she screamed. 'Take them away, take them away!' she screamed, and ran from the room crying. My sister followed her. Then my friend said to my neighbour: 'Poor woman, she's still unnerved. That's the second time she's thought she's seen her husband carrying gulls' eggs . . . She must go away.'

I went into the study. So I was dead, was I? When will we dead awaken?

Anne Treneer

SHEEP MAY SAFELY GRAZE

I

Hay Charlie, in the disused fowls' house, drew an object out of its hiding place behind a block of granite, gazed at it, and put it back again. The time was not yet. But his mother was certainly very ill. 'Very bad', was the way Hay Charlie put it. Old Ann Destra was very bad indeed. And old Martin was dead. He had died two years ago. And Funny Maggie was dead, too. She had died more years ago than Hay Charlie could remember.

Funny in the head Maggie had been, and Hay Charlie also was funny in the head. His watery blue eyes never seemed to comprehend what they rested on. They passed uneasily over every object, unrelated and unpossessed. He was a hay-coloured man, looking as though he might, on some muggy morning, have been born of a haystack, with the wisps of hay still adhering. Perhaps that was why they had nicknamed him Hay Charlie, a name which was often shortened to Hay.

Boys used to tease Hay till old Martin took the gun to them one Saturday. They used to tease him about the fire which had broken out at Bosworthogga on Jubilee night, the night of Queen Victoria's Jubilee. It had broken out in Funny Maggie's room, and Maggie's leg had been scorched. She had sat down on the door-step, taken off her stocking, and, regardless of the mounting force of the fire, applied flour to the wound! Hay had done nothing but babble and try to fill a bucket held the wrong way up. Neighbours had gathered to help put out the flames, and had heard Martin shout at his son, 'Hould thee'st tongue, and holler out *Fire*.' That was enough for the boys of the place. 'Hould thee'st tongue and holler out *fire*' became a classical quip. But once the boys went too far in teasing Hay. They got hold, one dark night, of a truss of straw, strung it up on an elm tree not far from Bosworthogga, and set it alight. 'Hould thee'st tongue and holler out *fire*,' they shouted in at the windows of the cottage while the red glare lit the lane. Martin was stirred to fury.

'Give me the gun, Chearley' he said to his son.

Hay gave him the gun.

'Now bring me the cartridges.'

Hay brought the cartridges.

'I'll pepper their asses,' said Martin, and fired the gun in the dark night in the direction of the retreating boys. And wouldn't have cared if he had hit them either. Boys were more circumspect after that. 'Martin's dangerous; best leave he alone,' they said. But Hay Charlie had no defence when they caught him.

That was not often. Hay's mother kept such a hold on him that he seemed only to live within the circuit of her eyes. He had nothing that was not hers. She took all his earnings. Once, as a boy, he had tried to keep the 'big card' he had had from Sunday school. He had had a ticket every Sunday, and the fifty-two tickets could be exchanged for a 'big card'. Lovely these big cards were. Pictures of flowers and birds and beasts, surrounding illuminated texts they had. Some were decorated with wild roses; some with poppies and corn; some with little girls and angels; some with daisies; some with lambs. Hay's big card was wonderful. It had marguerites and singing birds, and green pastures, and water, and, under shady trees, sheep and lambs.

SHEEP MAY SAFELY GRAZE

was printed across the card in glorious letters. Hay had bit and scratched when his mother had taken his card away. She had stitched a border of red ribbon round it, and hung it up by red ribbon to a nail in the wall of her bedroom. Hay could get another big card for himself with fifty-two more tickets, she said. But Hay had not saved up tickets any more. He had 'minchied' from Sunday school after that.

2

The doctor had been to Bosworthogga, so had the district nurse to tend old Ann. Now they had gone. Hay stood outside his mother's room and listened at the door. He thought he would fetch the young preacher. But first he went out again to look at his treasure which, this time, he transferred from its hiding-place to his poacher's pocket. The pocket bulged. He passed his hand over it lovingly.

The young preacher was ready enough to come. He was ready to help and sustain anyone in trouble, and he had known Hay from boyhood.

'You go up,' said Hay as they reached the cottage. 'Mawther is very bad sure 'nuff.'

The young preacher went up the winding stair which led from the kitchen to the bedroom above. But soon he had returned to the kitchen.

'Your mother is not only very bad, Charlie,' he said, 'she is dead.'

Hay Charlie rose silently. Then he went up the staircase, followed by the young preacher. He stood by his mother's bed. The room was crowded with furniture. On the wall opposite the bed was the text, still bound in faded red ribbon,

SHEEP MAY SAFELY GRAZE

Hay's eyes travelled wanderingly over it, then they came to rest on his mother's face. For a moment he stood contemplating the still form; then he moved slowly towards it. He knelt up on the mattress; with one hand he turned his mother's head, then he brought his mouth on a level with her ear.

'Be you dead, mawther?' he shouted.

There was no sound, no answer, no movement. Hay Charlie waited. Then, very deliberately, he went to the other side of the bed, knelt on it, and again turned the lifeless head.

'Mawther, be you dead?' he shouted again, placing his head as before on a level with the dead woman's ear.

Silence pervaded the room. The young preacher, petrified by the strange spectacle, did not move.

Hay stood upright now. A wild light lit his features and wandering eyes.

'She's dead,' he said. 'And everything that's in this house is mine.'

With that he drew from his pocket the object which he had taken from its hiding place. The young preacher watched him draw the loosened cork from the bottle and raise it to his lips. His eyes rolled, his Adam's apple moved rhythmically. Hay was drinking. Then he went unsteadily to the wall on which the text hung and tried to remove it from its nail. He could not. He gave it a mighty jerk and the nail came out of the wall, leaving a gaping hole in the plaster. He stood swaying for a moment, the text in one hand and the bottle in the other.

'Sheep ... may ... shafely graze,' he said to the young preacher. And, lurching into his own bedroom, he shut the door.

Donald R. Rawe

THE DEEP SEA DREAM

As a boy Neil was a funny little chap with shy secretive ways and probably too much imagination. He did not often join in coussers or conkers with other boys. He used to read a great deal, and books older than some people thought he should read. Queer books like Malory's *Morte d'Arthur*, Hunt's *Popular Romances of the West*, even *The Golden Bough* of Frazer.

Fortunately for Neil none of those around him at Hayle knew much about books, so they let him go his own way. In spite of his reading nobody ever called him clever. He might have been, but at school he was lazy; a proper dreamer. He had quick penetrating eyes and pointed pisky-like ears. A few tongues idly whispered he was a changeling.

It was near one Christmas when Neil had his deep sea dream. It was easy enough for him to piece together events and scenes which reappeared vividly linked in it so as to realize what had given rise to the dream; though these did not explain why it all stayed with him in accurate memory all his life.

They had been practising carols at school: mainly the normal ones that children sing from door to door, knocking after the first verse and vanishing in the middle of the second, once they had the coppers. But this year they had some that were new to Neil, and one of them – 'I saw three ships a-sailing' – delighted him with the Cornish simplicity of its words and tune. For no reason that he could see it made him want to cry; so he hardly ever sang it himself but sat listening to the others around him.

> I saw three ships a-sailing
> On Christmas Day, on Christmas Day:
> I saw three ships a-sailing
> On Christmas Day in the morning.

In the evenings he had been reading some ancient traditions and had been captivated by that series of conjectures, half hints and unproved assertions, about Lyonesse, the district between Land's End and Scilly and once part of Cornwall, which is supposed to have abruptly and inexplicably sunk or become flooded in the year 1099. Historians balanced and counterbalanced what evidence existed: some believed, some disbelieved there ever had been such a land. Nobody *knew*. It had not been proved that Lyonesse once flourished: but it had not been disproved. Neil only hoped the tradition was true.

And then the Sunday before at chapel there had been a sermon about Billy Bray. The minister's eyes and voice seemed to glow with admiration, in rising revivalist fervour as he sketched the character of the miner evangelist who was born at Twelveheads, buried at Baldhu, and who built several chapels almost unaided. He used to work eight hours down the mine, eight building a chapel and four tilling his own plot of land. He would walk scores of miles in a Sunday to preach, dancing and jigging all the way for sheer joy of 'doing the Lord's work'. The last Cornish saint, the minister called him.

The deep sea dream that followed all this was so powerful that in his later life Neil could remember everything and see it all exactly as he had dreamed it. Other dreams leave mere threads of their stories with us on waking which stay in the memory for a month, a year or even several years, then suddenly seem to turn to dust like the golden hair of Guinevere when her body with Arthur's was dug up five hundred years after their deaths. But this vision (he could call it even that) was one of the memorable moments of Neil's life, and he treasured it intensely.

Sometimes he wondered whether it really had been only a dream.

He stood on Hayle quay very early in the morning, looking down at the mudflat and green seaweed. The tide was coming in, sweeping across the flats: grey, frothy, bearing scum.

There was only the sound of tiny hisses and crackles under

the mud as the water seeped down into it. They were made by cockles opening. There was no one else to be seen; Hayle was a dead town. The only living creature was a heron standing like a verger some way out in the water, solemn and unmoving. The sun hovered over the hills toward Camborne and the red ruined engine houses of tin mines.

The tide mounted rapidly, becoming an opaque green; the seaweed on the walls waved hazily through it. And there Neil stood on the quayside, waiting.

He heard a flapping of heavy wings and a guttural call – Kronk-kronk! The heron had risen, unhurriedly but disturbed by something.

There was a ship coming up the estuary, without sails, yet noiselessly. A man leaned over the bulwark smoking a pipe. The heron fled up the river and nothing stirred except this black ship looming up, gliding soundlessly on the green water.

When she came near enough Neil saw a familiar figure-head beneath the bowsprit, and he recognized the schooner. A painting of the *Gipsy Maid* had hung on the wall at home for as long as he could remember. The master was his grandfather, whom he vaguely knew from his earliest recollections – he had died when Neil was six – but whom he remembered best as the subject of numerous stories. For years the *Gipsy Maid* had sailed from Hayle to Swansea taking tin over and coal back.

Alongside the quay came the schooner, his grandfather regarding him intently, smoking his pipe all the while. Neil felt shy of meeting the old man.

'Come aboard, me handsome,' said the captain at last.

Neil came aboard. They shook hands. Neither said anything more, and they both turned and regarded the town. The sun was high now and the shadows gone from the roofs. Yet it was deserted, with not even a dog in the streets. The tide was high and impassive. The captain knocked out his pipe on the bulwark and the sound seemed to echo across the empty quayside. Slowly he went aft to the wheel, still looking at the town and shaking his head cryptically.

The *Gipsy Maid* began to move, to glide astern without sail in the still morning air. The quay receded. Now the tide was ebbing, leaving a wet rim around the wall showing dank seaweed and rusty rungs of ladders.

The ship went ahead and started downstream to the open sea. A flag began to wave lazily on the mizzen-mast high above. There were no clouds.

Neil turned and glanced back at the town. On the quay stood a figure in white skirts and red petticoat. It was his mother: she was calling to him, but he could not hear her words. He was not curious to know what they were.

'Look,' he said to his grandfather. He said it without urgency, merely as a matter of passing interest. But the master stared straight ahead and would not look back.

' 'Tis mother,' Neil said. She was the captain's daughter: he ought to look. But he would not. The boy watched her growing smaller with the houses and the slipway. She waved farewell to him, timidly, reluctantly.

They heard a squawk above them: – Y-aak! – and looking up they saw a seagull perched on the foremast head.

'Ha!' said the old man approvingly. 'Good boy! Good boy!'

The gull looked around with wicked brittle eyes, poking its yellow beak from side to side.

'No storms with he up there,' remarked the captain.

Neil said nothing. There was still an awkwardness between the two; they were not behaving as grandfather and grandson should. But there was nothing he could do about it.

They were now well out in St Ives Bay and making for the outside ocean. Looking back towards Gwithian, Neil saw that the great sandy Towans had gone. There were now glowing fields and hedges sloping down to the water. He could see the village, the church spire, several fields of ripe wheat and green vegetable patches; there was even an orchard. These were fat and fertile lands; and yet they too seemed empty, forsaken: lonely fields on a lonely shore. Save for their brightness they were desolate.

It was not that he was surprised to see them, for he had heard about the rich meadows of Lelant and Gwithian, covered up by sand in a single night centuries ago. He looked across to port to see whether St Ives showed signs of life; but there was no St Ives as he knew it. Only a grey church, a few ancient cottages, and the long yellow beaches: and nothing stirred there either.

All this reminded him of the castle of Sleeping Beauty before the prince came. It was a day which the world was sleeping through and would never know existed. Perhaps each week actually had eight days, but the eighth day was unknown because everybody slept through it. It was probably the day reserved for the dead to walk on earth. Certainly grandfather took it calmly enough, as though he were used to sailing the *Gipsy Maid* around single-handed, having the earth to himself.

Suddenly and with something of a shock Neil became aware of two other schooners, one on each side of them. They were of the same type as *Gipsy Maid*; three-masted fore-and-aft. All three ships were now on the green ocean with the shore merely a vague blue line to port: they were sailing westward. They all had full sail now, and the great white canvases were taking the wind. But the seagull was still there on the foremast glancing around vigilantly.

The ship on their port side was full of men. Perhaps an emigrant ship going to Canada. Neil could see a small figure standing on the poop evidently haranguing the crowd on board. From time to time he heard a long drawn 'Aaah!' from them, and caught fragments of speech from the orator. Then perhaps the schooners came a little nearer each other or perhaps the wind changed slightly; at any rate he was soon able to hear whole sentences.

'You'm all workin fer the biggest company of all – the company of the Feyther, the Sonne, an' the Oly Ghost – an' brothers, I tell 'ee thet company wunt never go scat . . .'

'Well now, look 'ere. Ef the Lord 'ad meant fer men to smoak, 'ed've maade us all wid chimleys in our 'ades . . .'

'Hess now, I do mind that there Prodeegal Sonne arunnin off 'ome from the far contry: I can see onn now, a-coussin over they moors with 'unger in the belly of'n, an' 'is shirt tail 'angin out o' the hass of 'is trousies: and d'ye knaw, brothers, we'm all the saame as 'ee? I tell 'ee, we'm all of us Prodeegal Sonnes a-'ungrin an' athirsting fer our Evveenly Feyther. Then come in brothers, come in to the Kingdom uv Evveen, ragged hass or no!'

Neil heard another gasp of abasement and repentance from the listeners, and then the voice went on, speaking simply and not loudly over the waves.

'Well, the Lord put et into me 'ade to build a chapel: so me an me little sonne, us went to work an got some stawn ...'

The voice faded and became again unintelligibly removed. Still the little man on the poop talked and gesticulated, sometimes lifting his hands to the skies, sometimes bowing his head. He was not still a moment but jerked back and forth all the while. And still Neil watched, fascinated. The figure and some of the words were familiar to him, but who, who was it? He had the name rising like a fish in his mind but he could not catch it –

In desperation he turned to his grandfather.

'Who's that on th'other schooner, Grandad?'

The old man did not reply immediately. After a space he pulled off his peaked cap and said humbly, 'Why, now you mention it, thass Billy Bray.'

Of course: Billy Bray. Admiration and respect welled up in Neil; they were followed by something like remorse. He wanted to apologize, beg somebody's pardon for an error, a sin – some shadowy blunder he had made: what was it? He did not know, it had gone from him ... neither did it matter so long as forgiveness was given. O shrieve me hermit – O little missionary grant me grace – Saint Billy Bray pray for me pray for me, bring me to eternal –

The gull screeched and flew off the masthead. It did not go far but circled round the schooner making a kind of yodelling barking sound. The sky was stormy to starboard: big brown cloud masses hunching together, bearing across towards them. The wind was getting up, the canvas flapping and cracking like gunshots. Then the gull settled again on the masthead and though the atmosphere had become intense the clouds stood off to starboard, poised but for the moment only brooding.

At this point Neil noticed the schooner on that side. She was farther away than the other, an ill-defined black shape against the dark clouds, so that there was no opportunity to see who or what was on her. She was travelling with full sail and seemed to have no difficulty in encountering these splenetic seas: she slipped easily through them, loping along like a sea-panther. Neil knew there was someone on board her, someone powerful, possessed of a vibrant personality that made itself felt across this distance of rearing waves, through the enveloping air of inclemency. It was some giant or more than human creature; it was almost incomprehensible, yet something that lurked back there within the scowling clouds for a purpose ... it dared not be revealed, but could only be understood vaguely by being hidden.

Neil looked around. His grandfather was no longer with him. He looked upward; no seagull either. Across to port. Billy Bray's schooner – gone. And the other? He turned back to starboard.

The great bulk of cloud was turning slowly from brown to red, producing vivid gashes of purple and green that flared into the mass, mingled and were lost. The wrack swelled: it must soon disgorge violence. But still it went on spreading across the sky, Neil suffering in the suspense. He knew that one thing was certain: he could not escape the coming anger. The seagull had vanished and he was doomed.

There was no land in sight; he ran to the wheel. According to the compass the *Gipsy Maid* was sailing southwest. He was past Gurnard's Head and Cape Cornwall. He was beyond Land's End and the Scillies could not be far off. He was sailing above the sunken lands of Lyonesse.

The wind abated in an instant leaving a heavy brooding calm. The dark green ocean ceased chopping and clashing, and dropped into a thick turbid swell. The sky hung tremendous above like a precipice.

There was a faint rumble, then a yellow stab of lightning.

Thunder. Rain hissed down, a million sharp furies on the green sea. Wind tore at the ship from all directions; she plunged and rose like a whale. The sails gave and the mizzen boom came flying around, kicking Neil overboard. He saw the foremast snap off as he struggled in the cruel water.

Then he was sinking slowly and restfully down through the green glassy sea; descending with relief in silence and coolness. Fish flicked past him through the greenness and faded. Peace, unbreakable peace.

A shape grew vaguely toward him. It had long hair swirling behind it; a white body and arms, a woman's smooth breast. A red-gold tail, a beautiful lazy tapering thing curving from side to side. Blandly, heedlessly she passed, swimming slowly with a dreamy motion. The beautiful tail receded into the gloom. Goodbye siren, goodbye merrymaid . . .

Falling, falling gratefully, serenely, silently.

Lyonesse!

He remembered. By the rocks of Lethosow on a calm day you can see the houses of a sunken city below the waters.

Yes, but how many have seen it?

Fishermen have brought up pottery and slates from the bed of the sea.

But how long ago? Where are these things now?

A hundred and forty churches and parishes drowned in the storms of A.D. 1099 . . .

A hundred and forty? After the Doomsday Book was compiled? Where are the records?

A man on a white horse escaped the flood and landed at Sennen to tell the tale . . .

The sea is too deep. The cliffs at Land's End are too old. All this happened too long ago.

St Michael's Mount: Caragclewse en Couze: the Grey Rock in the Woods. The Towans covered the meadows of Lelant. Submarine forests all around the coast. Languna too was lost . . .

Sinking slowly, coolly, greenly. The sea bed is a long way but O when I touch it I shall know whether or not –

At first Neil considered that whoever had awakened him at this point had done him the greatest disservice they possibly could, and he wept a long time in his child's rage and disappointment. But later he was able to bear this fate well enough. After all, though he was so chagrined at being denied what he believed would have been the truth about Lyonesse, what would his feelings have been if it had been revealed to him that it had never existed? What was not proved was still not disproved.

He realized the truth about the third schooner when they next sang the Three Ships carol:

> Our Saviour Christ was in those ships,
> On Christmas Day on Christmas Day . . .

As for the rest of the dream's events, he could connect them, account for having dreamed them. And as for Lyonesse – well, we all still dream about Lyonesse.

CONTRIBUTORS

Jack Clemo: Was born in 1916 at St Stephens, St Austell, where he has lived all his life; was related through his father, a kiln-worker, to the Cornish novelists Joseph and Silas K. Hocking. He received no formal education after the age of twelve when he left Trethosa village school through a temporary attack of blindness. Blindness and deafness have been with him ever since, but he has triumphed magnificently over these drawbacks to produce a mass of work. Well known in Cornwall as the author of humorous dialect tales in the *Almanacks* issued in Truro, Camborne and Penzance during the thirties, he later built up a national reputation as a poet. Among several books published, including a novel, *Wilding Graft*, an autobiography, *Confessions of a Rebel*, and a spiritual autobiography, *The Invading Gospel*, are several books of collected poems, *The Map of Clay*, *Cactus on Carmel* and a new one, *The Echoing Tip*. He was represented by twenty poems in the Penguin Modern Poets series, 1964. Awarded a Civil List Pension, 1961, recently renewed.

Charles Lee: Coming to Cornwall in his early twenties, Charles Lee settled in the western end of the peninsula and wrote a number of sharply humorous stories and novels about Cornish life, the most notable being *Dorinda's Birthday*, *The Widow Woman* and *Our Little Town*. Many of his stories were broadcast by the B.B.C. and others turned into plays. He captured Cornish life and dialect as no other non-Cornish writer has done.

Daphne du Maurier: The second daughter of the famous actor and theatre manager-producer, the late Sir Gerald du Maurier, the much-loved *Punch* artist and author of *Trilby* and *Peter*

Ibbetson. After being educated at home with her sisters, and then in Paris, she began writing short stories and articles in 1928, and in 1931 her first novel, *The Loving Spirit*, was published. Two others followed. Her reputation was established with her frank biography of her father, *Gerald: A Portrait*, and her Cornish novel, *Jamaica Inn*. When *Rebecca* came out in 1938 she suddenly found herself, to her great surprise, one of the most popular authors of the day. The book went into thirty-nine English impressions in the next twenty years and has been translated into more than twenty languages. Sir Laurence Olivier starred in the film under Hitchcock's direction.

Other novels followed, each with a Cornish setting. *Frenchman's Creek*, *The King's General* and *My Cousin Rachel* were all widely read. Inspiration came from France for *The Scapegoat* and *The Glass-Blowers*, and from a hill city in Italy for *The Flight of the Falcon*. During the last decade Cornwall has claimed her loyalty once again, with *The House on the Strand* (1969) and *Rule Britannia* (1972). Amongst her short stories, *The Birds* was made into a film by Hitchcock, while *Don't Look Now*, from the collection *Not After Midnight* (1971), has also been adapted for the screen.

Daphne du Maurier was made a D.B.E. in 1969, and is the widow of the late Lieutenant-General Sir Frederick Browning, K.C.V.O., D.S.O., wartime commander of Airborne Forces, Chief-of-Staff to Earl Mountbatten in S.E.A.C., and until 1958 Treasurer to the Duke of Edinburgh. She has two daughters and a son, and five grandchildren.

'Q': Not only in Cornwall but in the world of English letters this single initial was enough to identify Sir Arthur Quiller-Couch, novelist, short story writer, poet, critic, anthologist, essayist, journalist – and Cornishman. Born at Bodmin in 1863, his life was always bound up with Cornwall and Cornish affairs. For many years he lived at Fowey, where in fact he died as a result of an accident during the Second World War. Fowey was the setting for the famous novel, *Troy Town*, and Cornish settings were featured in most of Q's stories. At the end of the last century he helped to found, and edited, the *Cornish Magazine*, which set a brilliant standard during its short life. Apart from Cornish affairs, 'Q' achieved eminence in the literary world, and was Professor of Literature at Cambridge for many years.

Charles Causley: Born 1917 at Launceston, where he has spent most of his life, writing and teaching. After serving six years as lower decker in the navy during the last war, he began contributing poems to a wide variety of magazines, and still does; meantime several collections of his poems have been published, including Penguin's. Many of his poems have been broadcast by the B.B.C. Western Region and the Home and Third Services, and he has also scripted and introduced broadcasts and appeared frequently on television. Apart from his naval service he has travelled extensively, including a visit to Russia, and these experiences have been reflected in his poems. Recently he published a book of fables.

A. L. Rowse: Born 1903 at St Austell and educated at St Austell Elementary and Council Schools, afterwards winning a scholarship to Christ Church, Oxford. Lecturer of Merton College from 1927 to 1931, and at the London School of Economics from 1931 to 1935, and now at All Soul's College, Oxford. An outstanding figure in contemporary Cornish literature, he has achieved a national reputation as a historian and as a poet. Among his publications of special interest to Cornish readers are *Sir Richard Grenville of the 'Revenge'*, *Tudor Cornwall*, *Poems of a Decade*, *A Cornish Childhood*, *Poems Chiefly Cornish*, *Poems of Deliverance* and *West-Country Stories*. He has also written many authoritative history books, among them *The Use of History* and *The End of an Epoch*. Best known for his books about life in Shakespeare's time, he recently created a furore by claiming to have identified the 'Dark Lady of the Sonnets'.

Winston Graham: Although born and educated in Lancashire

he has spent the greater part of his life in Cornwall. He lived for many years at Perranporth and it was during this period he produced the now famous *Ross Poldark* quartet – *Ross Poldark*, *Demelza*, *Jeremy Poldark* and *Warleggan*, presenting a fascinating and very well documented picture of life in the early days of Cornish mining. Since the Second World War he has published nineteen novels, one book of short stories and a history of the Anglo-Spanish war of the sixteenth century. His novels have been translated into fifteen languages and have been major book club choices in four countries. Six have been filmed. An ex-chairman of the Society of Authors and a Fellow of the Royal Society of Literature, he now lives at Buxted, Sussex.

David Watmough: Born in Cornwall, and served a journalistic apprenticeship on the *Cornish Guardian*, Bodmin. Later emigrating to Canada where he has twice been a winner of the Canada Council's Arts Bursary in Theatre and Creative Writing. He has written several plays for Canadian theatres, and also T.V. documentaries for the Canadian Broadcasting Corporation. Recently visited Britain on a tour reading his stories – some of them taking place in Cornwall – to live audiences.

Howard Spring: Born in Cardiff in 1889, Howard Spring worked for many years as a journalist on the *Yorkshire Observer* (1911–15), *Manchester Guardian* (1915–31) and then on the *Evening Standard*, on which paper he succeeded Arnold Bennett as literary critic. After that he began writing the novels that have made him famous, and settled at Mylor, near Falmouth in Cornwall, later living until his death at the White House, Falmouth. Cornwall features in many of his novels, as well as in autobiographical writings. Among his best-known books are *Shabby Tiger*, *Rachel Rosing*, *My Son My Son*, *Fame is the Spur*, *Hard Facts*, *All the Day Long*, *These Lovers Fled Away* and *Winds of the Day*.

J. C. Trewin: Born in 1908. Comes from the Lizard; went to Landewednack School, later to Plymouth College. Descriptive writer for the *Morning Post*, then sixteen years with the *Observer*, six as literary editor, ten as second drama critic. Has been drama critic of *Punch*, *John O' London's*, *Illustrated London News*, *Birmingham Post*, *The Listener* and *The Lady*. Edited the regional literary magazine, *West Country Magazine*, and also editor of more than forty anthologies of various sorts, including the annual *Plays of the Year*. He has written some forty books, including two volumes of autobiography, *Up from the Lizard* and *Down to the Lion*, biographies of Robert Donat and Peter Brook, *Portrait of the Shakespeare Country* and *Portrait of Plymouth*. Married to writer and critic Wendy Monk, with two sons, one of whom is literary editor of *The Times*.

Denys Val Baker: Although Welsh by descent he has spent the past thirty years in West Cornwall, with homes at Penzance, Sennan Cove, St Hilary, St Ives, Fowey and now in the Penberth Valley, not far from Land's End. Experiences of family life in Cornwall have formed the theme of a series of autobiographical books, *The Sea's in the Kitchen*, *The Door is Always Open*, *Life Up the Creek*, *An Old Mill by the Stream*, etc. Also well known as a short story writer, with nearly 100 stories broadcast by the B.B.C. and stories in leading magazines here and abroad. Several volumes of his stories have been published, the latest being *The Woman and the Engine Driver*. In 1949 he founded the *Cornish Review*, a regional literary magazine which recently celebrated its twenty-fifth anniversary – as the result of his work editing the *Review* he accumulated the material for *The Timeless Land*, subtitled 'the creative spirit in Cornwall', a survey of how and why so many artists come to work in Cornwall. Married with six children: his wife Jess has been a studio potter in Cornwall for the past twenty years.

C. C. Vyvyan: Born in Australia, but her mother was Cornish and she has lived at Trelowarren, near Helston, from the age of two. After earning with distinction a social science degree at the London School of Economics, she travelled widely – including a journey with one other woman to the Arctic Circle, up Rat River with Indian guides and over the Divide into Klondike country by a route only once before traversed by a white woman. Married in 1929 to Colonel Sir Courtney Vyvyan, C.M.G., C.B., D.L., J.P., tenth baronet of Trelowarren, Cornwall. Author, under maiden name of C. C. Rogers, of *Cornish Silhouettes* and *Echoes in Cornwall* (Bodley Head). Under her married name of C. C. Vyvyan she has written extensively for national magazines, and also published an anthology on birds, *Bird Symphony* (John Murray), *Gwendra Cove* (Jordan), and *Our Cornwall* (Westaway Books Ltd.).

Frank Baker: Associated with Cornwall since pre-war years when he was organist at St Hilary Church during Father Bernard Walke's time there: later he lived for a decade at Mevagissey, and now has a family home at Porthleven. He is well-known for *Embers*, *The Downs so Free*, *My Friend The Enemy*, *Teresa*. His recent book, *I Follow But Myself*, a collection of essays about friends and literary figures who influenced his life, included a section on Mary Butts. He has had several television plays produced and for some years worked as a script editor with the B.B.C. at Welsh Region, Cardiff. Recently returned from a year as writer lecturer at Central College, Oklahoma, U.S.A.

Ruth Manning-Sanders: Born in South Wales and lived in the north of England as a child. Studied for an English Honours degree at Manchester University. Began by writing verse, and was first published by the Hogarth Press. Has published novels, short stories and verse in England and America, including *Swan of Denmark, A Biography of Hans Andersen* (Heinemann), *A History of the English Circus* (Werner Laurie), *The Seaside* (Batsford), *The River Dart* (Westaway Books) and numerous children's books. Since the 1930s she has lived in Cornwall, mostly at Sennen Cove, near Land's End. Now lives quietly in Penzance.

Ronald Duncan: For many years farmed at Morwenstowe, now at Welcome, just over the border, and has written on country life in such books as *Journal of a Husbandsman* and *Jan's Journal*, and in articles in the *Evening Standard*, etc. However, is best known as a poet and playwright, notable among his works being *This Way to the Tomb*, a masque and anti-masque that has been widely performed here and abroad. Wrote the libretto of Benjamin Britten's second opera, *The Rape of Lucretia*, also the film script of *The Girl on a Motor Cycle*, and has contributed short stories to various collections, including *Thy Neighbour's Wife* and *The Ghost Book*. Now working on a mammoth poem, *Man*.

Anne Treneer: Like A. L. Rowse, whose work she greatly admired, Miss Treneer came from the St Austell area, and her most successful book, *Schoolhouse in the Wind*, was a vivid account of life at Gorran, where her father was schoolteacher. One of those quiet but very effective writers, Anne Treneer achieved considerable literary success, following up her earlier autobiography with *A Stranger in the Midlands*, *Cornish Years* and a book of short stories, *Happy Button*. She also wrote a number of biographical books, notably *Charles M. Doughty*, and a more recent life, *Sir Humphry Davy*. Her death in the late 1960s deprived Cornwall of one of her most talented writers.

Donald R. Rawe: Cornish playwright and novelist, was born at Padstow in 1930 and lives there still. Author of *The Happening at Botathen* (*Cornish Review*, Winter, 1970); a stage version of *In the Roar of the Sea*, by Baring-Gould; *Petroc of Cornwall*, etc. Contributor to various Cornish magazines, *Western Morning News*, first series of *Cornish Reviews*, etc. Made a Bard of Gorseth Kernow in 1970 in recognition of his services to drama (*Scryfer Lanwednok – Writer of Padstow*). Publishes books on Cornish subjects under the imprint of Lodenek Press.